Children from the Light:
A Tori Cooper Novel

By Vicki Stewart

Books written by Vicki Stewart

The Tori Cooper Novels:
First Sight, 2013
The Enlightenment, 2014
Guardians of the Chosen, 2015
Children from the Light, 2016

This book is dedicated to God. He knows why.

Children from the light,
see into the night,
fear and darkness creeping.

Bring them 'round,
safe and sound,
the fearless who are sleeping.

~ Vicki Stewart

Chapter 1

The morning sun emerged on the horizon, just as Wade rounded the bend on the path along the curve of the lake.

He loved being here this time of day. The crispness of the morning air and the serenity of the birds singing as the earth woke from its evening slumber always put him in the right frame of mind for the rest of the day.

He knew from experience that a few hours from now, this harmonious scene of tranquility would be completely different as the invasion of teenagers and parents, toting small children by the hand, would swarm upon the beautiful little lake and the calm glass-like water would become infested with screaming children and worn out parents. All the while, everyone would be hoping to escape the summer heat during their hour rental while they paddled around in the water, praying for the occasional lake breeze to cool their blistering skin.

A shudder ran through him as the memory filled his mind, again thankful for the calmness surrounding him now.

Keeping a steady pace, he passed the strip of beach separating the water from the trees, catching the rainbow of colors from the row of canoes and kayaks lying on the sand in front of the rental shack in his peripheral vision.

Mentally checking off another mile marker in his head, he placed his fingers on his inner wrist and counted the beats for ten seconds. Then quickly multiplying that number times six, he nodded to himself, satisfied. *"One hundred seventy and steady, good job Wade,"* he thought inwardly.

While he ran, the sun filtered through the branches overhead, casting a spotlight on a patch of dirt to his right where one of the groundskeepers had placed a layer of straw on the ground, attempting to regenerate the soil with new grass seed. The light, casting off of the golden straw, triggered a memory in his mind, as he found himself thinking back to the day when he first met his wife, Wendy.

It was her long, thick, honey-gold colored hair that first caught his eye. And when she had turned to face him, her beautiful smile and laughing blue eyes were all it took for him to be completely captivated by her.

They were at a pub in Boston, each with their group of friends, and with the help of a little liquid courage from behind the bar, he had walked up to her table and introduced himself to her. By the end of the night, she had given him her number and from that day on, they had been inseparable.

That's where their fairy-tale had begun. Once upon a time, Wade and Wendy Hackett were the couple everyone wanted to be. Once upon a time, she was a beautifully confident, happy woman, with a quick and friendly smile for everyone she met. Everyone loved her. He had loved her.

Then something happened. Something to this day he still couldn't figure out. Wendy became critical and judgmental of their friends and him. She began finding flaws in herself that he simply just couldn't see; which made her angry at him for being so annoyingly blind.

That's when she began to change. First it was small things like when she dyed her beautiful honey-gold hair to a bleached platinum blonde, which now hung lifeless and straw-like over her shoulders - like doll hair.

Then came the tanning bed sessions where her skin glowed like a Halloween pumpkin afterwards. Next were the bright red, fake fingernails, excusing her from making dinner because didn't he know how damaging preparing food could be to her manicure?

When the too-tight fitting clothes that looked like they belonged to their daughter and not his wife started to show up, he began to worry.

But even that wasn't enough. Then the bigger changes happened. When she could no longer quiet her inner demons, she turned to a plastic surgeon.

First it was a few tucks by the eyes to smooth out the crow's feet; then it was minor alterations to the shape of her nose and chin. But that still wasn't enough.

Then the talk, which turned into an argument, about breast reconstruction happened. When she cried pitifully and tried to convince him that being a B cup was absurd and didn't he know every woman wanted to be a DD? And if he truly loved her, he would support her and her decision. After all, she was doing this for him too. At least that's what she told him.

Afterwards, once she healed, she had encouraged him to touch her; to feel her new body and love it as much as she did.

But he didn't.

The once soft, supple flesh that used to stir his thoughts and desires, now felt foreign, hard, cold and lifeless in his hands. She looked un-natural, felt unnatural, like a human cartoon. She was no longer the once beautiful woman she used to be.

He saw the looks when they went out together in public. The glares from the women when they caught their husbands looking at Wendy embarrassed him. He became tired of giving those women looks of apology in reply, which immediately became looks of sympathy back at him.

Wendy seemed oblivious to it all. She enjoyed the attention she received from other men and soon, people stopped asking them over for dinner parties. No one invited them to join them on weekend trips anymore. They were no longer the couple everyone wanted to be.

The moment he knew he lost her was the day she finally turned her eyes to his, and her once bright, beautiful blue eyes, stared back at him through filmy, green contact lenses. Emotionless; dull; and empty. The once wide-open windows to her soul were now clouded over by her fear and insecurities. He couldn't see his reflection in her eyes anymore so after a while; he stopped looking.

Then he met Julia. Beautiful, exotic Julia.

They met at the health food store one day when he was buying whey protein. He remembered turning down the aisle and nearly stopping in his tracks at the sight of her.

She was that beautiful.

She had been reading the label on a container of the same brand of powder that he used. That had given him the perfect opening to talk to her when he took a container off the shelf beside her, barely avoiding brushing up against her hand in the process.

Then she had turned to look at him and in an incredibly soft, sexy voice she had asked, "I see that you're buying this same brand. Is it good? I'm not sure which one to try. Perhaps you could help me?"

One look from those incredible brown eyes had been all it took and for the second time in his life, he had been captivated. She was one-hundred percent all natural; no preservatives; no artificial fillers; a voluptuous all-American beauty.

In the beginning, they were just running partners. After he had introduced himself as a personal trainer, she asked for his help so when he offered she happily accepted. They began meeting twice a week in the mornings for an hour, here at the lake. Within a few weeks, she had matched her pace to his, and they were running seven and a half miles, stride for stride.

It was nice having someone to run with when she was able to meet him. She was easy to talk to, not to mention easy to look at. She hadn't seemed to mind that he was married. He told her everything. And instead of looking at him with pity afterwards, he had seen compassion and understanding in her eyes.

Then one day, they got caught in a downpour and had to wait out the storm in a section of the woods under the protection of the trees. They laughed at each other, at first; seeing each other soaked to the skin. But he couldn't keep his eyes from wandering over her. The shape of her body through her wet clothing set his pulse racing and when her eyes met his, the mutual desire he saw reflecting back at him was too overpowering. The storm of emotions raging inside of each of them unleashed as they grabbed one another into a passionate kiss; that turned into a lust-filled hour in the back seat of his Town Car.

Did he love her? Maybe; he wasn't sure. All he knew was when he was with her; he felt alive again like he was a part of something special. And when he touched her, she was warm and soft and real. Everything a woman should be.

Completing another pass by the kayaks and canoes, he checked his pulse again and realized he was up to one-hundred and ninety beats per minute. *"Easy, man,"* he warned himself. *"Stop thinking about the girl and focus on your stride."*

Laughing at himself, he adjusted his pace, blew out a deep breath and locked his eyes on the path ahead, trying not to think about her.

Distracted by his thoughts, he didn't notice the red dot on his shirt, located where is heart was racing at one hundred and ninety beats per minute.

When the bullet struck him, there was no time to react. With his veins and arteries wide open, he felt his heart faltering at the sudden loss of blood, and his legs gave way beneath him.

As he fell to the ground, the last image in his mind, were Julia's beautiful chocolate brown eyes.

Chapter 2

Piper smiled to herself wryly as she watched the bullet hit her target, dead center from fifteen hundred yards away.

"Dang it!" Logan cried out, knowing he had just lost twenty bucks.

Ben chuckled under his breath, as Logan slapped the bill into Piper's open hand. "You can't say I didn't warn you, buddy! I told you not to bet her. I learned my lesson the hard way."

"Fifteen hundred yards, are you kidding me? Who does that?" Logan argued, looking back at the target area.

"Apparently, I do," Piper chirped happily, snapping the bill taut between her hands. "It's a pleasure doing business with you, sir."

"Oh, shut up and quit gloating," Logan mumbled, positioning his rifle for his next shot. "You've obviously been practicing since we graduated. I had no idea you improved your range that much!"

"Yeah, those were good times; I've missed these little moments," Piper teased gently. "I think I'm going to like having you on our team."

"Well, don't get too used to your little extortion ring. I've learned my lesson. You're not getting any more money out of me," Logan advised.

"We'll see about that," Piper giggled, tucking the bill into the pocket of her jeans. "So where are you aiming?" she asked, innocently.

"Same place as you, sunshine," he smirked, lying down prone on the ground to line up his scope.

"Ha! I'll bet you twenty bucks you miss," Piper goaded.

Logan looked up at Piper and shook his head in disbelief. "Are you kidding me? Did you not just hear what I said?" He looked over at Ben, who was doing his best not to laugh out loud, witnessing the exchange between his friends. "Oh, yeah, go ahead and laugh. You're next, buddy!"

Ben raised his hands in surrender and choked out, "Oh no. I'm out. This is between the two of you. Go ahead. Take your shot."

"Yeah, I'll take my shot. Don't you worry about that," Logan grumbled as he turned back to his target and adjusted his position. Visually calculating the drop and drift he needed to account for at this distance, he positioned his eye behind the riflescope, squeezed the trigger and watched the clump of dirt fly up from the ground, two hundred yards in front of the target.

"Hey! That was really close!" Piper praised, kicking him gently on the leg.

He looked back up at her, preparing to fire back a mild obscenity when he noticed the look of praise on her face was genuine. Closing his mouth firmly, he grunted in reply and stood up.

"I'm serious; that was the closest you've come today! Come on, you have to be happy about that!" she exclaimed.

Brushing the dirt from the front of his clothes, he grimaced and replied, "I guess. Thanks."

"Do you want to keep going?" she asked, turning to look back at Ben to include him in her question.

"I'm done," Ben admitted.

"I've had enough for today too," Logan frowned, picking up his rifle.

"Cool. Let's grab a beer. I'm buying!" Piper offered, heading towards the car.

"Yeah, with my twenty bucks," Logan chuckled, following her.

~~~~~~~~~~~

"Ah! That's good stuff," Ben exclaimed, setting down his bottle of beer. "Thanks, Piper – I mean Logan!"

"You're very welcome, Ben!" Piper giggled, glancing over at Logan's sullen expression.

"You both suck," Logan quipped, taking a long draw from his bottle.

"Okay, we'll stop," Piper agreed, rolling her eyes. "Change of subject. How are you settling into your new pad? Do you like our humble little apartment complex?"

"Yeah, it's fine," Logan admitted. "At least until I figure out where I want to live permanently."

"Well you helped Tor and me out a lot by taking over our lease, man," Ben added. "Thanks again for doing that. With the baby coming and stumbling over Goliath all the time, we needed to find a bigger place."

"I still can't believe you two are expecting!" Piper gleefully replied. "I'm going to be an aunt! How cool is that? Too bad the baby is due in August and not in June. He or she would have been a Gemini like me! When are you going in for the sonogram so we know whether it will be a boy or a girl? You two are still planning to find out, right?"

"Yep, that's still the plan. Considering the long line of daughters of Remiel though, it seems silly to have a sonogram when we're fairly certain it will be a girl," Ben replied. "Our appointment is Friday at three o'clock."

"Well, at least you'll be able to see her and count her ten little fingers and ten little toes!" Piper sighed, dreamily.

Logan looked at Ben's expression and smiled. "I'm still trying to wrap my head around the fact that you're going to be a dad," he admitted. "Here I was hoping that joining Agent Hunter's team was going to give us a chance to have some Bro time and hang out like we did at the Academy!"

"We will!" Ben argued. "Come on, this is going to be great! You were miserable with your team in Boston. And with Tori being pregnant and not being able to be in the field anymore, this will not only give her the opportunity to be more of a forensic analyst; which is what she prefers; it fills a hole on our team with someone we know will be a good fit. As long as you and Piper have resolved your past relationship issues," he teased.

"We're fine!" Piper interrupted. "It's not weird, right Logan?"

Logan flashed a quick wink at Ben and smirked at Piper mischievously, "Not more weird than usual. Considering your little color-wheel carnival act and everything."

Piper rolled her eyes again and scowled at Logan. "You can be such a jerk sometimes; you know that? Luckily your aura is your normal deep red color which means you are just your normal jerkish self. Your puny words do not bother me."

"Wow!" Logan laughed. "So what are you saying, you're rubber, and I'm glue?"

"If the shoe fits," Piper taunted.

"Is this Piper – our Piper? Where is the pixie-warrior who's always ready to charge into the heat of the battle? Was there a pod under your bed last night before you went to sleep and now there's a body somewhere being disposed of?" Logan chuckled.

"Shut up!" Piper laughed along with him. "I've matured a lot since our time at the academy! Agent Hunter is a wonderful mentor for teaching self-control, and Agent Hughes has been helping me find a healthy balance between my spiritual side and my intellectual side. He thinks I'm gifted."

"Hmm, yes I believe I've heard something along the lines of how much Agent Hughes has been uh, helping you," he teased, using air quotes with his fingers.

Piper scowled at him in frustration, trying to control her temper. "Just what is that…,"

"What matters," Ben interrupted, "is that it's all starting to work out, and we're all getting along, right?"

"It's working for me," Logan agreed, winking at Piper. "Hey, I've got nothing against the guy. From what I've seen and heard, he seems cool. I'm just a little surprised that you would be interested in a guy like that."

"Interested in a guy like what, exactly?" Piper challenged testily.

Logan raised an eyebrow in surprise at her immediate defense and said, "He seems a little too straight-laced for someone like you."

"Like me how?" she glared at him through narrowed eyes.

Logan flicked a look over at Ben, who was looking at him with a blank expression.

"Don't look at me, you started this one. I'd hand you a shovel, but you seem to be doing a pretty good job digging yourself into that hole you're standing in," Ben chuckled.

"I'm just messing with you, Pip," Logan attempted to tease. "Here, let me make it up to you. Next round is on me!" he added as he quickly got up from the table and headed for the bar.

Watching Logan walk away, Piper turned to Ben expectantly who gave her a crooked smile in response. "He's just messing with you; you know Logan."

"We'll see," Piper replied, unconvinced.

Chapter 3

Tori stared at the screen of her laptop, saddened by the details around the brutal killings of their latest victim. As she read through the list of evidence, her eyes stopped on the description of a small silver heart-shaped necklace, found in one of the vehicles.

Suddenly feeling sentimental, she reached down to the silver heart charm necklace around her neck and held it up so she could see it. Turning it over, she gently traced the engraving that read 'Always Sisters' and thought of her sister, Aubrey, who had a matching necklace to hers. It was a companion necklace that their mother now kept, along with Aubrey's cremated ashes.

The murder of Tori's sister had shaken their small community. For years, no one knew what happened to her. The Cooper's became 'that family who lost their little girl' that everyone wanted to talk about, yet not talk directly to. It worked out well for everyone as the Cooper's didn't really have anything to say.

Even after Tori discovered the body of her sister, years later, the Cooper's still couldn't talk about their daughter;

a daughter whose spirit was still among them, seen only by Tori and her mother; each woman possessing the ability to communicate with the spirits of victims of violent deaths.

Sliding the charm slowly back and forth along the chain, Tori awakened from her reminiscing by a sudden movement from the baby. She drew in a surprised breath and ran her hand over her stomach as she felt the flutter more intensely than she had earlier. "Easy, baby girl," she quieted softly, leaning back in the swivel chair to stretch out her torso.

Sensing her discomfort, Goliath rose from his curled position on the floor beside her, looked up at her and nudged her hand gently.

"Need Remy?" she heard him ask.

Extending her other hand to pat the dog gently on his massive head, she smiled at her companion and replied, "No, I'm okay, Goliath. The baby is moving around a lot right now; that's all."

Hearing her comment, Riley looked up from his laptop across the table and eyed her with concern. "Is everything okay?"

Tori smiled and replied, "We're fine, thanks."

He paused and looked over at Goliath for confirmation. When he saw the dog's demeanor calm and relaxed, he smiled at Tori and replied, "You promise you'll let me know if ever the two of you are ever not fine?"

Laughing lightly, Tori nodded and said, "I promise I will."

"All right," he conceded. "So, how far have you read through the case information I sent you earlier? Are you at a point where we can start working up the crime board?"

Tori glanced back at the screen of her laptop and said, "I read through everything start to finish so I could get a general idea of the overall picture. Then went back to each case in particular and made some notes where I had questions. Before I do that, where are the case evidence items being held? I would like to see if I can pick up any additional clues from any of those items, which might help answer some of my questions."

Agent Hughes gave her a wry grin and admitted, "I had a feeling you would ask that question, so I've arranged to have them delivered here. The courier should be arriving early this afternoon. Do you want to take a break now, and stretch your legs a bit? You've been sitting in that chair for a couple of hours, and that can't be good for your circulation."

Tori gave him a surprised look and replied, "Wow, you're getting pretty good at playing babysitter, you know that? But you're right sitting in this cushy chair probably isn't helping. I think walking around a bit will help," she replied as she stood from her chair and began walking around the table.

He chuckled, good-naturedly and said, "How many times do we need to tell you that we're not babysitting, Agent

Cooper! We all just want to ensure that you're comfortable, now that you're expecting."

"And you're all making it quite obvious that someone has been assigned to be with me at all times when Ben's not with me, which I would assume is his idea!" Tori exclaimed. "Look, I appreciate what everyone's doing but I am capable of being alone without fear of Luc trying one of his death games. Besides, Goliath can sense him when he's near so everyone needs to relax!"

Agent Hughes gave a heavy sigh and admitted, "Okay. I'll come clean. Ben did ask that we all keep an eye on you. And before you say anything," he added when she opened her mouth to speak, "for me personally, I'm actually enjoying this chance to spend more time with you. It's given me an opportunity to learn more about your abilities and how effective they are in honing your skills as a profiler."

Tori grinned and readily admitted, "Thank you for saying that! I really am enjoying it and was hoping you didn't feel like you had to work with me due to the new arrangements."

"Not at all!" he assured her.

"Then would you mind if we referenced each other on a first-name basis when it's just us? I know Agent Hunter likes us to be formal outside of the team, but you can call me Tori, you know," she offered.

"Fair enough," he agreed, inclining his head. "From now on we're Tori and Riley."

"Perfect!" Tori replied.

As Tori approached the wall where a large whiteboard was attached, Goliath's head whipped up towards her, and he began to whine, nervously.

"What's wrong, Goliath," she paused, looking at him curiously.

Suddenly she heard a cracking sound on the wall behind her. As she turned, she saw the whiteboard falling towards her. "Oh!" she exclaimed in surprise.

"Tori look out!" Riley yelled, quickly rushing forward to grab the edge of the frame.

 Jumping backward, she barely cleared the board's path as one corner crashed to the floor. "Whew, that was close," she breathed heavily.

Lowering the board to the floor against the wall, Riley came to her and gently placed his hand on her shoulder. "Are you okay?" he asked worriedly.

"I'm fine," Tori replied. "Just give me a minute to catch my breath."

Glancing back at the whiteboard, Riley looked up at the mounting brackets and shook his head slowly. "That was too close," he decided angrily. "Those brackets should have held better than they did."

"It's not the brackets fault, and you know it," Tori replied with a scowl. "I was wondering why Luc has been so quiet lately."

Pausing briefly, Riley took one last look at the board and then turned to Tori. "Still feel like you don't need someone with you at all times?"

Chuckling quietly, she replied, "Okay, so maybe Ben did have the right idea."

"Odd timing that you mention Lucifer and then this happened," Riley thought out loud.

"That was his way of reminding me that he's always paying attention," Tori advised. "Evil never takes a break."

"I would have to agree. You're sure you're okay?" he asked.

"I'm fine, thank you. Nice footwork by the way. You jumped in there pretty quickly."

"Yeah, that was quite a jolt to my adrenaline. My pulse is still racing!" he laughed.

"Mine too!" Tori laughed with him.

"Tori is okay?" Goliath asked her quietly.

Tori looked down and saw Goliath standing beside her, his golden eyes filled with concern. Reaching down to pet his head gently, she replied, "I'm okay, Goliath. You tried to warn me when you knew it was Luc. Good boy."

"Tori doesn't need Remy?" he asked her.

"No, we don't need Remy this time," she smiled.

"Well, I'm going to call facilities right now and tell them what happened. They need to make sure this board is securely re-hung on that wall." Riley exclaimed.

"I'm sure under normal circumstances, even a building inspector would confirm that there was nothing wrong with the way that board was hung. Don't try to find logic in an illogical situation," she gently suggested. "Piper tried to do the same thing the first time something like this happened when she was with me. Remember? When we were in San Francisco, and I almost walked into an elevator shaft thinking there was an elevator car?"

Nodding agreeably he replied, "Yes I do recall that. Piper tried to explain it to me afterward but you know how hard it is sometimes to understand her when she's excited about something. She starts talking so fast; you almost need to record her and play it back later at a slower speed!"

Tori smiled and nodded, "Yes, she does have an amazing level of energy about her, doesn't she?"

"Yes she does," he laughed.

Tori watched the smile on his face soften as a memory seemed to come back to him and his eyes took on a distant look. *"He really does care for her,"* she thought to herself happily. *"It's nice to know he feels the same way about her as she does about him."*

Suddenly aware of the silence in the room, his eyes regained their focus, and he glanced at her, embarrassed at being caught in his daydream. "Ahem, yes well," he cleared his throat, nervously. "I'm going to make that call. In the meantime, while we wait, why don't we have some lunch?"

Tori smiled at him, nodded and replied, "Okay. Lunch sounds great!"

Chapter 4

When they returned, the whiteboard was back up on the wall, and two large cardboard boxes were waiting for them on the conference table.

"Ah, I see the facilities team put our board back up while we were out," Riley announced, pulling gently on the edge of the board to make sure it was secure.

"And the courier delivered the evidence boxes," Tori noted checking the delivery receipt. "So based on what I read earlier, the matching bullets are the only evidence linking these two cases together. Is that correct?" she asked as she broke open the security seal and removed the lid from the box closest to her.

"That is correct," he replied.

"And the forensics on the bullets indicated they were both fired from the same long-range rifle," she recalled.

"Also correct," he confirmed.

"Okay then, let's see what we've got," Tori declared, placing her hands inside the box. "It looks like this evidence belonged to Mr. Grant Albertson since I recall reading that he was killed while walking his dog," she added, removing her hands from the box holding a dog leash.

Placing the looped end of the leash in her left hand, she closed her eyes in concentration and took a deep breath as the images began flooding her mind.

Already familiar with this behavior from her, Riley waited for a few moments and then quietly asked, "Tell me what you see."

With her eyes still closed, Tori tilted her head to one side and calmly replied, "I see many walks with the same dog, a black Labrador. I'll assume it's Brady, Mr. Albertson's dog. I'm having visions of walks at different times during the day; sometimes it's sunny outside, other times it's raining. Both Mr. Albertson and Brady seemed to enjoy their walks, and the weather didn't bother them."

"Does he ever stop and talk to anyone?" Riley prodded her.

"A few quick conversations, mostly in passing with other people walking their dogs," Tori replied, still watching. "Wait," she announced and then paused.

"What?" he asked.

"I keep seeing a woman with dark hair walking a Dalmatian. At first they simply pass one another, and their conversations are brief. Then, there are a few times they're both sitting on a bench in the park, and the dogs are lying on the ground by their feet," Tori stated then paused again.

"Well Mrs. Albertson has blonde hair, and they only had the one dog," he noted.

"Yes, I recall that as well," Tori agreed, her eyes still closed, watching the scene in her head.

"Are they touching? Like they could be having an affair?" he asked.

"No, I haven't seen anything that would lead me to think they were having a physical relationship. Quite the opposite, like she's very sad about something, and he's comforting her," Tori replied.

"Well, he was the manager of the local grocery store in LaGrange, Kentucky. Perhaps he worked with her or she was a frequent customer, and they were friends," he thought out loud.

"Perhaps," she quietly replied.

A few minutes later, Tori opened her eyes and looked down at the leash in her hand, thoughtfully. Then she looked over at Goliath, who had returned to his curled sleeping position on the floor beside her chair.

"What are you thinking?" he asked curiously.

Meeting his eyes, she replied, "I'm thinking that if I was killed while walking my dog, what would happen to the dog? I don't recall reading anything in the police report that mentioned what happened to Brady."

"Well, taking you and Goliath out of the equation of being a typical owner and canine, considering the telepathic bond the two of you share," he reasoned, which Tori inclined her head in agreement, "I would assume Brady would have stayed with the body until someone showed up. Why is this important?"

"It may not be," Tori admitted. "But since it wasn't mentioned in the police report, I might want to talk to the responding officer or Mrs. Albertson to see if either of them recalls if Brady was found with Mr. Albertson's body or if he was found with someone else."

"As in found with a dark haired woman with a Dalmatian?" he asked, realizing what she meant.

"Exactly," Tori nodded.

"Hmmm…good question, let's add that to our list of follow-up items," he agreed, making a note on his notepad.

After checking the remaining items, including Mr. Albertson's house key, wallet, cell phone and clothing, Tori returned everything to the box and placed the lid back on top.

"Pick up anything else from the other items?" he asked as he finished writing the last entry on the whiteboard beneath Grant Albertson's name.

"Nope, the leash had most of the clearest memories," she admitted, reviewing what he had written. "What you have there on the board is a good start."

"Okay, good," he nodded.

Breaking the seal from the second box, she removed the lid and said, "Let's see what this one has to offer from Mr. Wade Hackett, our personal trainer from Shelbyville, Kentucky."

As before, she carefully removed each item, picking up fragments of images but it wasn't until she picked up the car keys that the picture became clear. "Whoa," she exclaimed, doing her best to keep her surprise from breaking her concentration.

"What? What do you see?" Riley asked with concern.

"Um...Mrs. Hackett is a platinum blonde, right?" she asked, her face beginning to flush.

"Yes, why?" he asked cautiously.

"Because there's some pretty steamy sex going on in the back seat of this car and the woman is definitely not Mrs. Hackett," Tori exclaimed. Setting the keys down carefully on the table, she looked at Riley and declared, "Wow! That was one X-rated vision. I need to sit down."

"Really?" he laughed, handing her a bottle of water as she eased down into the chair. "Dare I ask that you tell me what you saw?"

Tori winced as she unscrewed the cap of the bottle and replied, "Would you mind if I didn't tell you everything on this one? I'm not sure I would be comfortable telling you everything."

"Okay, give me the G-rated version," he chuckled. "So we now know Wade Hackett was having an affair. What else?"

"Well, she's gorgeous whoever she is," Tori admitted, taking a drink from the bottle. "She had olive complexion, long dark hair, and beautiful dark brown eyes. And Mr. Hackett was very fond of her."

"Hmm, okay, so another unanswered question to add to our list," he replied while adding another entry on his notepad. "Who is our mystery brunette?" Looking back at Tori he asked, "What else?"

"We already knew Wade Hackett was a jogger, and he was found by another jogger on the path at the lake he was known to frequent. I didn't get a sense of anything going on with him but again, the images were pretty fragmented on everything except for the keys. I'm not sure I picked up anything else that will help on this one."

"Well, the discovery of an affair is a pretty big piece of evidence, which implies motive for at least Mrs. Hackett if not as well as our mystery brunette's possible husband or partner," Riley suggested.

"True," Tori agreed. "I think the best course of action at this point will be for me to meet with both of the victim's spirits and see if they'll talk to me. That's the only way to find out for sure what really happened."

"You know Agent Hunter will want you to clear any travel plans with your doctor before we make any arrangements. I would be willing to accompany you if you wouldn't mind me tagging along," he replied.

Narrowing her eyes slightly at him and giving him a wry smile she asked, "As a fellow colleague and not as a babysitter?"

He laughed and shook his head replying, "Strictly as a fellow colleague, I assure you. Other than the time we found Agent Neviah, I haven't had the opportunity to be with you when you've interviewed the spirits of our victims. I'm still fascinated with your ability and would like to join you if that's okay."

Nodding her head in agreement, Tori replied, "In that case, Goliath and I would enjoy your company."

"After your doctor clears you for travel," he cautioned.

"Absolutely!" she agreed. "So, what's next?"

"I think that's it for today," he admitted. "We've gone through all the evidence we have and have started working up the white board comparison of our victims."

"Well, why don't I make some calls and try to find out who returned Brady to Mrs. Albertson and you can do some digging on our mystery brunette," she suggested.

"Sounds like a plan, let's do it!" he agreed.

Chapter 5

Sarah pushed the last box on top of the others and then stepped back to stretch out her back. "Whew! Last one! And just in time. I don't think my back could have handled much more!"

"I told you to let Dad do all the lifting, Mom!" Aubrey chastised as her spirit shimmered semi-transparently beside her mother.

"It's not fair to expect him to do everything, honey," Sarah assured. "A couple of ibuprofen before bed and I promise I'll be fine."

Aubrey looked at the stacks of boxes along the wall of the room and asked, "So what are you going to do with all of this stuff from Meda's house?"

"Well," Sarah paused, thinking. "This is all the historical documentation Meda had about both hers and our lineage to the Archangel Remiel. We need to preserve this for Tori and her family. For now, we'll keep it here in the loft apartment above your father's office, until we have a more permanent place for it."

"What about the house in Hereford? Meda left everything to you, right?" Aubrey asked.

Sarah nodded and replied, "Yes, she did. We were her only remaining family, God rest her soul. For now, your dad and I agreed to keep the house. It's a beautiful location, and the house is paid for and fully furnished, so all we need to do is pay taxes and the occasional maintenance. Besides, it will be like having a vacation home when we want a change in scenery."

"Good. I like it there. Being there makes me feel closer to Meda, Karla and Tobias; like they're still with us. I miss them, Mom," Aubrey admitted sadly.

"I know you do, sweetheart. I miss them too," Sarah agreed.

"What do you think happened to Karla and Meda once they crossed over? Do you think there's a special place in heaven for Remy's children?" Aubrey asked curiously.

Sarah shrugged and replied, "I honestly don't know, honey. Agent Sullivan believes that since Remiel had an agreement with God to be cast out of heaven along with Lucifer, in hopes of bringing the fallen angels back to Him; it's possible that we, as daughters of Remiel, and the special abilities we were given using the statue and the amulet, might mean we'll have those same abilities when we cross over. I personally feel that just going to heaven is reward enough. I wouldn't think we should be given any special treatment than anyone else. But since we don't have any proof one way or the other, we'll just have to wait and see. Why do you ask?"

Aubrey hesitated for a moment and said, "Do you ever feel like there should be more to our lives that what we have?"

"What do you mean, sweetheart?" Sarah frowned.

"Well, for years, while my body was hidden in Mr. Cole's basement, all I knew was my spirit was still here, trapped on earth and I didn't feel like I had a purpose. I was just there. Then after Tori found me and I saw you and Dad again, I thought maybe the reason I didn't leave was because I was meant to be with you again, you know? Not just to have closure before I went to heaven, but maybe that was only part of it?"

Sarah nodded. "And?" she encouraged.

"And then we met Meda and Karla and discovered that we had a whole other family we never knew about, and we're part of this big prophecy and descendants from an Archangel that is still here on earth and can appear to us at will. It's all so random yet at the same time, not. Does that make any sense?" Aubrey asked.

"Yes. It does sound very surreal when you hear it spoken out loud, which is why we don't talk about it around others outside of the family and certain people from the FBI and Agent Hunter's team," Sarah replied.

"I get that," Aubrey agreed. "But since Meda and Karla are gone and now it's just you and Tori; she's the only one left to carry on the lineage of Remiel through her children. It just feels like that can't be all there is. Does it seem that way to you? Don't you ever think about another purpose to us being here that we haven't discovered yet?"

"What do you mean? I'm not sure I'm following you, honey," Sarah asked, puzzled.

Aubrey ran her hands through her hair in frustration, and her image began floating around the room as she spoke. "I mean me, Mom! Is this all there is for me? Was that all there was for Karla before she decided to cross over with her parents? If we're part of this great prophecy, then when do I get to play my part in it? I didn't even know I was part of this whole thing until two years ago when Remy made contact with Tori. I want to know more, be more than I am right now! There has to be something more than this for me!"

Sarah's face fell into despair as she realized she could neither embrace nor comfort her daughter. "Oh, sweetie, I wish I knew what to do or say to help answer your questions! I know you feel you were dealt a bad hand, and I'll admit, those years when you were gone, and we had no idea what happened to you were the darkest days of my life! I was so angry at God, and I shut myself off from your sister and your father. Believe me, I wish I could undo all of it so you never would have gone through any of that."

"We all know it was my fault," Aubrey interrupted. "If I hadn't been such a brat and snuck out of the house that night, none of this would have happened."

"We don't know if that's true, honey," Sarah replied, softly. "If it was truly meant to happen, it would have whether it was that night or another one. What matters is here and now. I am so thankful for these past two years, sweetheart. It's been an answer to my prayers, having had this time with you, even under the circumstances. You don't have to go until you are ready."

"I know, Mom," Aubrey whispered, her eyes brimming with tears. "I haven't given up, I promise. I'm not ready to go yet."

Sarah smiled at her daughter and replied, "Good because I'm not ready for you to go yet either. All I can say is to try to be patient, honey. We're all learning about our roles in the prophecy and there are many questions we just don't have the answers to right now. I do believe that God will reveal those answers to us when He's ready. Okay? We just have to be patient. Can you do that?"

"Yeah, I guess," Aubrey relented.

"Honey, I could use a hand down here," Tanner called out from the bottom of the stairs.

"Oh my goodness, I forgot about your father!" Sarah laughed apologetically. "You're okay if I go help him?"

"Yeah, I'm fine," Aubrey murmured.

"I'm on my way sweetheart!" Sarah called out, rushing from the room.

Surrounded in silence, Aubrey looked around the room, wishing there was something she could do to help her parents. "I hate feeling so useless," she grumbled out loud to no one in particular.

As her eyes continued to wander, they stopped at the hall table where her mother had set her purse and a small notepad and pencil. Slowly approaching the table, she looked down at the pencil and focused all of her concentration on it. "Okay, since I have nothing else to do, let's try this again. Practice makes perfect," she declared, fiercely as the pencil slowly began to move.

Chapter 6

Reagan shielded her eyes with her hand from the morning sun as she glanced at the row of canoes and kayaks lying along the sand in front of the small rental station.

"What exactly are you hoping to find here that our other agents weren't able to, sir?" she asked curiously.

Agent Hunter looked around them, surveying the tree line and replied, "I'm not convinced we have the proper point of origin where our shooter was positioned. I wanted to see the area for myself to be sure."

"What makes you think the calculation is off?" she frowned. "The estimated range and condition of the bullet seemed consistent with what we've seen in the past."

"True," he agreed, "however the angle of the wound was not consistent with what we've seen in the past. The coroner stated that the angle of the wound indicated the bullet entered the body at an eighteen-degree angle."

"Right," Reagan nodded, "which would indicate that the shooter was approximately five hundred feet away and about a twenty-five-foot elevation."

Agent Hunter smiled at her, knowingly and asked, "Are you sure about that, Agent Nichols? What about the Rifleman's Rule?"

Reagan rolled her eyes and chuckled lightly. "You mean the one that states a rifleman needs to accurately calculate not only the usual forces acting upon a projectile like gravity, drag, and wind; but also horizontal and vertical elevations?"

His smile broadened, pleased with her answer. "Exactly," he stated.

Reagan frowned again as she thought about what she'd said and then turned back to the tree line along the jogging path. "Wait," she paused, debating.

"Whenever you're ready," Agent Hunter smiled patiently.

As her mind raced through the calculations in her head, Reagan gasped, and she turned back to her mentor with a surprised look. "They had the wrong tree!"

Nodding in confirmation, Agent Hunter replied, "They had the wrong tree." Scanning the tree-line and doing a bit of math of his own in his head, he suggested, "Let's talk this through and see if we come to the same conclusion. Shall we?"

"Okay," Reagan agreed.

"Where exactly was the victim found?" he asked.

Reagan opened her notebook and reviewed the report details she had pulled up on the screen. "The GPS coordinates of that location are 38° 13.692119' by -85° 13.323784'."

Entering the numbers into an app on his phone, Agent Hunter leaned over towards Reagan, looked down at the screen to confirm the coordinates and began walking forward slowly. When he reached the destination, he looked at the spot in the path around them and then back towards the tree line. "This should be the spot where they found the body."

Following his line of sight, Reagan scanned the trees until she saw the red marker and then pointed towards the tree. "There's the tree the assessment team noted as being the location where the shooter was positioned."

"All right," he confirmed as he reached into his jacket pocket and pulled out a neon yellow evidence marker. Placing it on the path by his feet, he stood upright and began walking toward the trees. "Let's go."

As they walked, they mentally paced off the distance between the marker and the tree and when they reached the base, they turned to one another and confirmed their estimate.

"Four hundred eighty-six," she stated firmly.

Agent Hunter smiled and replied, "My feet are a bit longer than yours, so I'm right at four hundred ninety-four. Close enough."

They both looked upwards at the red marker twenty feet above them and surveyed the base of the trunk and a large branch, big enough to support a grown man.

Allowing her time to re-evaluate her original calculations, Agent Hunter began looking beyond the tree for a more suitable option.

Scrolling through the report pages on her notepad, Reagan furrowed her brow in frustration. "We don't have any information on the weather the day of the murder."

"It was a morning almost identical to this one," he replied casually.

She snorted a laugh, shaking her head and muttered, "Of course you already checked that."

"So...," he prompted.

"So...," she sighed looking back and forth between the tree and the yellow marker on the path, "the height from that branch, along with the distance to the marker, doesn't work. Especially after taking into account the downward gravitational acceleration of the bullet along with the proportional force against velocity. I don't see how the bullet could have entered the body at an eighteen-degree angle. We would need a taller tree."

"I agree," he replied.

Scanning the remaining trees before them, Reagan spotted one in particular and frowned again, thinking. "Well, the next tallest tree able to come anywhere near that trajectory would be that oak tree over there. But that's almost another five hundred yards away!"

"And why does that surprise you?" he asked.

"Well, that would mean the shooter would have fired from almost a thousand yards away; which would mean we're not talking about the average hunter here. We're looking for someone like Piper. Or at least someone with military experience, like a sniper."

Reagan turned back to Agent Hunter and noticed the lack of surprise on his face. "But you've already thought about that, haven't you?" she added grimly.

Agent Hunter shrugged and shook his head slowly, "I'm not ruling anything out. Don't let frustration cloud your thinking. We've seen people in our team, yes specifically Piper, who are true marksmen at that distance, but that doesn't mean the person we're looking for has had any sniper training or military experience. For now, we have to keep the options open. In the meantime, let's take a look at that tree and see if we've guessed correctly."

As they approached the large oak tree, Reagan walked around the base of the trunk and as suspected, about three feet off the ground, she saw two small chips missing from the bark. "This is it. These are spur climber marks. Look — you can see two of them, about two feet apart, every couple feet going up the trunk."

"Good eye, Agent Nichols," he commended. "What else do you see?"

Reagan craned her head upwards, but the shadows from the branches overhead made it difficult to see how far up the marks went. Retrieving a pair of binoculars from her bag, she focused the lenses and scanned the vertical field. Repositioning her stance around the trunk, she checked three times and announced, "I see the last set of marks right at the large bough with the circular knot at the base. Do you see it?"

Agent Hunter nodded and replied, "Yes, I see it. Looks like about sixty or seventy feet up. Would you agree?"

"That looks about right," she confirmed.

Realizing there was little more they could do at this point, Agent Hunter removed his cell phone from his pocket and initiated a call.

"Who are you calling?" she asked curiously.

He held up a finger as the call connected and said, "Hello may I speak to Sheriff Wallace, please? Yes. Please tell him Agent Gabriel Hunter from the FBI is calling."

While he waited for the call to transfer, he placed his hand over the speaker and advised Reagan, "I contacted the Sheriff before we arrived to let him know we would be visiting the crime scene and told him I would let him know of any new developments."

Reagan looked at him with a puzzled expression and said, "But we don't really have any new developments yet, do we? Other than this tree and the spur marks?"

He winked at her humorously and asked, "Are you prepared to climb this tree and look for evidence?"

Craning her neck upward again, she shook her head and admitted, "Actually no. No, I'm not."

"I didn't think so," he chuckled removing his hand from the phone. "Hello, Sheriff Wallace! It's Gabriel Hunter from the FBI calling. Yes, it's nice to speak with you again as well. I hope I haven't caught you at a bad time."

Pausing to hear the Sheriff's reply, he continued. "Good. Glad to hear it. I was wondering if you wouldn't mind meeting me at the park where the body of Wade Hackett was found. Yes, right now. Oh, and if you could also bring a few of your officers along with some tree climbing equipment, that would be extremely helpful."

Pausing again, he smiled at Reagan and added, "Yes sir you heard me correctly. I said tree climbing equipment. Does your local fire department have a truck with an extended ladder?"

Trying to imagine hearing both sides of the conversation, Reagan chuckled as Agent Hunter added, "Oh I would guess about seventy feet high. Yes, you heard me correctly."

Chapter 7

Enjoying the rare opportunity of being completely alone, Tori sighed contentedly from her reclined position on the couch and pulled another pretzel stick from the bag beside her. Dipping the pretzel into the bowl of ice cream resting on her stomach, she angled the stick strategically, trying to get as even of a ratio of caramel sauce and ice cream on the stick as possible.

Just as she had the perfect scoop and was about to take a bite, she heard the sound of Ben and Goliath returning from their walk. Pausing in mid-air, she realized she wouldn't be able to move quick enough to hide the evidence, so instead she took a bite and savored the beautiful blend of flavor she had accomplished while she watched the door, waiting for it to open.

"Here we go, buddy," Ben announced as he pushed the door open, removing his key from the lock.

Noticing Tori on the couch, Goliath eyed the bag beside her and quickly rushed in ahead of Ben to see what she was eating.

"Goliath treat?" she heard him ask as he looked at the bag of pretzels expectantly while wagging his tail.

She laughed, reached her hand into the bag and extended a pretzel towards him. "Seriously Goliath, do you practice that face in the mirror when we're not here? You are so cute! I absolutely cannot resist you when you do that!"

"Thank you," she heard him reply as he gently opened his mouth and took the pretzel from her. Hardly chewing it, he swallowed and continued staring at the bag.

Ben set his keys on the hallway table and walked over to greet her. "Hi!" Looking down at the bowl, he raised his eyebrows in surprise. "Really, ice cream and pretzels? That's what you came up with for breakfast today?" he teased.

"Actually my first thought was a chocolate shake and a large order of fries but I was too lazy to get dressed and drive around town trying to find a place open this early that serves non-breakfast food. Then I thought salted caramel pretzel ice cream. We didn't have any of that either, so I dug around in the pantry and got lucky! So I decided to be creative and came up with this!" she applauded herself. "It's delicious!"

Ben grinned and sat down beside her. "Okay, You sold me, I'm curious. My hands are dirty, may I try a bite?"

Recreating the pretzel to ice cream to caramel ratio she achieved earlier, she held a pretzel up to Ben and watched his face eagerly as he took a bite.

"Wow, okay," he mumbled as he chewed. "That is seriously good! Although I feel like I still have to point out that it's not the healthiest thing you should be eating for breakfast." Stopping in mid-chew, he stared at Tori in surprise and swallowed hard. "Wait. Did those words just come out of my mouth? What have you done to me, woman! You're always the one correcting me on my poor eating habits! What's going on?"

Tori laughed and patted his arm, comfortingly. "Don't worry, your secret's safe with me. I won't tell if you don't."

"It better be," he frowned. "I have a reputation to keep up you know."

"Uh huh," Tori eyed him speculatively, laughing. Handing him the now nearly empty bowl, she asked, "Here, Mr. Bad Influence, will you hold this and help me up?"

"Of course," he replied, taking the bowl from her with one hand and pulling her up from the couch with the other.

Temporarily off balance, Tori braced herself against Ben's shoulder and growled in annoyance. "Man! It's getting harder to get out of that couch lately! Thanks!"

"You're welcome, beautiful," he smiled, taking advantage of her proximity to kiss her gently on the lips.

Glancing down at her midriff, she slowly rubbed her hand over the growing mound of her belly and asked, "I'm really starting to show lately, aren't I? Do you think I'm starting to show too much too soon?"

Ben's face froze, knowing he had just heard a trick question. He glanced down at the bowl in his hand, realizing if he replied, he was a dead man. Since there was no way he was going to make it out of this conversation alive, he quietly turned around and headed for the kitchen.

"Hey, I caught that," she cried out, following him.

"I have no idea what you're talking about!" he replied innocently, as he rinsed the bowl and spoon in the sink.

"Coward," she laughed as she returned the bag of pretzels to the pantry. "I'm serious. These cravings are insane! I'm already thinking about what I want for lunch!"

Still cautious of saying the wrong thing, he motioned to the clock on the stove and carefully noted, "Uh, shouldn't we be leaving for the office soon?"

Tori drew in a surprised breath when she noticed the time. "Oh! I didn't realize it was already so late. I'll be ready in twenty minutes!" she promised as she rushed from the room.

"No worries, babe," he chuckled, quietly; proud of himself for somehow managing to come out of the discussion without a single mark.

~~~~~~~~~~

Just shy of a half hour later, Ben was sitting at the kitchen table eating breakfast, and staring intently at the screen on his laptop when Tori emerged from the bedroom.

"What are you working on over there so quietly?" she teased as she came up behind him and wrapped her arms around his shoulders. "Ooh! Is that some of the stuffed French toast that you made the other day? How did I forget that was in the fridge?"

"You got me started with that ice cream earlier, and it made me crave something sweet. Then I remembered we had a piece leftover! Do you want a bite before it's gone?"

"Umm, as tempted as I am by the smell of the cinnamon and maple syrup, no thanks," Tori replied. "I'm still full from the ice cream. I really liked it though. Maybe we can make it again this weekend. Did it take long to make?"

Ben shook his head and replied, "Honestly no. All you do is cube some bread, layer it in the bottom of a pan, cut two rectangles of cream cheese into cubes and layer that on top, and then add another layer of bread. Then you mix a dozen eggs with cinnamon, maple syrup, and milk; pour it over the bread and the cheese and let it soak in the fridge overnight. Then you bake it the next day for about an hour, and it's done."

"Wow! That is a pretty easy recipe! Let's plan that for Saturday morning," Tori suggested.

"Can we have bacon too?" Ben pleaded with a hopeful smile.

Tori laughed and agreed, "Fine. You can have bacon too!"

"It's a deal!" Ben cheered.

"Seriously what are you working on?" Tori asked, looking over at the monitor screen.

Glancing quickly around them he whispered, "Where's 'you know who'?"

"G?" she quietly asked, using hers and Ben's code name for Goliath, so he didn't know they were talking about him.

Ben nodded, looking towards the bedroom.

"He's out cold on the floor by the bed," she whispered. "Why, what's going on?"

"I found them," Ben said in a low voice, giving her an intense look.

Tori drew in a surprised breath and whispered, "Are you serious – them as in G's former family?"

Angling the laptop screen for her to see, Ben nodded and quietly replied, "Here they are; the Cutler family."

"Cutler," she murmured, reviewing the page he had pulled up on his screen. "Nice job! And you're one hundred percent sure it's them?"

Ben nodded and affirmed, "It's definitely them. A family of three; husband, wife, and daughter, killed in a house fire a little over a year and a half ago in Pikeville, Kentucky. Investigators concluded the fire was accidental and due to a faulty gas line."

"Yeah, well we know better than that thanks to Goliath," Tori argued as she read. "So how come it took you so long to find them?"

"Well, first of all, I'm not internet-girl like you who can find anything. Plus, it was a little trickier than I originally thought it was going to be," Ben admitted. "The father's name, Sam or Samuel as I assumed, actually ended up being a middle name. The father's name was Patrick Samuel, but his father was also a Patrick Samuel so instead of going by Patrick Jr. or Pat, he preferred to be called Sam."

"What about the mother and the daughter?" Tori asked, as she sat down on the chair beside Ben and began scrolling down the page.

"Ashlyn, the wife, isn't as common, and it doesn't seem to be shortened from anything, so her name was constant in the search filters," Ben admitted. "What became challenging was Mandy. I was searching for a child named Amanda because that's what I thought Mandy was a shortened version of but as it turns out, it's also a shortened name for Miranda. So once I added that name to the filter, I found them!"

"What happened to their bodies afterward?" Tori asked.

"Ashlyn's sister took care of the funeral arrangements," Ben replied. "They were all buried together in a family plot at a small cemetery outside of Pikeville."

"Mandy Cutler," Tori whispered, thinking back to the dream she had several months ago of a little red-haired girl riding on Goliath's back. "Wait, is this their picture?"

"Yes," Ben confirmed.

Tori frowned and looked at Ben, confused. "But the picture of this little girl is blonde."

"So?" Ben asked, puzzled.

"So remember my dream? The little girl in my dream had red hair, not blonde," she replied.

Ben smiled and gently rubbed his hand up and down Tori's arm. "Sweetie, didn't you also say the little girl in your dream had green eyes and called you 'Mama'?"

Tori blinked as the realization hit her. "Oh," she breathed, absently rubbing her belly. "You think that was....."

"Couldn't it be?" he asked gently.

"But I've never had visions that far ahead before. They've always been present day or memories of the past," she argued.

"Your gifts are continually evolving all the time, honey," Ben reminded her. "Once you claimed ownership of the statue and the amulet; invoking your part in the prophecy, the era of the enlightenment began. Even Remy agreed. Since you are the first of his descendants in many generations to have possession of both items, we have no idea yet what that means or what will happen."

61

"True," she conceded. "But why that dream? Why that particular vision if it wasn't Mandy?"

"I don't know, Tor. I guess we'll just have to wait and see," Ben admitted.

Glancing back at the laptop, she asked, "So what do we do now that you've found them?"

"Well, we agreed that we would tell Agent Hunter when we found them before planning anything, so let's tell him what we found today and see what he thinks," Ben suggested.

"Do you think he would let us pursue this on our own?" she wondered.

"He probably won't while we're actively working a case but maybe afterward when the case is closed. It's worth asking," he reasoned.

Tori nodded and agreed, "Okay. But let's not tell 'G' yet. Not until we have a plan. I don't want to get his hopes up."

"Agreed," Ben replied. "We have to get going. I'm going to power down my laptop and get packed up. Do you want to wake Sleeping Beauty?"

Tori laughed and replied, "Sure, I'll get him."

Chapter 8

When Ben, Tori, and Goliath arrived at the FBI office in Quantico, in typical Goliath fashion, all of the garbage cans between the front door and the conference room were thoroughly examined and purged of any food items along the way. Fortunately, Ben and Tori had planned ahead for their companion's ritual, so they arrived just in time as the team was sitting down at the table.

"Good morning!" Tori greeted, as they entered the room.

"Good morning Agent Cooper, Agent Vincent," Agent Hunter replied, pleasantly. Glancing down at Goliath he added, "Goliath."

"Good morning, sir!" Tori heard in response.

"Goliath said good morning, sir," she advised.

"Good morning," Riley nodded.

"Hi!" Reagan greeted.

"Hey, guys!" Logan waved from across the table.

"Well don't the three of you look like a happy little family?" Piper smiled, enjoying the bright, colorful aura's surrounding her friends. "Come here, you big, beautiful boy," she encouraged Goliath, who eagerly approached her.

Taking his massive face in her hands, she began to rub his head and ears, rendering him helpless to do anything than succumb to her power over him. "How is my sweet, sweet boy today?" she cooed softly.

"Goliath loves Piper," Tori heard him contentedly sigh.

"He says he loves you," Tori laughed, as Goliath's eyes closed, enraptured.

"I love you too, Goliath," Piper giggled. She looked up as Tori approached the chair beside her, and quietly studied her friend as she sat down.

"What?" Tori asked, catching the look.

"There's something different about you today," Piper replied, concentrating on the air around Tori.

Concerned, Tori asked, "Different how? Do you see the darkness again? I don't feel anything if you do and Goliath isn't acting like Luc is nearby."

Hearing Luc's name, Goliath's eyes opened, and he quickly looked around the room. *"Goliath does not feel the darkness near Tori."*

Patting Goliath's head to settle him, Piper quickly replied, "No, nothing like that. It's okay. Tori is fine, Goliath."

"What do you mean, Piper?" Ben asked, sitting beside Tori.

Looking back at Tori's aura, she squinted as she saw the colors changing and replied, "I'm not sure exactly. Tori's typical bright green aura is still there, but every once in a while, thin ribbons of yellow and violet circle around her and then they just disappear."

"What does that mean?" Tori asked curiously. "What do yellow and violet represent?"

"Well, the shade of light yellow I see usually represents emerging psychic or spiritual awareness, which is strange because I would have thought that color would have shown up a long time ago, especially when you claimed ownership of the statue and the amulet."

"Maybe it's a latent evolution of a new gift that's just now showing up?" offered Riley.

Piper shrugged and admitted, "I guess that's possible."

"What about violet? What does that mean?" Tori asked.

"That's the strange part, and I may have to do a bit of research on that one because I personally have never seen violet in an aura before. A violet aura is extremely rare. From what I've read, violet is the most intuitive of all colors and reveals complete psychic power," Piper replied.

"Complete psychic power? What's that supposed to mean?" Reagan asked.

"I'm not sure. Let me do some research to make sure I remember correctly," Piper admitted, directing her reply to Tori. "I don't want you to worry in the meantime, okay? Nothing that I'm seeing feels bad or evil. It's just different than normal. Okay?"

Not sensing anything negative from her friend, Tori smiled and nodded. "Okay, I promise I won't worry."

"Good," Piper smiled. "Besides, today's the big day isn't it? You're going in for your first sonogram, right?"

Tori's smile broadened, and she nodded. "Yes. My appointment is at three."

"That's so exciting!" Piper exclaimed, grabbing Tori's hand. "Promise me you'll call afterward and tell me how beautiful your little girl is!"

"Well we're guessing it's a girl," Ben reminded Piper.

"Right, of course," she agreed. "Either way, it will be wonderful!"

Tori squeezed Pipers hand and promised, "I will call you as soon as we're done."

"Thank you," Piper replied happily.

"We will all look forward to hearing from you, Agent Cooper. In the meantime, why don't we get started?"

Agent Hunter interrupted as everyone's attention turned to him.

"Of course, go ahead, sir," Tori replied.

"As you all know, Agent Nichols and I traveled to Shelbyville, Kentucky earlier this week and went back to the crime scene where Wade Hackett was murdered," he announced.

Tori glanced at Reagan, who nodded in agreement.

"While we were there," he continued, "we discovered some conflicting information from the original report that led us to reevaluate the details of the crime scene."

Tori frowned and looked back and forth between Reagan and Agent Hunter, puzzled. "What do you mean?"

"Would you like to explain, Agent Nichols?" he asked.

"Yes sir," Reagan replied, turning her attention to the rest of the team. "As we were recreating the crime scene, Agent Hunter reminded me of the conditions around the Rifleman's Rule and how you can't just estimate the distance of a gunshot based upon gravity, drag, and the wind; you also need to take into account horizontal and vertical elevations."

"I'm familiar with the concept," Tori nodded.

"Well," Reagan noted, "The coroner's initial determination was that the bullet entered the body at an eighteen-degree angle from a twenty-five-foot elevation. As we were standing in the exact spot where Wade Hackett was shot, we could not visualize the tree or any other structure that would have given the shooter that vantage point. At least not from the tree the police had marked as the shooters location."

"So what changed your mind?" Logan asked.

Reagan smirked and glanced at Piper. "As a matter of fact, it was Piper."

"Me?" Piper exclaimed. "What did I do?"

"You've been repeatedly hitting targets at close to fifteen hundred yards which technically puts you at the skill level of a military sniper," Reagan advised. "So we needed to consider the possibility that our shooter could be an advanced marksman and that the police had the wrong tree. After Agent Hunter and I recalculated the distance, we found the tree the shooter used."

"How do you know you had the right tree?" Ben asked.

"Because we found spur climber marks on the trunk of one tree, in particular, which went up every two feet up to a seventy-foot elevation," Reagan replied proudly. "And before you ask," Reagan added as Logan leaned forward and opened his mouth to speak, "the area is a state park where hunting is strictly prohibited so no, it couldn't have been used by a hunter."

Accepting her response as reasonable, Logan sat back in his chair and said, "Fair enough."

"And," Reagan paused as she reached into a box on the table in front of her, pulling out an evidence container, "We found this."

Tori squinted at the container and asked, "What is it? I don't see anything."

Handing the container to Tori, Reagan replied, "It's a hair that the forensics team found caught in a branch near the place the spur marks stopped. We were hoping it could be a hair from the shooter, and you could pick up something from it."

"I guess I could try," Tori agreed, "but it could also just be a hair that was picked up in the wind and snagged in the tree."

"We've considered that possibility," Agent Hunter admitted. "So we brought back one other item we would like you to try, after this one."

"Okay, let's give it a shot," Tori agreed as she tore open the seal from the container and removed a small plastic bag from inside. Breaking open the tape at the top of the bag, she held her right hand out and gently tipped the bag forward in her left hand.

Meanwhile, Logan, who hadn't yet had an opportunity to see Tori's gift in action, leaned forward anxiously in his chair, holding his breath.

As the hair landed in the center of Tori's palm, she slowly closed her hand and her eyes at the same time and drew in a deep breath.

The room became completely silent as everyone waited in anticipation for what would happen next.

A few moments later, Tori opened her eyes and let out a deep sigh. "Sorry boys and girls, there's no memory associated with this hair."

Disappointed, Reagan frowned and asked, "Nothing? Not even a twinge of any memory?"

Returning the hair to the evidence bag, Tori shrugged and said, "Nope."

"That is unfortunate," Agent Hunter frowned. "Agent Nichols, let's try the other item."

Reagan's eyes flickered over to a draped gurney in the corner of the room and cleared here throat, nervously.

"Okay," she replied, as she pushed her chair back and rose from the table. Glancing back at Tori she paused and said, "Now before you get upset because I know how much you love and appreciate nature, I want you to know that we really didn't have a choice other than bringing this particular piece of evidence to you. Obviously, since it was seventy feet high and in your condition, you wouldn't have been able to reach it."

Tori eyed the draped item in the corner and narrowed her eyes at Reagan, "What did you do?"

Walking over to the gurney, Reagan pulled away the drape, revealing a large section of a tree bough that must have weighed over a hundred pounds. "We brought you the bough we believe the shooter rested on when he made the shot."

Tori gasped in surprise as she noticed several smaller branches growing from the section of the tree, displaying several tender green leaves, now beginning to shrivel up at the ends. She looked accusingly between Reagan and Agent Hunter and exclaimed, "You cut down the tree?"

"N-n-not the entire tree," Reagan stammered. "Just the one bough, the rest of the tree is still standing!"

"But look at the size of that bough!" Tori exclaimed. "Where's the rest of the limb?"

"Uh, the Sheriff said something about taking it home and cutting it up for firewood," Reagan sheepishly admitted.

"Oh!" Tori exclaimed, throwing her hands up in the air. "That's just great! I hope he enjoys those beautiful fires next winter after it seasons!"

"Tor," Ben interrupted, gently touching her arm. "They didn't take down the whole tree. Come on, just give it a shot."

"Fine," Tori muttered with a pained expression, gently rubbing her hand over her stomach.

"What's wrong? Are you okay?" he asked, noticing her expression.

"It's just a kick," she admitted, smiling weakly. "My outburst must have woken her up."

"But you're okay?" he clarified.

"Yeah, I'm fine," she confirmed, touching his hand gently. Turning to Reagan and Agent Hunter, she added, "I'm sorry I got so upset. Let's see if all the effort was worth it."

Approaching the gurney slowly, she angled her body between the smaller branches, so she was as close to the base of the tree bough as possible. Turning her head to see the angle of the branch, she asked, "Is this the location where you think his feet would have rested?"

"Yes," Reagan agreed. "We think his feet were at the place your waist is now, and then a couple feet above you, where the bough splits to the left, might be where he would have placed his hands to balance himself."

"Okay," Tori replied, eyeing the approximate area Reagan described. Placing her hands in the general area, she pressed her palms against the bark and closed her eyes. Almost immediately, a shot of energy went through her body, and she drew in a sharp breath. "Bingo," she breathed as the images began flooding her mind. Meanwhile, no one in the room dared to move or say anything to risk breaking Tori's concentration.

Agent Hunter silently motioned to Piper, who nodded her head, indicating she was watching Tori's aura closely. As she had seen before when Tori read an item from a crime scene, the normal bright green band of energy surrounding her friend, began to display threads of blackness, swirling around her.

Once he felt Tori had a solid connection to the visions, Agent Hunter quietly asked, "Can you tell us what you see Agent Cooper?"

Inclining her head in the direction of his voice, Tori kept her eyes closed and in a calm, steady voice, she began to describe what she was seeing. "I'm sitting in the tree," she began. "I-I mean, he's sitting in the tree, I'm watching him," she corrected herself.

"Piper," Ben said quietly.

"There's a lot of darkness around her, but she still has control," she replied to everyone in a hushed tone.

Noticing that Tori's breathing was becoming more labored, Agent Hunter asked, "What else do you see? Is the person you're watching our shooter? Are they male or female?"

"Definitely male," Tori replied, panting slightly. "He's dressed in camouflage gear. Even the rifle is camouflaged. He's watching his mark; a man jogging along a path by a small lake."

"Do you see any determining landmarks or visuals to confirm where you are?" he urged.

"I see a small building, like a shack," she replied. "And there's a row of brightly colored canoes and kayaks by the shore of the lake. The lake is to the left; the jogging path is on the right by a row of trees."

"That's it," Reagan nodded.

"Are you picking up any thoughts or emotions from the man?" Agent Hunter continued to press her.

Tori's face darkened as the man's thoughts became clearer to her. "I'm feeling a lot of anger and confusion," she announced, beginning to feel her head hurt. "He's confused, almost disoriented. He's thinking Semper Fidelis repeatedly in his head."

"That's the motto of the United States Marine Corps," Reagan exclaimed.

Noticing Tori's labored breathing Agent Hunter looked at Piper again and asked, "Agent Stirling?"

"Her aura has gone almost completely black. I don't know how much longer she can remain in control, sir," Piper advised with concern.

"Should we pull her out?" Ben looked to Agent Hunter for direction.

"Not yet!" Tori cried out in frustration as a new series of images began to come to her. "The man jogging is Wade Hackett. I can see him clearly through the scope. Oh my goodness, this guy is so angry. He's cool as a cucumber on the outside but here in his head it's pure chaos."

Seeing all but a small thread of green energy remaining around Tori, Piper asked, "Tor, you're losing control. You need to pull back."

"I can't," Tori whispered, openly struggling as she felt herself getting pulled deeper into the visions.

"Okay, that's enough," Ben announced. "We need to break the connection."

"That could do more harm than good," warned Agent Hughes, equally concerned for Tori. "We don't know how that will affect Tor; I mean Agent Cooper."

An audible gasp from Piper interrupted the discussion as she stared at the air around Tori, amazed. "Wait!" She called out, extending her hands towards Ben.

"What is it? What's wrong?" he asked, ready to pull Tori's hands away from the tree.

"It's amazing!" Piper breathed as she noticed Tori's expression soften and her breathing begin to become less labored. "Do you feel it, Tor?" she asked.

"I do!" Tori smiled, her eyes still closed. "What is it?"

"I don't know," Piper admitted in awe.

"What's going on," Ben demanded.

"The bright yellow and violet threads of color I saw around Tori before," Piper announced. "They've become bigger! They've blended into Tori's green color, like a braid, and they're pushing away the blackness."

"So she's okay?" Ben hoped.

"More than okay," Piper laughed. "She's brilliant! And I mean on the outside! I've never seen this kind of color around anyone before!"

Agent Hunter regarded Tori, curiously and asked, "Are you in control, Agent Cooper?"

"Very much so sir," Tori confirmed, opening her eyes and removing her hands from the tree branch. "Whew! That was weird."

"Are you sure you're okay?" Ben asked as he placed his hand on her shoulder, comfortingly. "Wow!" he exclaimed, pulling his hand away.

"What?" Tori asked, looking down at her arm.

"You shocked me!" he replied with a surprised look, rubbing his fingers.

Piper walked over to Tori and watched as the bands of yellow and violet once again receded and only the green energy around her remained. Gently placing her hand on Tori's arm and feeling no shock, she asked, "How do you feel now?"

Tori blinked and replied, "I feel great! I was starting to feel the beginning of a headache, but now it's gone!"

"What's going on?" Logan exclaimed, totally blown away by what he just saw.

Looking around the room at everyone's calm expressions except Logan's; Tori eyed him humorously and sarcastically replied, "Welcome to the freak show, Logan!"

"Well I have told you on many occasions that I think you're completely crazy," Reagan chuckled as she sang out the last word.

"And yet you still admit to others that you're my friend," Tori teased back.

"Yeah, well," Reagan shrugged as she reached over to the chair beside her and closed Logan's gaping mouth. "Careful there or a bug might fly in."

"What was all that just now?" Logan asked, looking around the room. "Did all that just really happen?"

"Really, really, buddy," Ben replied, patting Logan on the back as he sat down in the chair beside his friend. "We tried to warn you when you joined the team that ours was a special unit of carefully selected individuals."

"Well, honestly I thought you were making all that stuff up! When you said special individual, I had no idea you meant this!" Logan exclaimed. Turning to Ben, he narrowed his eyes and studied Ben's face carefully. "So what do you do? Turn into a werewolf during a full moon or something?"

Ben wiggled his eyebrows ominously back at Logan and whispered, "I guess you'll have to wait for the next full moon to find out, won't you?"

"Let's get back on track," Agent Hunter advised, reigning the discussion back in. Turning to Tori, he asked, "What do you remember? Did you pick up other images that could help us with our investigation?"

Tori blew out a deep breath and ran her hands through her hair, thinking back. "Gosh, where do I start? I guess I'll start with the last memory and work backward. That would probably be easier. Agent Hughes, do you want to man the board and make some notes?"

Riley immediately jumped from his chair, picked up a dry erase marker from the tray and replied, "Ready when you are!"

"Okay," Tori paused, organizing her thoughts. "The images that I saw were very fragmented and chaotic, but at the same time, I had a sense that at one time, this guy was very disciplined and organized. He kept thinking Semper Fidelis, and as Reagan noted, that's the motto of the United States Marine Corps – always faithful. He feels very strongly that his belief in that motto has been compromised, and he's punishing people for not upholding it."

"Did you get the impression that he personally knew Wade Hackett?" Agent Hughes wondered.

"I think he did," Tori admitted. "This wasn't some random sniper in the trees, picking off joggers at a state park. This guy knew who he was aiming at and timed his moves very carefully. He watched Mr. Hackett for some time. He knew his routine, and he planned the shooting very carefully."

"What else did you pick out?" Agent Hunter inquired.

Tori looked at Riley and asked, "Agent Hughes, remember the day we were going through those evidence boxes?

When I picked up the leash and mentioned a Dalmatian associated to the memories on the leash of Mr. Albertson from LaGrange?"

Riley nodded his head and replied, "Yes, I remember. Mr. Albertson's dog was a black lab named Brady, and you recalled seeing Mr. Albertson talking to a dark haired woman with a Dalmatian. Why? What did you see just now?"

"I believe our shooter also knew the woman with the Dalmatian," Tori advised.

"Well, that would make sense considering both of our victims were killed with what we believe to be the same gun. The ballistic reports are a complete match," Reagan pointed out.

"In my vision, the Dalmatian came to the man obediently when called. The dog recognized him, and the man was petting him," Tori replied.

"Which could mean he also knew the dark-haired woman," Riley surmised, seeing where Tori's point was headed.

"What do you mean Agent Hughes?" Agent Hunter asked, not seeing the connection.

"Agent Cooper recalled seeing a woman with dark hair walking a Dalmatian, at the same times when Mr. Albertson, our first victim, would walk his dog, Brady," Riley replied, pointing out the notes on the board under Mr. Albertson's name. "The encounters began informally, passing each other during those walks, however at some point their meetings became more casual and they seemed to be meeting each other in certain locations, both walking their dogs."

"Do you think they were having an affair?" Piper asked.

"No, I didn't see or feel anything that led me to think they were having a physical relationship. I had the impression that the woman was very sad about something, and he was comforting her," Tori replied.

"Mr. Albertson was the manager of the local grocery store in LaGrange, wasn't he?" Reagan asked.

"Yes," Riley replied.

"Maybe they knew each other, and they were friends," she suggested.

"That's what we considered as well," Riley agreed as his glance stopped on Goliath, who was sleeping on the floor beside Tori's chair. Turning to Tori, he asked, "Did you ever find out who found Brady after the shooting?"

Tori nodded and replied, "I spoke with the detective working the case, and he said Brady remained with Mr. Albertson's body until Mrs. Albertson, and the coroner showed up. Then a neighbor came by and took Brady to their house while Mrs. Albertson went with the police."

"Why is that significant?" Agent Hunter asked curiously.

"It was a hunch we both had that didn't play out," Riley admitted.

"So who is the mysterious dark haired woman with the Dalmatian?" Logan asked.

"That is one of our open questions," Riley noted, pointing to the notation on the board. "Anyone want to pick this one up and start digging?"

"I'll do it," Logan offered. "I could use a little solid fact-finding work after what I've seen today."

"Sold to the non-believer at the end of the table," Riley announced, noting Logan's initials beside the comment.

Piper stifled a giggle as she caught Agent Hunter casting a stern look in Agent Hughes's direction.

"Is there anything else you remember, Agent Cooper?" Agent Hunter asked patiently.

"Other than the feeling this guy is broken, no," Tori sighed, meeting his gaze. "Do you know anyone suffering from PTSD, sir?"

Agent Hunter raised his chin, proudly and admitted, "I have a few friends, former Marines whom I served with who have been diagnosed with the condition. Why do you ask?"

"Because I really don't know that much about it and maybe I should. I'm wondering if the brokenness I'm feeling from this man and the sense that he may be former military means he's suffering from PTSD and needs help," she admitted sadly.

"If he is, he's still a murderer, Agent Cooper," he reminded her calmly.

"I know that sir," Tori replied. "You of all people have taught me that not everything is black and white, and we need to remember there are gray areas that may tell another side of the story we don't know."

Smiling proudly at her as a father would, he nodded his head and replied, "I'll reach out to a couple of my friends and see if any of them would be willing to talk to you."

Tori nodded and smiled, "Thank you, sir."

Chapter 9

"So are we done for today?" Piper asked, hopefully. "It's getting close to lunchtime."

"Yeah, I could eat," Ben admitted.

"Shocker," Tori whispered, laughing. Ben winked and laughed with her.

"That's all I had scheduled for today. Does anyone else have anything they wanted to discuss?" Agent Hunter asked the group.

"Oh, shoot! That reminds me!" Tori immediately replied, grabbing her phone. "Just give me one minute, Agent Hunter. There's one more thing I wanted to ask you."

Opening text window on her phone, Tori quickly typed and sent the following message.

Tori: Hey, Piper. Would you mind taking Goliath outside for a few minutes? Ben and I have news about his family but don't want him to hear what we've found out yet. I'll explain later...

Hearing the vibration from her phone of an incoming message, Piper looked down at the device and picked it up. She frowned at first when she saw the message was from Tori, but after reading the text, her expression relaxed. Briefly looking up and making eye contact with Tori, she typed her response.

Piper: Sure, no problem!

Walking over to the spot beside Tori's chair where Goliath was sleeping, Piper reached down and began gently petting him on his side. "Hey big guy, do you have to go outside? Would you like to go for a walk, Goliath?"

Immediately, Goliath's eyes opened, and he jumped up to his feet.

"Walk?" Tori heard him excitedly ask. He looked up at Tori, making sure she was okay with him leaving. *"Goliath go outside with Piper?"*

Patting him affectionately on the head, Tori laughed and replied, "Yes, it's okay Goliath. You can go outside with Piper."

"Yay!" He replied, bounding happily from the room.

"Hey, wait up Goliath!" Piper called out, laughing, as she chased after him.

Riley chuckled, watching Piper attempt to catch the large dog and turned to the group questioningly, "I think I'll grab some fresh air too as long as your question to Agent Hunter doesn't require my involvement?"

Tori shook her head and replied, "No go ahead. Ben found out some information about Goliath's family that we wanted to run by Agent Hunter. We're just not ready to tell Goliath yet."

"Ah, understood," Riley nodded. "Is there anything else you need from me, sir?" he asked Agent Hunter.

"No. Thank you, Agent Hughes. We're done here," he agreed.

"I guess we'll see you guys later," Logan announced, getting up from the table, slowly heading towards the door. "Call me later, Ben."

"I will," Ben waved as Logan left.

"Let me know how it goes today," Reagan whispered, gently touching Tori's shoulder as she passed by.

"I will," Tori smiled.

Once the others left the room and only Tori, Ben and Agent Hunter remained, they took adjacent seats at the end of the table facing each other.

"Why don't you go ahead and share what you found, Ben," Tori encouraged.

"Okay!" he quickly replied, reaching over to grab his laptop.

Plugging the device into the overhead projector, he opened a document and displayed it on the screen. "It took some digging, but I finally found Goliath's family," he began, giving Agent Hunter time to read what was on the screen. "They were Patrick, or Sam as he preferred to be called; Ashlyn and Miranda Cutler. The little girl's nickname was Mandy, but her full name was Miranda."

"Like your wife," Tori smiled.

"Quite the coincidence," Agent Hunter noted, smiling back.

"Agreed," admitted Ben. "The Cutler's were killed in a house fire a little over a year and a half ago in Pikeville, Kentucky. There was a full investigation of the fire, and it was concluded to have been accidental, due to a faulty gas line."

"Which we know is incorrect, based on what Goliath has told Agent Cooper," Agent Hunter surmised.

"Correct," Ben nodded.

"Since we agreed not to do anything before discussing how to proceed with you, we wanted to see what your initial thoughts are," Tori added, hopefully.

Agent Hunter scanned the rest of the page and sat back in his chair, considering the next course of action. "Do you know where their bodies are located now?" he asked.

"In a cemetery outside of Pikeville," Tori replied.

"And you have copies of both the coroners and police reports for me to review in more length?" he asked.

"Yes, sir," Ben confirmed.

"Does the police report go into detail about Mr. Cutler's job or anything that appeared as if the police were looking at any suspects initially, or does it appear that they thought it was accidental from the beginning and it was an open and shut case?" Agent Hunter asked.

"Interesting you asked that," Ben noted as he opened another document to the screen. "Detective Drew Daniels was the investigating officer on the case, and as you can see in that top section of the page noting people they talked to during the investigation, he had questions about a man named Pierce Andrews, who worked with Sam Cutler. He was never able to find any concrete evidence against him, but his gut seemed to keep telling him to look at that guy."

"And all the information related to Mr. Andrews is in your information as well?" Agent Hunter asked.

"Yes, sir," Ben nodded.

"So for the time being, there isn't a rush to make any arrangements to see the Cutlers?" Agent Hunter stated.

Disappointed where the discussion was leading, Tori shook her head and frowned, "No sir."

Seeing her reaction, Agent Hunter sighed and leaned forward in his chair. "I'm not saying no, Agent Cooper, just not right now. We're in the middle of an investigation and for the time being, that takes priority. There is no urgency to act upon this information about Goliath's family at this time."

"Yes sir," Tori agreed, meeting his eyes. "I understand."

"Do you?" he stressed. "I don't want you or anyone else from the team, mainly Piper, coming up with another loophole in something I've said, making you think you can go off on your own and follow up on this lead. I need to know I can trust you to honor my decision to wait."

Tori snorted a laugh and smiled at him sheepishly, "I promise I will honor your decision and not do anything until you've said it's okay."

"Very good," he replied. Turning to Ben, he added, "Nice work, Agent Vincent. It looks like some of Agent Cooper's knack for navigating the internet is rubbing off on you."

"Thank you, sir," Ben smiled. "And thank you for listening."

"You're welcome. I promise we'll circle back to this again and discuss how we want to proceed once we've completed this case. In the meantime, please forward me what you've found and I'll look at it in more detail later, okay?"

"Yes, sir. I'll do that," Ben agreed.

"Now, if I'm not mistaken, your appointment with the doctor is at three today, right?" he asked them both.

"Yes!" they replied in unison.

Chuckling good-naturedly, Agent Hunter pointed towards the door and ordered, "Good. Then have a nice relaxing lunch and good luck at your appointment. Miranda keeps reminding me to let her know if she'll be buying lots of pink as we suspect! She's as excited about this baby as I'm sure both of your folks are!"

"Oh, my mom has gone totally overboard, believe me," Tori laughed. "She's already started shopping!"

"Her and my mom both," Ben grinned, rubbing Tori's back affectionately.

"I bet," Agent Hunter replied, rising from his chair. "I'll look forward to hearing from you."

"Thank you, sir," Tori replied, giving him a quick wave as he left the room.

Turning back to Ben, she met his eyes and smiled sadly. "Well, we gave it a shot."

"Yes, we did," Ben agreed as he began packing up his laptop. "And remember, he didn't say no. He said not yet. It'll be okay, Tor. We'll give Goliath the closure he needs, just not right now."

"I know," Tori sighed, watching him. "I guess we can wait a little bit longer."

"There's my girl," Ben smiled, bending over to kiss her tenderly on the lips. "Come on, let's get some lunch. I think I recall someone saying something about hot, salty fries and a frosty chocolate shake?"

"Oh, can we? That sounds so good right now!" Tori exclaimed as her expression brightened immediately.

"Absolutely!" he laughed. "Let's go!"

Chapter 10

"Oh, maybe eating all of those fries and that chocolate shake weren't a good idea right before our appointment," Tori groaned, rubbing her stomach. "I ate too much."

Ben smiled and glanced over at her while he drove. Reaching over to pat her hand gently, he replied, "We should probably focus a bit more on nutrition and healthier eating for the rest of your pregnancy, but a few fries and a chocolate shake every once in a while is fine, honey. That is until you start sending me out at three in the morning for pickles and ice cream, then we may need to reconsider."

Tori laughed at the thought of her doing that and said, "You know what's funny? I don't think I've really had any of those types of cravings yet. I realize the fries and chocolate shake craving is a bit out of the ordinary, but it's not keeping me awake at night thinking about it. Maybe I'll be lucky and won't have a food fixation that most women talk about."

"I guess we'll have to wait and see," Ben agreed.

"There's the building," Tori pointed, as they approached the row of medical offices. "Number five hundred on the right."

"I see it," Ben nodded, engaging the turn signal and slowing down to enter the parking lot. "Look at us, five minutes to spare!"

"Mr. and Mrs. Punctuality," Tori teased.

"I hate being late for appointments," Ben exclaimed as he parked the car. "It's a sign of disrespect for the person waiting for you."

"I know, I'm just teasing you," Tori smiled. "I love your wonderful mix of responsible and mischievous. You always keep me on my toes."

"It's never a dull moment with you either, my love," he smiled, leaning over to kiss her. "Are you ready?"

"Yes!" she exclaimed excitedly. "Let's go see our little girl!"

"All right," Ben agreed as he removed his seat belt and grabbed the keys from the ignition. "Wait right there!" he warned as he exited the car and shut the door.

Tori smiled as she watched him jog around the car to her door and waited as he opened her door for her.

"My lady," he smiled, extending his hand to her.

"Why thank you, sir," she giggled, taking his hand as he helped her out of the car. "We're so weird."

"Maybe, but I don't care," Ben replied. Pausing long enough to pull her into his arms, he hugged her tightly and said, "I love you so much."

Hugging him back, Tori smiled and replied, "I love you too, Ben."

Taking her hand in his, Ben heard the buzz of his cell phone as they began walking toward the entrance of the building. Noticing he wasn't paying any attention to it, Tori asked, "Aren't you going to check to see who that is?"

"Nope," he replied firmly. "The last time we walked together hand in hand, a car almost hit you. I'm not letting Lucifer ruin this moment for us. Besides, whoever it is will just have to wait until after our appointment."

"Wow, I'm impressed," Tori laughed as they walked through the doorway leading into her doctor's office.

"Chivalry is not dead, fair maiden," he chuckled lightly. "That is, at least not as far as I'm concerned."

"Indeed not," she agreed.

"Good afternoon," the receptionist greeted them as they approached the counter. "May I have your name, please?"

"Cooper," Tori replied. "We have a three o' clock appointment with Dr. Matthews."

"Yes you do," a woman's voice announced from behind them. Turning towards the voice, they saw Tori's doctor standing in the open doorway to the interior office. "Right on time as usual!" she added, smiling.

"Hi," Tori greeting her, warmly. "You remember my husband Ben, don't you?"

"I do!" Dr. Matthews replied. "It's nice to see you again, Ben."

"It's nice to see you too, Dr. Matthews!" Ben smiled.

Glancing down at Tori's stomach briefly, Dr. Matthews' expression showed a slight surprise. Then just as quickly, she looked back up at Tori and met her eyes intently. "How have you been feeling?" she asked curiously.

"Great!" Tori replied, caressing her stomach gently. "The baby has been moving around a lot lately but nothing painful or anything like that. She's just very active."

"Hmmm," Dr. Matthews paused. "And the last time I saw you we estimated you were about twelve weeks along at that time, right?" she asked.

"Yes, why do you ask?" Tori asked, having noticed her doctor's expression earlier.

"No reason, just making sure that's what I had written on your chart," Dr. Matthews replied casually. "Shall we go take a look?"

"Yes, please!" Ben exclaimed. "We've been waiting for this for weeks!"

Tori nodded in reply, smiling broadly.

"All right, then," Dr. Matthews smiled. "Follow me!"

As the trio made their way into the exam room, Dr. Matthews began setting up the sonogram machine while she gave Tori and Ben their instructions. "Ben, you can take the seat beside the table, over there. Tori, there's a changing area behind that partition in the corner where you can change into one of our gowns. There should be a hook on the wall for your clothes. Make sure the opening of the gown is in the front. When you're ready, come on out."

"Okay," Tori agreed as she stepped behind the partition as instructed.

"Is this your first time seeing a sonogram, Ben?" Dr. Matthews asked as she continued to calibrate the machine.

"Yes," Ben replied, watching her as he sat down.

Noticing his curiosity, she explained, "Okay. I'll go over a few highlights while we wait for Tori then. What we're going to look at today is the overall size of the fetus, take some measurements and check the level of amniotic fluid. Hopefully, if your little one is cooperative, we'll be able to determine the baby's gender. You do both want to know, right?"

"Yes," he nodded.

"We absolutely do!" Tori exclaimed as she emerged from behind the partition, fully gowned.

"Wow, that was quick!" Dr. Matthews laughed. "You are excited about this!" Motioning Tori to a scale, she said, "First we'll need to check your weight and your blood pressure so step over here to the scale and let's see where you are."

Grimacing guiltily at her, Tori sheepishly replied, "I was kind of hoping you'd forget that part. We stopped for lunch on our way over, and I have to be honest and admit that it wasn't an entirely healthy lunch."

Dr. Matthews smiled, appreciating Tori's honesty and tightened the blood pressure band. Squeezing the bulb, she asked, "Fudging every once in a while is fine, Tori, as long as you don't make it a habit. What do you consider not entirely healthy?"

Wincing, Tori confessed, "A large order of fries and a chocolate shake."

"Oh! How funny! That's what I used to eat when I was pregnant with my daughter," Dr. Matthews laughed. "Isn't that the best combination?"

"It is!" Tori exclaimed as she waited for the doctor to read her blood pressure.

"One twenty-five over eighty-five, a tad high but still in range," Dr. Matthews advised, motioning Tori to the scale.

Relieved she wasn't going to be chastised for her lunch choice, Tori added, "The salty and the sweet mixture is the best! I've been thinking about it for days, and it was so good! I promise I'm not eating like that all the time."

"No worries, everything in moderation is fine," Dr. Matthews replied as she pushed the metal bar over until it hovered and balanced over Tori's weight. Glancing down at the chart on the counter beside her, Dr. Matthews glanced back at the scale and made a note on the paper.

Once again, seeing her doctor's expression change, Tori glanced down at the scale and drew in a surprised breath. "Does that really say one hundred seventy pounds?" she asked. "That can't be right!"

Meeting her eyes, Dr. Matthews shrugged and replied, "I'm afraid it is."

"But that's sixteen pounds in almost eight weeks!" Tori exclaimed. "I realize that I've been looking bigger lately but I thought that was normal! I swear I haven't been eating like I did today since I last saw you! How could I have put on sixteen pounds?"

"Try not to focus on the weight," Dr. Matthews assured, patting Tori gently on the arm. "Every woman is different, and some gain their weight in spurts instead of gradually over the course of their pregnancy. Maybe you're one of those women. Just to be safe, I'll want to get a blood and urine sample before you go to make sure we don't need to be concerned with gestational diabetes or anything like that."

"Oh!" Tori gasped, looking at Ben fearfully.

"It's okay, sweetie," he assured. "It's just to make sure."

"Absolutely, nothing to be worried about," Dr. Matthews agreed, gently guiding Tori towards the table. "Now, lie down and let's take a look at your baby."

"Okay," Tori nodded hesitantly, sliding the silver heart charm along the chain around her neck while she gently caressed her stomach.

Once Tori positioned herself comfortably on the table, Dr. Matthews opened the gown and applied a small amount of warmed gel to Tori's lower abdomen. Noticing the look of concern on Tori's face, Dr. Matthews paused and asked, "Are you ready?"

Nodding, Tori reached over to take Ben's hand and whispered, "Yes, we're ready."

Gently pressing the transducer wand against Tori's stomach, Dr. Matthews began moving it around while she carefully watched the screen. Within moments, she understood the reason for Tori's dramatic weight gain. "Well, I think it's safe to assume your food choices are not the cause of your weight gain."

Once again becoming alarmed, Tori asked, "What do you mean? Is there something wrong?"

Smiling slowly at what she was seeing, Dr. Matthews reached over to engage the ultrasound and waited as the audio speaker picked up the sound of the heartbeats.

"Oh Ben," Tori whispered, as her eyes filled with tears. "Is that not the most beautiful sound you've ever heard?" She looked over at Ben and saw his eyes were also brimming with tears as he smiled in awe, hearing his child's heartbeat.

"It is," he breathed, squeezing her hand.

Never tiring of this part of her job, Dr. Matthews remained silent, staring at Tori and Ben's faces, wondering if they would pick up on what she already knew. Then she saw Tori's expression change.

"Wait," Tori exclaimed, quickly looking at the screen. "Are there?" she stopped and looked at Dr. Matthews questioningly.

Dr. Matthews smiled broadly and nodded. "There are."

"What are?" Ben asked, his eyes darting back and forth between Tori and her doctor. "What's wrong?"

Tori laughed and looked back at Ben, happily. "Nothing is wrong! It couldn't be more perfect!" Stopping herself, she looked back at Dr. Matthews and said, "Wait, are they okay? Do they look healthy?"

"They?" asked Ben, now very confused. As the realization sunk in, he stammered, "D-d-do you mean? A-a-are you saying there are t-t-two of them? We have t-twins?"

Tori and Dr. Matthews nodded, and Tori exclaimed, "We're having twins!"

"Are they fraternal or identical?" Ben marveled, staring at the screen.

"Identical," she replied. "They're sharing the same placental sac."

"We're having identical twins," Tori breathed.

"Yes you are," Dr. Matthews smiled. "And from what I can see they both look very active; which is probably why you've felt so much movement lately. Let me do a few measurements and then we'll take a peek behind the curtain and see if we can determine gender."

While they waited for her to assess the babies, Tori and Ben smiled at one another, still in shock.

"Your mom's going to freak when we tell her," Ben laughed, remembering how excited Sarah was that she was going to be a grandmother.

"Yes, she is. I can already see my dad bouncing each of them on his knees at the same time," she replied, smiling.

His face suddenly becoming serious, Ben exclaimed, "We're going to need another crib! And another car seat! We're going to need a bigger car!"

Tori shook her head, laughing at his expression and replied, "Slow down! Enjoy the moment before you start freaking out about stuff like that! We have plenty of time to make adjustments to what we've already set up in the nursery."

"Ah, you might need to move some of that up a bit," Dr. Matthews noted, rechecking her last measurement.

"What do you mean?" Tori asked, the smile leaving her face. "What's wrong?"

"Nothing's wrong, per say," Dr. Matthews replied, studying Tori's face. "Let's go back to our earlier conversation about when you conceived. Are you one hundred percent sure you conceived last November?"

Tori hesitated, thinking back and replied, "I'm ninety-nine percent sure. I realize that my cycles weren't regular, and I had skipped a few months before I realized I was pregnant but when I saw you in December, that's what you and I both decided was the approximate date of conception. Why? What's making you question that now?"

"Well," Dr. Matthews sighed, glancing back at the screen. "Based on the measurements I'm seeing, the babies both appear to be closer to thirty-two weeks old, not twenty-eight weeks as we first thought."

"Thirty-two weeks!" Tori cried out. "Are you saying I'm actually seven months pregnant? That's not possible!"

Dr. Matthews shrugged and replied, "It certainly looks like you are! I don't have an explanation other than what I'm seeing. Unless you're aware of some mystical power at work here causing the babies to have some kind of accelerated growth or something like that! Both of your baby's head sizes and body measurements indicate they are about thirty-two weeks old."

Tori laughed, nervously glancing at Ben and said, "Ha! Mystical power, huh? That would be crazy, wouldn't it, Ben?"

"Y-yes, that would be totally crazy!" Ben stammered, avoiding her look. "And you can see twenty fingers and twenty toes?" he asked, the doctor hopefully. "They both appear to be healthy?"

"Both your daughter and your son appear to be in perfect health," Dr. Matthews smiled.

"What did you just say?" Ben argued.

"I said both your daughter and your son appear to be in perfect health," Dr. Matthews repeated.

"D-did you say, son?" Tori whispered, her eyes widening in surprise.

"I did!" Dr. Matthews exclaimed. "Congratulations! I'm printing off copies of the images now so you can take them with you to show your family and your friends. The printer is in the room next door. I'll be right back."

As Dr. Matthews left the room, Tori turned to Ben, whose eyes were equally as wide as hers. "We're having a son, Ben," she whispered.

"How is that possible?" he whispered back.

"Mystical powers, maybe?" Tori raised her eyebrows, questioningly.

"Heck if I know!" Ben replied. "The lineage of the Remiel has always been daughters. There's never been a recorded birth of a boy before."

"That we know of," Tori pointed out.

"That we know of," he repeated. "What does this mean?" he asked, searching her eyes.

"I don't know," she admitted. "I need to talk to Remy."

Unseen by either of them, Remy stood silently in the corner of the room, equally shocked by what he had just heard. Looking upward towards heaven with troubled eyes, he quietly asked, "Father, what have You done?"

Chapter 11

"Well, it's official," Tori chuckled, ending the call on her cell phone. "My parents are totally freaking out about the news!"

"I bet!" Piper exclaimed. "Identical twins and the first reported Remiel boy! When you make news, you really make it big!"

"I guess," Tori shrugged. "Have you heard anything from the guys yet?"

Piper nodded and replied, "I talked to Riley. He, Ben and Agent Hunter are with Agent Sullivan doing research on whether there have ever been any male children recorded in the Remiel line before or not."

"Well, I guess the best source would be for me to ask Remy," Tori admitted.

"Have you seen him today?" Piper wondered.

"No, not yet," Tori yawned. "What an exhausting day!"

"Look at you! You're asleep on your feet. Why don't you lie down and get some rest? I'll let you know if the guys find anything," Piper suggested.

"A nap sounds so good right now. Are you sure you won't mind?" Tori hoped.

"Of course not," Piper promised. "Get some rest! You have cable, and I saw a bag of chips in the pantry earlier, so I'm all set! Now go!"

"Okay," Tori laughed. "Thanks, Piper. Come on, Goliath."

Piper smiled as Goliath slowly rose from his curled position on the floor beside her, yawned and obediently followed Tori into the bedroom. "You are such a good boy, Goliath."

"Goodnight, Piper," Tori heard in her head.

"He says goodnight!" she advised her friend.

"Goodnight, Goliath!" Piper called out after them.

Closing the door behind her, Tori turned and jumped when she saw Remy standing in front of her. "Oh! Don't do that! You startled me! I am seriously going to have to consider putting a bell on you the way you pop in sometimes!"

"Sorry," Remy replied guiltily. "I've been waiting for you to be alone so I could talk to you."

"Did you hear our news?" Tori exclaimed happily. "We're having identical twins!"

"Yes, I was there. I heard the news," he confessed.

"You were there? Why didn't you let me see you?" Tori exclaimed.

"Well, it was a private family moment between you and Ben. I didn't want to interfere," he admitted.

Tori reached out and touched Remy gently on the arm. "You're family too, Remy. You have just as much right being there as anyone."

"Well I thought about letting you know but then I heard what the doctor said, and I guess I have to admit, I was a bit shocked," he replied.

"Us too," she exclaimed, exhaling deeply. "So, what do you think of our news?"

"I honestly don't know what to think," he blurted out.

"So it's true? There haven't been any male children in the Remial line before?" she asked.

"No!" Remy declared defiantly, his wings fluttering behind him.

"What does a male child in your line mean?" Tori wondered.

"I don't know!" he exclaimed in frustration. "I asked Father, but He hasn't answered me."

Tori studied Remy's face thoughtfully, thinking about how difficult it must still be for him being so far removed from God and the other angels. As she felt the movement of the babies, a thought came to her. "Can you communicate with them? With the babies, I mean. Have you ever spoken to one of your children before they've been born?"

"I don't know; I've never tried," he admitted, glancing down at her stomach nervously.

"Would you like to try now?" she asked.

His eyes flicked briefly to hers and then back to her stomach. "I-I guess I could try," he stammered, slowly stepping forward, placing his hands gently on her stomach.

Tori watched Remy's face and smiled as he registered surprise feeling the movement under his hands. He looked up at her and laughed gently.

"Well I'll be," he drawled softly.

"You've never felt that before?" she whispered.

"Never," he breathed. "What an amazing feeling! And this is what it's like for you all the time?"

"Not all the time," she admitted. "Sometimes they're sleeping so they don't' move much at all. Sometimes music will make them more active, or they respond to my voice when I'm talking."

"They definitely know who you are," he remarked, smiling at her.

"You can hear them?" she exclaimed in amazement.

Remy's smile broadened as he nodded in reply. "The female, your daughter," he paused.

"Gemma," Tori advised.

"Gemma," he smiled. "That's a pretty name. Her thoughts are very strong. She's definitely the more dominant of the two."

"What is she saying?" Tori demanded, excitedly.

"She's saying hello. She called me Father," Remy replied.

"She knows who you are?" Tori marveled.

Remy nodded and said, "She knows who I am; who you are, and she knows who Ben is. She understands the difference between us already. She knows that she has a heavenly Father; that I am her spiritual father and that Ben is her earthly father."

"How could she know that already?" Tori exclaimed. "She's so little!"

"All of my children are created with the knowledge of who I am, of who the Lord God is and of good and evil, Tori," he advised. "They have to be to be prepared for their role here on earth."

"So I knew all of this when I was still in my mother's womb as well?" she asked.

Remy nodded and replied, "Yes, you knew, however since your mother didn't teach you your heritage after you were born, and what you were capable of, you forgot."

"That's so sad," Tori frowned. "I wish it could have been different. All those years, you watched me grow up, and I didn't know who you were. I'm sorry."

Remy gave her a small smile and replied, "That wasn't your fault, Tori. The choices your mother made were what she felt was right at the time, and I believe that all things happen for a reason. You were destined to discover your role in the prophecy when God intended and not a moment sooner."

"I guess," Tori agreed quietly. Seeing Remy's face light up with a comical grin, she asked, "What?"

"The boy, your son," he chuckled.

"We haven't had much time to talk about a boy's name yet," Tori admitted. "I've been thinking about RJ."

"RJ?" he frowned.

"Remy Jackson," Tori replied, hesitantly. "I thought we could use the R for Remy, in honor of you, and the J for Jackson, in honor of Ben. Jackson is his middle name."

"RJ," Remy replied quietly, smiling again. "He likes it."

"Do you?" Tori hoped.

"Does Ben?" he asked.

She nodded and replied, "I suggested it to him earlier, and he said he did."

"Then RJ it is," he agreed, chuckling again.

"What is he saying?" she asked curiously.

"He's quite the comical one. He's clever too. Not to mention a bit mischievous like Ben. He thinks his sister is a little bossy," Remy grinned.

A thought occurred to Tori as she watched Remy's face. "Remy," she paused until his eyes met hers. "Earlier today at the office when I was touching a piece of evidence from a crime scene, Piper saw my aura mix with two colors she hadn't seen before."

"Is that a question?" he teased gently.

"Was that them?" she asked curiously. "Were the bright yellow and violet bands of color my children?"

Remy nodded and replied, "Yes, they were protecting you."

"Protecting me? Protecting me from what?" she worried.

"You mean from whom," he corrected her.

"You mean Luc?" she puzzled.

"Who else would I mean?" he replied dryly.

"He's been pretty quiet lately," Tori noted. "I was kind of hoping he forgot about me."

Remy gave her a stern look and warned, "Don't you dare think that way! Just because he hasn't appeared to you lately doesn't mean he's not watching you, waiting for you to slip up. That's exactly what he's hoping for! He wants you to get so wrapped up in this pregnancy that you stop being careful. That's why Gemma and RJ helped you earlier today. You have to be strong and be on your guard at all times, Tori!"

"I know that!" Tori argued, stepping away from him. "I of all people know what he's capable of, Remy! My gosh! Do you actually think I would be so foolish as to forget that the devil has tried to kill me on multiple occasions? That doesn't mean I can't still enjoy this moment in my life without having to worry about him stalking me!"

Sensing her frustration, Goliath nuzzled Tori's hand and looked up at her with eyes filled with concern. "Is *Tori angry at Remy?*" she heard him ask.

Petting him gently on the head, Tori looked down into his deep golden eyes and sighed. "I'm not angry, Goliath. It's okay. I'm just really tired."

"That's my queue," Remy replied, preparing to leave.

"Wait!" Tori cried out, reaching out to grab Remy's arm. "Promise me that when you know more about RJ's part in the prophecy, you'll tell me? Please? Good or bad, I need to know."

Remy patted her hand, affectionately and replied, "I promise that I will."

"Thank you," she smiled, meeting his eyes.

"You're welcome," he replied. Giving Goliath an affectionate pat on the head he added, "Keep an eye on our girl, big guy."

"*Always,*" she heard Goliath promise.

A flutter of his immense wings later, Remy was gone.

Chapter 12

"What?" Tori mumbled in her sleep, hearing the sound of children's voices chanting a hauntingly familiar nursery rhyme. "What are you saying?" she mumbled again, turning over in her sleep.

The rhyme sounded familiar to her, yet it stayed just far enough outside of her conscious to keep her from recognizing it. Just as she began to fall deeper into sleep, the chanting started again.

"...Children from the light, see into the night, fear and darkness creeping. Bring them 'round, safe and sound, the fearless who are sleeping...."

Ending their rhyme, the children began to laugh gleefully; the sound of their laughter circling around inside of Tori's head.

As the sound began to fade, it was quickly replaced with the sound of what must have been hundreds of buzzing cicadas. The sound was so overpowering, it woke her abruptly, and she stared up at the vast open sky above her instead of what should have been her bedroom ceiling.

Sitting up, she looked around an open field, not recognizing where she was. Then her gaze stopped on the elegantly dressed man in the Italian suit, smiling at her from an oddly placed leather wingback chair in the middle of the grass.

"Great. I'm still asleep," she thought to herself.

"Ah, Sleeping Beauty has woken," Lucifer crooned, smoothly. "Well, you know what I mean."

Scowling at him with narrowed eyes, Tori replied, "Oh, it's you. I guess I shouldn't be surprised that it's you creeping into my dreams. It was only a matter of time until you showed up." Further annoyed by the overpowering sound of the insects, she shouted, "ENOUGH!" Instantly, the sound ceased.

Nodding in approval, Lucifer applauded, "Impressive! You're becoming stronger in your abilities, even while sleeping." Hesitating for a moment, he glanced down at the obvious rounding in her stomach and added, "It makes me wonder if you're doing it on your own or if you have a little help."

Covering her stomach protectively with her hands, Tori glared at him and warned, "Don't even think about it, Luc. You do, and you'll have to go through me in the process."

Irritated by the casual use of his name, which she knew annoyed him; he raised his chin indignantly, then like a flash, gave her his most charming smile. "Fear not, my

Queen," he crooned. "I won't harm your little princess. Or your little prince," he added challengingly.

Startled, Tori drew in a sharp breath, revealing her surprise.

"What? You didn't think I'd heard the big news?" he laughed, heartedly. "I'm still connected, my dear Tori. The almighty God may have tossed me down here on earth like heavenly garbage, but that doesn't mean I'm not aware of what's going on! All of the heavens are abuzz with the news of the prodigal Remial son! You're quite the celebrity. You're like the latest and greatest Virgin Mary!"

Taken aback, Tori gasped and replied, "Shame on you! That's blasphemy, even for you. You take that back!"

"Why should I? It's not like my soul is any danger," Lucifer shrugged, straightening the crease on the leg of his dress pants. "Besides, what are you going to do to me if I don't, hmm?"

Tori blinked, realizing she had no answer for him. Further realizing she was in control of her dream and not him, she simply glared at him and replied, "Goodbye Luc." Instantly, the dream began to change, and she watched his face begin to dissolve.

"You can't ignore me forever, Tori...," he calmly replied, his voice fading until it was gone.

Watching in satisfaction as he completely dissolved into her dreamy mist, a new image emerged; the familiar image of the little red-haired girl with bouncing curls and laughing green eyes; riding Goliath like a pony. The frills on the hem of her dress bounced in a wavelike motion as Goliath galloped in a large circle around a wooded backyard with lush green grass.

"Is that Gemma?" she wondered.

As in her previous dream, when Goliath felt his young rider beginning to lose her grip, he slowed down and stopped beside Tori so she could help the girl down. The little girl gave Goliath a final hug before she was pulled away, and turned her angelic face up towards Tori. "That was fun, Mama!"

"It looked like fun, baby girl!" Tori smiled, kissing the little girl on the cheek.

The girl pressed her face against Tori's, hugged her tightly and said, "I love you, Mama."

Returning the hug, Tori smiled and replied, "My beautiful Gemma. I love you too, my sweet angel."

Suddenly, the little girl began to giggle, pointing at something across the yard. "Look, Mama!" she laughed.

Tori's gaze followed the direction the child was pointing and saw a young boy, the same age as the girl, with wavy dark auburn hair, standing at the base of a large water fountain. His denim jeans were soaked from the knees down, indicating at some point he had been playing in the water. The scene didn't seem unusual to Tori until she looked up at the fountain itself. For the second time, she drew in a surprised breath.

A cherub statue in the middle of the fountain, which should have been pouring out water from a large cement seashell in its hands, was instead holding what appeared to be a frozen band of water, starting at the shell and ending in the basin of the fountain.

The little boy turned his mischievous face to Tori, and she saw the mirrored male image of the little girl, except his eyes were the color of a blue sky on a cloudless day.

"I know that look," Tori thought. *"That has Ben written all over it."*

"RJ?" she whispered, amazed that she was actually seeing the faces of her unborn children. She looked back down at the little girl, still snuggled tightly in her arms and searched her eyes.

"It's okay Mama," Gemma smiled. "Don't be scared."

"I'm not scared honey, just a little overwhelmed," Tori admitted as she lovingly stroked her daughter's auburn hair.

"He won't hurt you as long as we're together," Gemma promised, turning back to RJ. "Isn't that right, RJ?"

Tori looked back up at RJ, who nodded, smiling affectionately at her. "That's right." Glancing briefly at the fountain, he made a slight motion with his hands and the ice instantly melted. Once again, the cherub resumed the job of pouring the water into the basin of the fountain.

"Who won't hurt me? How did you...," Tori began to ask when suddenly the image of her children's faces began to dissolve into the mist. "Wait!" she cried out in frustration, but it was too late, the image was gone. Still feeling the warmth of her little girls embrace, Tori felt a sudden loss and her heart ached to have the dream return.

As the feeling of despair consumed her, the mist began to clear. The new image was of an elderly man with vacant eyes, dressed in a worn military suit, sitting in a wooden rocking chair on the front porch of a dilapidated old house. The faded suit sagged on his thin frame; the buttons and medals once shiny and worn proudly with honor; were now tarnished and dull.

"Hello?" Tori greeted the man hesitantly, but he didn't look up or acknowledge her. She looked around, wondering what significance from this part of her dream should be. Then the mist washed over her again, and the scene changed to a much younger version of the man.

The condition of the home showed better care and attention revealing a freshly painted porch and large ceramic pots of beautiful flowers flanking either side of the front door. The blanket of sadness began to lift, and a new feeling of contentment took its place.

She looked over at the man who now stood proudly on the porch in his uniform, which was crisp and fitted, the buttons and medals polished to perfection, revealing his reflection. Still only a spectator in the dream, Tori saw the man smile as a taxicab approached the house.

"Honey, Zander is here!" the man called out behind him, in the direction of the screened front door.

"I'll be right there!" a woman's voice replied from inside the house.

The cab stopped at the end of the driveway, and a young man in a Marine Corps Dress Blue uniform stepped out. "Hi Pop!" the young man greeted as he approached the house.

"Welcome home, son," the man grinned proudly.

Suddenly a dark shadow passed overhead, and a blinding flash of light filled the sky. Instinctively, Tori shielded her eyes with her upturned hand, and she looked up at the darkened sky above her. She flinched as another flash lit up the sky, quickly followed by a deep booming clap of thunder that shook the porch beneath her feet.

The images were now overwhelming her, as her eyes and mind frantically tried to take them all in. All of a sudden, the clouds parted, and she saw a human form falling from the sky, plummeting towards the earth. She tried to see if she could see the person's face or anything recognizable but it was too far up above her to see clearly. Then she heard the sound of a baby crying, and the blinding light turned to completed darkness. Terrified, she began to stumble forward, her arms outstretched before her, searching for the source of the sound.

"Hello? Is somebody there?" she cried out in frustration.

"The baby's heart rate is dropping, doctor," a female voice called out in the darkness. "We're running out of time!"

"We're going to lose them both!" another voice exclaimed.

"Somebody, do something!" she heard Ben's voice plead.

"What's happening?" Tori screamed, waking herself from her dream.

Recognizing the ceiling above her, she lay completely still as her heart galloped inside of her chest and her mind replayed the images from her dream.

She looked over at the pillow beside her, expecting to see Ben's face but instead, she saw the note with his handwriting.

"Hey sleepyhead, I took Goliath out for a walk. Be back soon. I love you," the note read.

Tori sighed and laid her head back against her pillow. "I don't understand," she accused the ceiling above her. "What are you trying to tell me?"

Feeling the gentle movement of the twins stir, she gently caressed her stomach and quietly soothed, "Shhhh, I'm sorry I woke you. We're okay. Everything is okay."

No longer able to hold back the tears creeping from the corners of her eyes, she lay there weeping quietly.

"God, please help me understand," she pleaded. "Please don't take my babies away from me."

Chapter 13

Sarah rolled over and looked at the clock, sighing when she saw it was only an hour later than the last time she looked. *"Well there's no sense in lying here if my mind has obviously decided I'm not getting any sleep tonight,"* she thought to herself.

Slowly swinging her legs down to the floor, she eased her body out of bed, careful not to wake Tanner, who was sleeping soundly beside her.

Hearing her get up, Corkey immediately popped his head up from inside his bed and looked at her expectantly.

"It's okay Cork," she whispered quietly. Patting his head gently she added, "Go back to sleep."

The little dog yawned, licked his nose a few times, nestled back into his bed and closed his eyes.

"It's nice to see everyone else getting a good night's sleep tonight," she muttered to herself as she padded barefoot from the room down the hallway towards the living room.

As usual, the glow from the television screen was serving as the only source of light in the room. However, something seemed different this time. It took her a few seconds to realize the flickering light she was seeing wasn't from the scenes changing the current channel it was actually due to the channels being changed to new shows.

She glanced over at the Aubrey, whose ghostly form was hovering in front of the television and she could tell by the expression of concentration on her daughter's face that she was the one changing the channels.

"Bree?" she asked, curiously.

"What?" Aubrey exclaimed, her concentration broken. Turning towards her mother, she replied, "Oh! Hi, Mom! What are you doing up?"

"I couldn't sleep. Wait. Were you just….," Sarah blurted out, pointing towards the TV. "Did I just see what I thought I saw?"

Aubrey winced at her guiltily and quickly replied, "Please don't freak out, Mom. I promise I was going to tell you but I wanted to practice until I had better control over it before I showed you."

Sarah blinked at her daughter in confusion and asked, "Better control over what, honey? Were you just changing the channels? How is that possible?"

Aubrey shrugged her shoulders and excitedly replied, "I have no idea! It just started a few months ago, right after

Tori and Ben's wedding. One night while you and Dad were sleeping, I was bored with the channel you set the TV to and I remember thinking, "*I wish I could change the channel myself.*" The next thing I knew, the channel changed! It was so cool! So I concentrated on doing it again, and the channel changed again! Once I figured out I could do that, I started experimenting with other things to see what else I could do!"

Sarah walked over to the couch and slowly sat down allowing her mind to take in what Aubrey just told her. She looked up at her daughter's elated face and hesitated, not sure how to react.

"Well? What do you think?" Aubrey exclaimed.

"I think it's amazing, sweetie," Sarah admitted.

"Then why do you look so worried?" Aubrey asked.

"Worried? Do I look worried? Oh, I'm sorry, honey. I think I'm just a little overwhelmed that's all. I need some time to let this sink in," Sarah replied. "Wait, you said you could do other things, what kind of other things?"

"Oh, right! I did say that didn't I?" Aubrey giggled as her imaged shimmered excitedly. Looking around the room, trying to decide what to show her mother first, she blurted, "Oh, this is so much fun! What should I show you first? Oh I know, hang on!"

Still thinking about the changing channels, Sarah stared at the TV screen, lost in thought.

"Mom," Aubrey interrupted.

"What?" Sarah replied, turning back to her daughter. As she did, she noticed the television remote control, floating about a foot above the coffee table, slowly moving in her direction. "Oh!" she exclaimed, jumping back against the sofa.

"Come on, be cool, Mom. Don't freak out!" Aubrey teased.

"I'm not freaking out," Sarah replied defensively.

"Hold out your hands," Aubrey encouraged.

Slowly extending her hands, Sarah drew in a surprised breath as the remote gently landed in her opened palms. She looked up at Aubrey, whose face was beaming.

"Pretty cool, huh?" Aubrey giggled.

"Um, y-y-yes," Sarah stammered, staring at the remote.

"Ooh! And watch this!" Aubrey gleefully chirped, turning around to face the doorway to the kitchen. Not hearing her mother's reply, she looked back at Sarah and demanded, "Mom!"

"What?" Sarah mumbled, meeting Aubrey's eyes. "I'm sorry did you ask me something, honey?"

"Watch this!" Aubrey demanded, turning back to the doorway.

Sarah's eyes moved towards the doorway, and she drew in another quick breath as she saw the door gently close. A few seconds later, she saw the handle turn, and the door opened again.

"What do you think?" Aubrey grinned.

"I think I must still be asleep, and I only think I woke up and came out here," Sarah muttered, looking back at the remote control in her hands. "How is any of this possible? How can you have any contact with physical things?"

"Hey, I'm not going to question it! I think it's cool! Wait until I can show Tori, she's going to freak!" Aubrey laughed.

Sarah regarded her daughter thoughtfully for a moment and asked, "Does this have anything to do with what you asked me about a few weeks ago when we were moving Meda's files into the office, honey? When you asked me whether you had a greater purpose? Did you know you had these abilities then?"

"Yes," Aubrey admitted, guiltily. "But I wasn't ready to show you then. That's why I didn't tell you."

"You should never be afraid to show or tell me anything, sweetheart," Sarah encouraged. "Please don't ever think you can't share something that makes you so happy with me again, okay?"

"Okay," Aubrey promised.

Sarah smiled, realizing Aubrey was looking for her approval and asked, "I think all of this is pretty amazing, sweetie. So what else can you do? Is there more?"

Aubrey laughed and shook her head. "That's pretty much it as far as I've been able to discover. But I haven't given up! I want to find out if there's more I can do!"

"Well you'll have to let me know when you find out," Sarah replied as a thought suddenly occurred to her. "Bree," she paused, searching her daughter's eyes carefully. "When did you say you first noticed you could change the channels?"

"Right after Tori got married, why?" Aubrey asked.

Thinking back, Sarah replied, "Which was the same time Meda and Karla crossed over."

"What do you mean?" Aubrey prodded.

"I'm not sure, I'm just wondering. What if your new abilities have something to do with their crossing over?" Sarah mused.

Considering her mother's theory, Aubrey admitted, "I guess that's possible. Do you mean some kind of cosmic balancing act like their energy crossing over and some of that energy coming back at me kind of thing?"

"I have no idea. I don't even know if any of this makes sense. I'm thinking out loud," Sarah admitted.

"Well, how do we find out if that's the case?" Aubrey offered.

"I don't know," Sarah debated. "I think I'll make a call to Agent Sullivan tomorrow and see what he thinks. He's the closest thing we have to an insider on our family prophecy so maybe he'll have some ideas."

"Are you going to tell Dad?" Aubrey hesitated.

"Well I guess I should, considering doors will be opening and closing all by themselves from now on," Sarah teased. "At least that will prepare him for what he may see, considering he never knows where you are."

"Right," Aubrey laughed. "It's not like he's not already used to having a ghost in the house!"

"You know I don't like that term, honey," Sarah gently scolded. "Your father and I don't consider you a ghost."

"I know, I know," Aubrey sighed, rolling her eyes. "I'm a living spirit, not a spooky ghost."

"Exactly," Sarah giggled as she watched the remote rise out of her hands and float back down to the coffee table.

"So when should we tell Tori?" Aubrey asked; making sure the remote landed softly on the glass.

Sarah sighed and replied, "I think we should wait for now. She's got a lot on her plate with the pregnancy not to mention having to plan for the babies being born much sooner than expected. Knowing your sister, she's obsessing over the details and putting more stress on herself than she should. As cool as this new ability of yours is, sweetie, I have a feeling that would start Tori off on another research project that she just doesn't have the time for right now. I hope you understand what I mean."

"Yeah, I get it. She does seem to be more manic than usual these days," Aubrey admitted. "I guess we can keep this our little secret for now."

Noticing a look of hesitation on her daughter's face, Sarah asked, "So what else is on your mind. Is there something else you want to talk about?"

Aubrey chuckled and gave her mother an appreciative nod. "You always know."

"Go on, spill," Sarah smiled.

"Well, speaking of babies, how come the babies are coming sooner than expected? Didn't Tori and her doctor determine her due date correctly? How does that work?" Aubrey asked curiously.

Realizing she never had 'the talk' with Aubrey before her death, Sarah sat back in her chair and tried to think how best to explain the situation to the spirit of a seventeen-year-old girl.

"Well honey, a normal pregnancy takes about nine months which is about forty weeks from conception to birth. Originally, Tori thought she was only twenty-eight weeks along in her pregnancy, however now that there are two babies and based upon the babies measurements, her doctor feels the babies are closer to thirty-two weeks old," Sarah advised.

"So who did their math wrong?" Aubrey demanded. "Tori and Ben got married the end of October, and we know she wasn't pregnant then because she and Ben were waiting until they were married to…ah, you know."

"Agreed," Sarah quickly interjected.

"That doesn't make sense! If Tori is thirty-two weeks into her pregnancy, that would mean she would have been pregnant before she and Ben were married!" Aubrey exclaimed.

"But we know that's not true," Sarah advised.

"So what does that mean? Are you saying the babies are growing faster than they're supposed to be? Like they have accelerated growth or something?" Aubrey argued.

Sarah shrugged and admitted, "I don't know what to tell you, sweetheart. All I know is I know for a fact that Tori wasn't pregnant the day she got married, and now her doctor is telling her the babies are due sometime mid-to-late June.

"Well, then she needs a new doctor!" Aubrey demanded. "This isn't your ordinary pregnancy! These babies are special! They're the new heirs in the Remiel legacy! We can't put their lives in the hands of some run of the mill doctor, especially one who can't even calculate a baby's due date! We have to do something!"

"Trust me," Sarah confessed. "I'm already working on that!"

Chapter 14

"The baby's heart rate is dropping, doctor."

"We're going to lose them both!"

"Somebody do something!"

Tori shuddered as she replayed the end of her dream again in her head. Blinking back the tears clouding her vision, she felt a small twinge in her back that lately was a sign that she'd been on her feet too long. A quick glance at the clock revealed she had just lost fifteen minutes standing in front of the kitchen counter, lost in her thoughts.

"Okay, enough of that!" she exclaimed, frustrated at how easily she was being distracted today. She stared down at the ground pork resting on the bottom of the mixing bowl in front of her and sighed.

"Is *Tori okay?*" she heard Goliath ask, who was as usual, holding a vigil on the floor by her feet, hoping for something edible to fall off the counter.

She gave him a small smile and quietly replied, "Everything is fine, Goliath."

Unconvinced, he cocked his head sideways and stared into her eyes. *"Goliath help?"* he asked.

Shaking her head, Tori turned back to the counter and replied, "It's nothing, Goliath. There's nothing for you to eat here, lie down."

Feeling the sting of her words, he lowered his head and skulked to the other side of the kitchen, out of her way but still able to watch her.

Deciding she didn't want to dwell on the dream any longer, she set her mind to what she knew would make her feel better, cooking therapy.

"A nice bowl of hot soup for lunch will make everything better," she reasoned out loud. "And pork meatballs in Parmesan broth is just what I need."

Focusing her attention on the ingredients, she measured out the ricotta cheese, breadcrumbs, nutmeg, salt, and pepper, adding each ingredient to the bowl, ending with a cracked egg. Then she rinsed her hands in cold water and began working the ingredients together with her hands until everything was fully incorporated.

With skilled fingers, she then rolled out identically shaped golf ball sized meatballs and set them on a plate beside her until the bowl was empty.

The hard part now done, she washed out the bowl, placed it in the dishwasher and then thoroughly washed her hands, mindful of removing the raw pork from under her fingernails.

Next, she poured some grape seed oil into a saucepan and placed it on the stove. Working in batches, she browned the meatballs on all sides and then transferred them to the pot of broth warming on the burner beside her.

When she was done, she tossed a large handful of freshly grated Parmesan cheese into the pot, covered it and set the timer for twenty minutes.

Filling another pot with water, she placed it on the stove, sprinkled in some salt and set the burner to high so she could cook the noodles; which if she timed them correctly would be done at the same time the meatballs were cooked through in the broth. While she waited for the noodles to cook, she chopped up some artichoke hearts and fresh spinach leaves and set them aside.

Once she was done and the kitchen was cleaned up, she looked at the clock noticing that she still had several minutes until she needed to drain the noodles to finish the soup.

"Okay, what else can I do while I wait?" she asked out loud, looking around the kitchen.

"Somebody do something!" Tori heard her mind reply.

Instantly, the dream came flooding back to her. Unable to stop them, tears welled up in her eyes and she gulped back a sob as they began streaming down her cheeks.

"Oh," she sobbed out loud, gripping the edge of the countertop. "Come on! I was doing so well!"

From the corner of the room, Goliath saw her struggling and knew he needed to do something. She obviously didn't want to share what was bothering her with him, and since Ben wasn't home, the only other person he knew he could turn to was Remy. Focusing all of his thoughts towards his heavenly benefactor, he called out to Remy for help. *"REMY!"*

Within moments, Remy appeared and quickly rushed to Tori's side. "What is it? What's wrong?" he cried out, looking for blood or a sign of injury.

Unable to speak, Tori threw her arms around him, burying her head in his shoulder, sobbing uncontrollably.

"Shh...It's okay," he murmured, holding her tight.

"N-n-no, it's not," she sobbed.

"Tell me what's wrong!" he pleaded. "Did something happen? Is it Luc? Did he do something to upset you?"

"No, it's not him," she mumbled against his shirt.

"Well then what?" he asked again. "Did you have another vision or a troubling dream?"

"N-no," Tori lied, quietly

Pulling away from her, he looked down into her anguished eyes. Gripping her shoulders gently, he said, "Talk to me, Tori. I can't help you if you don't tell me why you're upset."

"I-it's just a feeling I have," she continued to lie. "A feeling that something bad is going to happen."

"Something bad is always going to happen, darlin'," he drawled with a small smile, "which is usually followed by something good afterward. That's just the way the world works. You know that. So what's got you so worked up?"

"Well..," she paused, debating whether she should tell him.

"Hello?" Bens' voice called out from the front entry way.

Remy instantly backed away from Tori as she attempted to wipe away her tears and regain her composure.

Helping her stall for time, Remy motioned to Goliath who quickly trotted out of the kitchen to meet Ben at the front door.

"Hey, Goliath!" he greeted, patting the dog affectionately on his head. "How's my good boy today? It smells like Tori's been cooking. Are you keeping her company in the kitchen?"

As Ben walked into the room, he smiled at Tori who now had her back to him as she finished straining the noodles into a colander in the sink.

"Hello, beautiful! How's my favorite girl?" he asked, approaching her from behind and wrapping his arms around her. He spun her around to give her a kiss but then saw the red rims around her eyes. "Hey, what's wrong, sweetie? Have you been crying?" He looked around the countertops to see if there were any chopped onions nearby to explain the tears, but they revealed no clues.

"I'm okay. I just had a hormonal moment, that's all," she lied, attempting a smile. "You know me lately. A well written Hallmark commercial sets me off."

"Are you sure?" he soothed, rubbing her arms gently.

"Yep, everything's okay," she stated, purposefully avoiding eye contact with Remy, who was standing behind Ben, next to Goliath.

"Well, the house smells amazing. It hit me in the face the moment I walked in the door. What are you making? Can I help?" he asked, looking at the colander filled with noodles in the basin of the sink.

"I made a batch of pork meatballs in parmesan broth for lunch," she quickly replied, glad for the change in subject.

"Oooh, that sounds good! Want me to get out the bowls and set the table?" he offered.

"Sure, that would be great! I'm almost done. I just need to add the noodles, artichoke hearts, and the spinach and give the spinach time to wilt for a couple minutes and then lunch will be ready."

"That sounds awesome, thank you for making lunch. Here I was going to be all chivalrous and offer to take you out for Chinese. This is even better!" he beamed.

"Oh, Chinese sounds good! Let's have that for dinner!" she suggested.

"Deal," Ben agreed as he set the bowls beside the stove and then walked over to the table to set down the napkins and silverware. As he did, his cell phone started ringing in the living room. "Oh, that's probably Agent Hunter. He said he would call if he found anything."

"Found what?" she frowned. "What are you guys working on?"

"Hang on, I'll tell you in a couple minutes. Let me get that before he hangs up," Ben promised as he headed towards the living room.

Once again alone with Remy, Tori met his questioning gaze, and she shook her head at him. "Not right now," she begged.

"We're not done talking about this," Remy chided her. "I want to know what you're keeping from me and Ben. I'll be back later, and you better be prepared to talk to me."

As Remy disappeared, his words hung in the air, leaving her feeling guilty for not telling him the truth. She glanced over at Goliath, who was watching her closely. Narrowing her eyes at him, he remained fixed on her, not backing down.

"We're not done talking about this either by the way. Calling out to Remy like that," she whispered fiercely as she heard Ben ending his call.

"Okay!" Ben chirped happily as he returned to the kitchen. "Let's have lunch. I'm starving!"

"Shocker," Tori teased as she ladled out the soup.

"I know, right?" he chuckled.

Chapter 15

"Retreat, retreat, the guy's wired! Come on, move, move, move," Corporal Davies cried out, backing away from the window of the vehicle stopped at the checkpoint. The sound of the explosion, followed by the screams from the men as the impact tore the limbs from their bodies, woke Zander from the horrific nightmare of his past, thrusting him into the present with a violent jolt.

Lying there in the dark covered in sweat, his heart sprinted in his chest while his pounding head announced the onset of yet another massive migraine. "Not again," he moaned, fighting to choke down the bile in his throat and the overwhelming terror inside of him. He rubbed his hands over his bloodshot eyes while the sounds of the screams from his fallen comrades began to fade.

"Go away, go away, go away! Why won't they just go away?" he whispered into the darkness.

"They're a part of who you are, Lance Corporal Wells," the Darkness replied. *"They can't go away."*

Reaching over to the top of the nightstand, Zander grabbed the bottle of Prozac, unscrewed the cap and without counting, tossed several of the pills into his mouth. Numb to the familiar bitterness as he swallowed them down, he lay back against the pillows and stared at the blades of the ceiling fan slowly stirring the air above him.

"It's getting worse," he thought to himself. *"The pills aren't helping anymore."* Sighing, he lamented, *"I miss Rhea. She would know what to do. She always knew what to do."*

"There's no help for you; you're a broken man. You and your demons chased her away," the darkness continued to taunt him.

"Shut up!" Zander muttered. "You don't know me."

Unsure if he could go back to sleep or not, he looked around the darkened room for something to distract his thoughts when suddenly, his gaze stopped at the window.

At first he didn't understand what he was looking at. As the moonlight streamed in between the louvers of the window blinds, he realized he was looking at the outline of his rifle case leaning up against the wall.

"What's that doing there?" he wondered.

Pulling back the sheets, he climbed out of bed, swaying slightly as the pounding in his head increased while he shuffled his feet over towards the window. When he looked down, he saw his army boots lying on the floor beside the rifle case.

"What are those doing there? I didn't wear those yesterday, did I?" he puzzled, doubting himself even further.

He picked up the camouflaged rifle case, intending to put it back in his closet when all of a sudden he smelled a familiar smell. *"That's gunpowder,"* his memory announced.

Striding over to the nightstand, he turned on the light, wincing as it pierced his eyes. Doing his best to ignore the pain in his head, he laid the rifle case on the bed. When he unzipped the zipper, the smell of the gunpowder became stronger. As he removed the rifle from the foam padding, he knew something was terribly wrong. *"This has been fired recently,"* his logic told him.

"That's crazy! I haven't been to the range in months," Zander argued out loud.

"Then who has been firing your rifle?" his doubt asked.

"That's what I'd like to know!" Zander exclaimed.

Glancing back at his boots, he saw mud on the bottom of the soles. Leaving the rifle on the bed, he walked over to the boots and picked one up turning it sole side up. *"That's fresh mud on the soles,"* his logic reported again. *"And pine needles."*

"But I didn't wear these….," Zander started to argue back but then stopped as a new spear of pain surged in his head.

"Pine needles..." a voice whispered in his ear.

Feeling nauseous, he set the boot back down on the floor and slowly shuffled his feet out of the bedroom towards the kitchen.

Grabbing a glass out of the cupboard, he went over to the sink and ran the faucet for a few seconds, waiting for the cold water to arrive. Then he filled the glass, drained it and filled it a second time, this time turning off the faucet and walking into the living room.

Hearing nothing but the pounding of the drummer in his head, he sat down on the couch and hit the power button on the TV remote. As the square panel sprang to life, he took another long drink from the glass but stopped mid-swallow when he heard the sound of the news anchorman reporting a breaking story.

"…..the murder appears to have been a single gunshot wound to the chest from a 22 caliber rifle. The victim, Peyton Birch, died at the scene. His body is now at County Hospital awaiting an autopsy."

"Birch," Zander thought as a feeling of uneasiness came over him. *"Why does that name sound familiar?"*

"Your rifle is a 22 caliber," the voice in his head whispered.

"What?" he asked, distractedly.

He continued to stare at the screen as the reporter walked over to another man while continuing with his story.

"I have Peter Barnes with me, the man golfing with Mr. Birch at the time of the murder. Mr. Barnes, can you tell us what you remember?" the reporter asked.

"Yeah, sure," the man replied. "Me and Peyton were trying to get in a round of golf before it got too dark. I was standing over there by the cart, waiting for him to take his shot and then all of a sudden; he just went down. I didn't know what was going on! He wouldn't answer me when I called out to him and then when I went over to him and rolled him over onto his back, I saw the blood on his shirt. It nearly gave me a heart attack! So I immediately pulled out my phone and dialed 9-1-1."

"And you have no idea who would have shot your friend?" the reporter probed.

"No, not at all," Peter exclaimed. "I mean who does something like this? Peyton was a great guy! I've known him since we were kids! He was a former Marine and served his country! He wasn't rich or anything like that, so it's not like he had a bunch of money for someone to come after him. We were just out enjoying a nice Sunday afternoon together!"

"...*Semper Fi....,*" the same small voice told him.

"What?" Zander replied as his mind began to wander.

Suddenly, Zander snapped to attention. *"Sunday? Did that guy just say Sunday? What the heck's going on? Today isn't Sunday; it's Saturday."*

Setting the glass down on the table, he jumped up from the couch and strode back into the bedroom for his phone. Clicking the power button, he stared in disbelief at the date displayed on the screen.

"I don't understand," he quietly murmured. "What happened to Saturday? How did I lose an entire day?"

Chapter 16

"I'll get it!" Tori called out, hearing the doorbell chime. As she opened the door, she registered surprise when she saw who was on the other side. "Oh! Hi! You're both here, together. Come on in!"

"Hi!" Piper grinned handing Tori a covered plate. "We decided to drive in together since we live in the same apartment complex. It seemed silly taking two cars. Here, this is for you."

"Hey, Tori," Logan greeting as he followed Piper inside. "Umm, I smell bacon. Is Ben in the kitchen?"

"Yep, right through that doorway," Tori pointed, laughing at Logan's reaction to the smell. "What's this?" she asked, turning to Piper, nodding at the plate.

"I made you sweet zucchini cupcakes with cream cheese frosting," Piper beamed.

"Oh, you didn't," Tori exclaimed, her eyes widening in expectation. "Thank you! I love you!"

"You're welcome," Piper chuckled as she and Tori walked through the living room together towards the kitchen. "I remember you mentioning you never had one before so I asked my mom for her secret recipe; that is no longer a secret by the way. I made a batch so you could try one. Thank goodness you invited Logan and me over for breakfast, or I would have kept eating them. A word of warning, they're addictive."

"Ha, thanks for the warning. I'll keep that in mind!" Pausing at the doorway, Tori whispered, "So seriously, you guys just drove over together? You're not...,"

"No! No, no, no, absolutely not," Piper whispered back. "It's strictly professional now between Logan and me. This carpooling was merely for convenience, trust me."

"Okay," Tori replied. "You would tell me if...,"

"I promise, I would tell you if anything did, which it won't because we've already been there, and we all know how that turned out," Piper smirked.

"True, okay, subject closed," Tori nodded. "Thank you again for making these," she added as they entered the kitchen.

"Making what?" Ben asked as he poured scrambled eggs into a pan on the stove.

"Sweet zucchini cupcakes with cream cheese frosting," Piper replied, proudly.

"*Cupcakes?*" Tori heard Goliath ask as he turned from his post guarding the floor around the stove.

"That got Goliath's attention," Tori giggled.

"Hey Goliath," Piper crooned. "How's my big, beautiful boy today?"

"*Cupcakes?*" he asked again as his nose followed the new smell that just entered the kitchen.

"Not for you, Goliath," Tori advised the dog, firmly.

Giving Tori a raised eyebrow grin, Ben asked, "And how is that a healthy breakfast option for you and the twins?"

"They have zucchini in them! That's healthy!" Tori argued, trying not to laugh.

"Zucchini in a cupcake, that's chick food," Logan snorted, derisively.

"Don't worry, buddy, I've got you covered," Ben advised. "We also have scrambled eggs, bacon and hash browns."

Logan nodded in approval and said, "Awesome. Now that's man food!"

"Man food? Since when did eggs, bacon, and hash browns become man food? Women eat bacon too, you know. You're both such dorks," Piper sighed, rolling her eyes.

"Remember who drove here today, Pip," Logan teased.

"Don't worry, I would drive you home if he bailed on you," Tori promised.

"Thanks, Tori! See? That's how you treat a friend, Logan. You should take notes," Piper joked.

"She only said that because you brought her cupcakes," he teased back.

"That's not true, and she knows it," Tori defended her friend. "Hey, Piper, want to come and check out the nursery while Ben finishes up the eggs?"

"Oh, I'd love to!" Piper exclaimed.

"Right this way," Tori invited, motioning with her hands.

"I love your house," Piper sighed as they walked down the hallway towards the bedrooms. "It has such a great energy flow, and the big windows give you so much natural light."

"Thanks! That's why we chose it," Tori smiled. "We walked in, and it just felt right. Thank goodness it has an extra room. We were planning to use as an office, but now it will be RJ or Gemma's room. They'll still need to share a bathroom, but at least they'll each have their own room. Here we go," she added as they entered the nursery.

"Oh, Tori," Piper breathed, awestruck. "It's beautiful! You matched the colors of the room to the baby's auras! What a great idea! When did you do this?"

"Last weekend," Tori confessed. "So you like it? You're the first person to see it."

"Like it? I love it!" Piper exclaimed. "That lemony yellow color on the walls is so bright and happy! And the shade of plum you chose for the lettering along the border at the top of the walls is gorgeous! I love the colors!"

"You loving color, that's a shocker," Tori teased, glancing at Piper's bright red hair.

"I know, right?" Piper laughed. "What's the verse painted in the plum lettering?"

"It's a nursery rhyme," Tori replied. "At least I think it is. I had this dream where RJ and Gemma were repeating that nursery rhyme over and over again, and when I woke up, it stuck in my head. So I decided to paint it as a border along the walls around the room. Well, Ben did the painting. I did the stenciling of the letters."

"Children from the light, see into the night, fear and darkness creeping. Bring them 'round, safe and sound, the fearless who are sleeping," Piper read out loud as she slowly spun around the room. "It's kind of ominous and creepy yet strangely comforting at the same time. Do you think that's them? The twins I mean. Are they the children from the light?"

"I don't know," Tori admitted. "I've thought about that. I guess it could be possible. Or it's just a weird dream from my twisted mind, and it doesn't mean anything."

Piper scowled at Tori skeptically and asked, "Do you really believe that? Does anything that revolves around you ever happen without a meaning or a purpose?"

Tori shrugged, guiltily and replied, "No, not really."

"Then there's your answer," Piper affirmed, looking around the room again. "It will be interesting to see how the twins react when they see it. If they react at all that is. It's kind of exciting to think about the fact that they already have an awareness of who you; Ben and Remy are. You'll get to see what your life should have been like had your mother taught you about your ability from the beginning. Don't you agree?"

When Tori didn't respond, Piper turned around and faced her friend who now seemed frozen in a trance staring into space. "Tor? Are you okay?"

Hearing Piper but unable to move or respond, Tori stood motionless; as suddenly she realized she was looking through the scope of a rifle, focused on a man standing in the middle of a fairway with a golf club in his hands.

She could hear birds chirping in the branches above her head, and smelled the fresh pine wafting around her from the grove of pine trees where she was standing.

"Tor?" Piper asked.

Still unable to answer her friend, Tori tried to remain focused on the details of where she was. Fighting the chaotic, fragmented thoughts that kept redirecting her attention, she watched the man in the crosshairs and felt the weight of the rifle in her hands.

As the realization that her finger was on the trigger came to her, her first thought was to pull her hand away but it was too late. The power to do so was not hers, and seconds later, she felt her finger advance as the rifle fired.

"Tor?" Piper asked again.

Startled by the sound of the gunshot in her head, Tori looked up into Piper's concerned eyes. "We have another victim," she informed solemnly as the sound of a cell phone ringing at the other end of the house broke the silence. "Come on," she urged, "that's Agent Hunter calling us now."

Chapter 17

"Is it just me, or is this whole vision thing a little creepy?" Logan whispered to Piper as they all drove towards the office together. "How did she know there was another victim before we did?"

"You know I can hear you, right?" Tori interrupted from the front seat as she handed Logan an oblong object wrapped in aluminum foil.

"What's this?" he asked, guiltily.

"Your breakfast," she replied, handing one to Piper as well.

As he opened one end of the parcel, Logan's eyes registered surprise when he saw what was inside. "You made us breakfast burritos?"

"Well, why not?" she asked. "We were all hungry; the food was ready to go, and we had no time. So I wrapped everything up into burritos on the go."

"Wait," Logan hesitated before taking a bite. "You didn't put a cupcake in here did you?"

Tori snorted a laugh and replied, "Of course not! That's dessert!"

"Hold on," Ben demanded as he drove. "I thought you said the cupcakes were healthy because they had zucchini in them. So how does exactly does that now qualify them as dessert? You're changing the rules on me!"

"*Cupcake?*" Goliath asked Tori, hopefully.

"Oh for goodness sake, Goliath," Tori chuckled, reaching into the bag for a cupcake. "Here," she added after removing the paper liner and extending it towards him.

"You're not going to let him eat that in the car are you?" Logan exclaimed, eyeing his proximity next to the large dog. "He'll get crumbs and slobber everywhere!"

Piper giggled and advised, "Clearly you've never seen Goliath eat anything before. Trust me you won't see a single crumb fall from his mouth afterward, watch."

Still skeptical, Logan watched as Goliath gently took the cupcake from Tori's hand where it then completely disappeared into his mouth. Seconds later, Goliath turned his attention back to Tori eagerly, his mouth open in a huge grin, cupcake free. "*Cupcake?*" he asked again.

"No, Goliath, that's all you get," Tori replied firmly.

"Did he even chew it? I didn't see his mouth move. One second it was there and then it was gone!" Logan marveled.

"I told you!" Piper grinned. "He's better than any vacuum cleaner I've ever seen!"

"Hold on, I'm still waiting for the explanation of the health benefits of these cupcakes," Ben teased.

Laughing, Tori opened the foil on one end of one of the burritos and handed it to him. "Just be quiet and eat your breakfast."

~~~~~~~~~~

"So what did you find out, sir?" Tori asked Agent Hunter as the team assembled around the conference table a short time later.

"You were right," he advised, taking a seat at the end of the table. "It appears that we do have a third victim. I just spoke with the lead investigator in Crittenden, who is handling the case, and he confirmed the details match up to your vision. Well, at least what little I was able to share without going into much detail."

"Crittenden, that's in Kentucky right?" Ben asked.

"That is correct," Agent Hunter nodded.

"Well, that makes three victims all from the same state, which means we have an approximate idea of where our killer is focusing his time. That's a good thing, right?" Ben suggested.

"Agreed," Agent Hunter conceded. "Speaking of which, Agent Cooper, why don't we talk through what you saw so we can get an impression of the killer from your point of view before we go into detail about the victim. Agent Hughes, would you do the honors and make notes on our crime board please?"

"Yes sir," Riley quickly replied as he rose from his chair and approached the board.

"Okay. Let's see," Tori paused, thinking back to earlier while she and Piper were in the nursery. "First of all, this was definitely the same man who fired the rifle from the tree with our second victim. It's almost like I have an impression of him in my mind now."

"What do you mean by an impression?" Agent Hunter inquired.

"Well, it's hard to describe, but if I had to put it into words, I guess I would say it's like a signature or a feeling of him. The way he thinks, the way he feels, the way he reasons logic in his mind – it's familiar. I feel like I already know him somehow. Like I'm inside his head, looking out and seeing the world from his point of view," Tori explained.

"And this is different from other people you've read in the past," Agent Hunter proposed.

"Absolutely," Tori nodded emphatically. "This is too familiar to me, but I don't know how that's possible. And what's even more interesting to me is the feeling of conviction he has when he's watching his victims. I sense very little anger in him which is unusual considering the circumstances. He feels strongly convicted that these men are unjustly alive on this earth, and it's his responsibility to finish something."

"Unjustly alive?" asked Reagan. "Finish what? What does that mean? Do you mean he sees himself as an executioner?"

"Oh!" Tori exclaimed in surprise. "That's it! That's what I was trying to say, but I just couldn't find the right word! Yes! He sees himself as an executioner of these men who for whatever reason, he feels don't deserve to be alive like they've cheated death somehow."

"That's interesting," Agent Hunter murmured, deep in thought.

"What's interesting sir?" Tori asked curiously.

"Something that the investigator said about our third victim, Peyton Birch," he replied. Clasping his hands together, he began tapping his index fingers against his lips as he considered where his train of thought was going.

While they waited for him to continue, Riley quietly wrote the name 'Peyton Birch' under a new column on their crime board.

"Agent Hughes, do you recall any details with either of our first two victims related to any tragic events in their lives?" Agent Hunter asked quietly.

"Uh no, not that I recall off the top of my head," Riley replied. "What do you mean by tragic events? Like accidents or deaths in their families?"

"Something like that yes. Peyton Birch was a former Marine, and he was the sole survivor of an IED explosion. All of the men in his unit were killed, except for him," Agent Hunter informed the group.

"Semper Fi," Logan murmured quietly.

"But neither Grant Albertson nor Wade Hackett was a Marine," Reagan reminded everyone. "Neither of them had any former military experience. I checked for that."

"Just to be sure, let's go back into their files and see if there's anything we may have overlooked. We need to find the commonality to our victims and right now, we don't seem to have any connection; other than our killer and possibly the state of Kentucky as Agent Vincent noted," Agent Hunter replied.

"It would be much easier for me just to visit our victims and ask them myself," Tori winced as she felt a strong kick in her ribs. "I'm sure they would be able to answer a lot of these questions in a matter of minutes."

"Agreed, however considering your current condition and the fact that you are too far along in your pregnancy to travel, we'll have to use good old-fashioned investigative research like everyone else," Agent Hunter advised. "Why don't you put some of your expertise navigating the internet to use and do some of that research? See if you can find out anything the police may have overlooked."

"Okay," Tori shrugged agreeably. "I can do that. I have a few ideas on what I should look for so I'll see what I can find."

"I'll help you," Ben offered. "I've become a bit more familiar with using evidence filtering in our main database that should help."

"If you could use another set of eyes, I'll help too," Piper chimed in.

"Excellent. In the meantime, the rest of the team will travel with me to Crittenden, get the lay of the land and see what else we can find out about our newest victim," Agent Hunter advised. "Oh, and Agent Cooper, I've arranged to have Mr. Birch's personal effects delivered here once the police have released them. Our evidence management unit will let you know when they arrive so you can determine whether you can pick up any resonant images or details that might help our case. Keep me in the loop once they've arrived and if you pick up anything."

"Yes, sir," Tori replied.

"Okay, that's all I have for now. Everyone keep your cell phones on and check in with me at the end of the day. Phone, email or text are fine but at least one of the three, agreed?" Agent Hunter instructed.

"Agreed," everyone replied in unison.

Chapter 18

"Well don't you look all cozy lying there on the couch?" Piper remarked as she walked through the door carrying two large pizza boxes. "I hope you don't mind that I barged in without knocking. My hands were full, and these pizzas are hot!"

"Hi! Of course not, come on in!" Tori greeted. "I heard the door open but thought it was Ben and Goliath returning from their walk. I think Ben wanted to burn off some of Goliath's energy so we could focus on our research tonight. Thank you for offering to pick up dinner on your way over. That pizza smells amazing!"

"You're welcome! I'm probably way overdue from contributing to dinner the way you and Ben cook all the time. You're always feeding me, so it's my turn. Speaking of which, where should I put these?" Piper motioned to the boxes in her hands.

"Um, on the kitchen counter I guess for now," Tori thought out loud. "That would probably be the safest altitude away from Goliath considering he'll immediately go into food recon mode the moment he walks through that door! Do you need any help?"

"No, you stay right there," Piper insisted, heading towards the kitchen. "I have everything under control!"

"Thank goodness. I was hoping you'd say no. It's pretty comical watching me try to get off of this sofa lately," Tori chuckled as she gently rubbed her stomach.

"Oh you poor thing," Piper called out from the kitchen. "It won't be too much longer and then you'll be back to your old self!"

"I sure hope so," Tori replied.

Returning to the living room pizza free, Piper set her purse and laptop bag down on the floor along the couch and sat down next to Tori. Tenderly placing her hand on Tori's stomach, she asked, "So how are our little angels doing? Are they awake?"

"They're pretty quiet right now," Tori admitted. "I'll let you know when they start moving around so you can feel them."

"Okay!" Piper smiled as she sat back against the cushion. "So everything is good? No unexpected visions or disturbing visitations from you know who?"

Tori shook her head and replied, "Nope, neither a peep nor a blip since earlier this morning when we were in the nursery."

"That's good," Piper sighed in relief. "A little normalcy for you is a good thing."

"How about you, is everything okay? Did Logan get to the airport in time for his flight?" Tori asked.

Piper nodded slowly and then gave Tori a strange look. "Yep, everyone made their flight in time."

"What? Did you want to go with them?" Tori wondered.

"No, I'm cool staying here working on the research with you and Ben," Piper assured.

"Then what's bothering you? And don't tell me nothing because I can tell something is on your mind," Tori warned. "Is it Riley?"

Piper shrugged and said, "Yes and no. I don't know! He didn't call before he left, but then again it's not like he has to. It's just that he normally does. Then when he saw me dropping Logan off at the airport, he gave me a look that I really couldn't translate. And it's not like I could ask him about it with Logan standing right there. I don't know...," she trailed off quietly.

"Did he know you were taking Logan to the airport?" Tori asked.

"I don't think so," Piper admitted. "It's not like Logan and I are getting back together or anything like that. He needed a ride, and I was heading out to your house, so I offered to drop him off."

"But again, if Riley didn't know that, he may have misread what he saw," Tori offered.

"Well, it's not as if I gave him a big wet kiss goodbye or anything like that!" Piper insisted.

Exhaling a deep sigh, Tori looked at Piper thoughtfully before replying.

"What?" Piper demanded.

"You know, for two people who are so good at reading other people, you seriously don't have a clue how to read each other do you?" Tori remarked sarcastically.

"What's that supposed to mean?" Piper challenged.

"I mean the two of you are crazy for each other yet neither one of you wants to step foot over that imaginary line that got drawn somewhere along the way. What's the deal? I've seen the way he looks when he's talking about you or thinking about you. You can't tell me you haven't noticed changes in him when the two of you are together," Tori exclaimed. "Am I right?"

Grinning sheepishly, Piper nodded and admitted, "His aura changes when he looks at me when we're alone together."

"Changes in a good way I would guess?" Tori prodded.

Piper nodded in reply.

"To a color that indicates he's feeling affection for you by any chance?" Tori teased.

Embarrassed, Piper nodded again.

"Then what's the problem you, dork!" Tori chuckled. "Just rip the band-aid off and get it over with! My gosh! At the rate the two of you are going with this relationship, the twins will be in college before you hook up!"

"Hey!" Piper exclaimed.

"Am I wrong?" Tori prodded again. "Seriously, what's the holdup? Are you worried about what Agent Hunter would say? Or is this still about Riley's past feelings for Karla? Have the two of you even kissed yet?"

"He leaned once when we were in the conference room working on the Talman Mahmid case last fall. But then he stopped and pulled back," Piper admitted.

"He leaned?" Tori asked with raised eyebrows.

"Yeah, you know, as in leaned forward," Piper demonstrated, leaning towards Tori.

Unconvinced, Tori frowned at Piper and replied, "That's it. He leaned."

"Yes!" Piper exclaimed.

"Oh my goodness, you are positively hopeless," Tori sighed dramatically.

"What?" Piper cried out.

"Did you lean too?" Tori asked.

Pausing to think back before answering, Piper looked at Tori with panicked eyes and replied, "I don't know! I may not have. What does that mean? Was I supposed to lean? How do you know all of this? Did you and Ben do the lean thing when you were first dating?"

Chuckling at Piper's expression, Tori admitted, "I'm not sure if using Ben and me would be the best example. Especially considering it seems we dated many years before I even knew we were doing it! All I know is I've seen movies where 'the lean' is a significant moment in a first kiss. And since it seems that Riley has already made one attempt that you shut down; he's waiting for you to make the next move. What do you think?"

"I think the thought of doing that is terrifying," Piper groaned. "I've never done anything like that before."

"Not even when you were dating Logan?" Tori asked.

"Ah, no," Piper laughed. "Logan is like a bull in a china shop when it comes to romance."

"I'm not sure I want to know what that means," Tori admitted, ruefully.

"What? No, nothing like that!" Piper exclaimed. "Right after we graduated from the Academy, we went out on a date, and then the conversation led to us talking about how we felt about one another. Then suddenly he just grabbed me and kissed me. There was no leaning involved. Riley, on the other hand, is more reserved. Everything he does comes with careful thought and consideration."

"Hence my comment about it being your move," Tori remarked.

Hesitating long enough to consider Tori's statement, Piper slowly nodded her head and admitted, "You're right. I hadn't considered that could be the case, but you're right. What do I do next? What would you do?"

"Hmm," Tori thought. "Well, how about sending him a short text message? I wouldn't say anything too personal, say something neutral, so he knows's you're thinking about him."

"Neutral? What would you consider neutral? Like asking him if he had a good flight?" Piper scowled in frustration.

"No, that's still a little personal," Tori admitted, trying to come up with an example. "I know! Tell him you're at our house and that we're about to start researching the three victims. Ask him if he or Agent Hunter found out anything new since they left. Then after he replies, say something like, you hope he has a good night or good luck with their investigation in Crittenden. Something that will put you in his mind in a pleasant way."

"That's pretty clever. I like it," Piper admitted approvingly. "And pretty sneaky, I might add. Okay, it's worth a shot!"

Hearing the sound of the front door opening, both women turned their heads as Goliath and Ben returned home.

"Whoa, hang on, Goliath!" Ben laughed, releasing his hold on the leash as the large dog immediately lunged forward when he saw Piper. "Hey, Piper!"

"Hi, Ben! Hey there, Goliath!" Piper greeted as Goliath rushed over and began smelling her hands. "Sorry buddy! The pizza is in the kitchen."

Confirming her statement, Goliath's head turned to the direction of the kitchen as his nose picked up the scent. Instantly he began galloping towards the open doorway.

"Ben!" Tori cried out, trying not to laugh.

"I've got him, don't worry," Ben chuckled, jogging behind the dog. "Goliath, down!" he scolded as he entered the room. A few moments later, he returned to the living room, grinning as Goliath followed slowly behind him.

"Did you catch him in time?" Tori teased.

"Yep. I put the boxes in the oven so he couldn't get to them," Ben announced.

"Oh, that was a good idea. I should have thought of that," Tori applauded.

"No worries, we're good. Are you ready for me to bring out the dishes and we can eat before we get to work? That pizza smells great, and I'm starving!" Ben admitted.

"Shocker," Tori remarked.

"I know right?" he grinned. "So is that a yes?"

"Just a few more minutes," Tori advised, glancing at Piper. "Piper has a text to send first."

"Oh, right!" Piper replied, jumping to attention. "I'll do that right now!"

Chapter 19

"Oh, I want another piece but at the same time, I'm stuffed!" Tori announced, wiping pizza sauce from the corner of her mouth. "That was so good!"

"I second that," Piper groaned, setting her empty plate on the coffee table and leaning back on the couch. "I can't decide which is better, the crunchy crust, the tangy tomato sauce or the melted cheese!"

"I vote cheese!" Tori declared. "The answer should always be cheese!"

"I prefer not to choose. They're all my favorites!" Ben announced, tossing a piece of pizza crust to Goliath as he stood up from the couch. "If you ladies are done, I'll take your plates and clean up so we can get started. Piper, would you like another glass of wine?"

Handing Ben hers and Tori's plates, she replied, "Just a half glass, please. Anything more and I'll get too relaxed. I have to drive home later. Thanks, Ben!"

"You're welcome! Here you go," he replied, filling her glass half-way.

"You know you can always crash here if you don't feel like driving," Tori advised as she reached over and took a sip of wine from Piper's glass. "Oh, that's good. Did we have that in our wine rack?"

"Is it safe for you to be drinking that in your condition?" Piper cautioned her friend.

"A small amount of wine is okay, I already asked my doctor," Tori advised. "And chocolate, that's safe too. I made sure I covered the important things of course."

"You're funny," Piper chuckled.

"Okay, we're all set," Ben announced, emerging from the kitchen with a bag of dark chocolate M&M's in his hand. "Did I hear correctly and someone mentioned they wanted chocolate?"

"Oh, you're the best husband ever!" Tori exclaimed, reaching for the bag.

"Don't ever forget that," Ben advised, bending down to kiss her on the forehead while handing the bag to her. "Is there anything else I can get you?"

"No, I'm good. Thank you, honey," she smiled up at him, fondly.

"You're welcome. Okay. So how do we want to do this? Should we each take a victim's case file and work them individually or should we go through each one together as a team?" he asked.

"I vote we work each one together as a team," Tori mumbled through a mouth full of chocolate. "That way we can focus on the new information we know we need to look for, based on what we talked about earlier today with the others."

"I'm good with that," Piper replied, reaching into her bag for her laptop. "Let's start with Grant Albertson since he was our first victim. Do you have the copy of the official police report Agent Hunter said he was going to give you?"

"Right here," Ben advised, handing Tori her laptop, a notepad, and a manila file folder.

"Thanks," Tori replied, positioning herself on the couch where she could rest the laptop on her legs far enough away from her stomach as she could. Chuckling at her situation, she announced, "Look at me! I can barely see the keyboard over my stomach! I'm running out of lap for my laptop!"

"Oh, I didn't think of that, I'm sorry!" Piper exclaimed. "Would you be more comfortable at the table? We can move!"

"Don't worry, she can't work at the table either," Ben warned with a smirk. "Her stomach prevents her from getting the chair close enough to the table. The couch is the only option for her right now."

"Oh! You poor thing," Piper giggled. "Oh, I'm so sorry. I promise I'm trying not to laugh."

"No, that's okay, you can laugh," Tori grinned, wryly. "It is pretty funny."

"Well, here, give me that file folder so at least you don't have to try and manage that too. Do you want me to take notes, so you have more room?" Piper offered.

"No, thanks," Tori replied, setting the notepad and pen on the cushion beside her. "I like to have my notepad handy and jot down notes as I work."

"Right, I forgot about that," Piper nodded, recalling Tori's habit for always carrying a notepad with her.

"All right, let's get logged into the VPN and start digging," Tori instructed as she entered her username and password into a command prompt on her screen. "Piper, go ahead and relay what we know about Grant Albertson from the file notes and we'll start picking that apart."

Scanning through the first page, Piper replied, "Okay. Let's see. Mr. Grant Albertson. He was born and raised in LaGrange, Kentucky and was the former high school Quarterback for the South Oldham Dragons. At the time of his death he was thirty-five years old. He was the manager of his family's grocery store called Albertson's Grocery."

"What does it say about his immediate family?" Tori asked. "Was he married? Did he have any children?"

Flipping the page, Piper read through the top half of the page and replied, "It says he was a widower but he remarried two years ago. His first wife and five-year-old son were killed. That's sad."

"Does it say how?" Ben asked.

"It was from a single car accident," Tori announced, as she read from her laptop screen. "I found a news article here dated June 1, 2005. Grant Albertson was the driver."

"Oh, man," Ben replied, shaking his head.

"Yep, that's what the report says here too," Piper confirmed, sadly. "He was the cause of his wife and son's deaths."

Nodding solemnly, Tori replied, "He fell asleep at the wheel, as they were driving home one night." Reading through the rest of the article, she added, "It says here that his wife died at the scene of the accident, and his son died in the hospital a few hours later. He had massive internal bleeding and died during surgery. Mr. Albertson was in critical condition and was placed in a drug-induced coma to prevent swelling of the brain until they could operate. For several months, he didn't know what happened to his family."

"That poor man and his parents," Piper muttered.

"They lost their only grandchild and then had to wait all those months not knowing if their son would survive," Ben agreed. "How do you tell your son that he was the cause of something like that? How did Grant Albertson deal with all of that guilt?"

"Not very well from what it says here in this medical report," Piper noted, reading through the next page. "According to his doctors, he suffered from depression, and it took several months of both physical therapy and psychiatric counseling before they released him from the hospital. He never fully regained all of his motor function, so he was no longer able to drive, and since he was clinically depressed, it made it difficult for him to find work. His doctor's diagnosis indicates that he suffered from survivor's guilt."

"I'm not sure I could get behind the wheel of a car after that," Ben admitted.

"Was he working for his parents before the accident?" Tori asked, curiously.

"It doesn't say anything about his former employment history," Piper scanned through the rest of the file. "What are you thinking?"

"Just curious about something," Tori replied, as she began to type quickly on her keyboard. "Is Grant Albertson's father's first name Daniel?"

"Ah, yes. Daniel Joseph," Piper confirmed.

"Here we go," Tori declared triumphantly. "Mr. Daniel Joseph Albertson from LaGrange, Kentucky, former Manager of Albertson's Grocery, retired in August 2010. He has been collecting social security since then."

"You hacked into the IRS database?" Ben exclaimed in surprise.

"What? Like it's hard?" Tori replied, innocently.

"You're going to have to bring your children to the women's penitentiary to visit their mother in prison, Ben," Piper teased.

"You are scary sometimes; you know that?" Ben accused.

"I love you too, honey," Tori smiled as she began typing on her keyboard again. "Okay, so Grant Albertson's tax return for 2010 show's his title as Manager of Albertson's Grocery and his address matches that of his father's, so that makes sense."

"What makes sense?" Piper asked, now confused.

"You said that Grant Albertson had difficulty finding work and that he was clinically depressed. I suspect Grant's parents felt sorry for their son. They probably had him move in with them when he was released from the hospital. Then his father hired him at the grocery store and trained him to do his job. Then, when Daniel Albertson felt his son was ready to take over the store, he retired, and Grant became the new manager," Tori surmised.

"And what part of this is what you feel we need to focus on?" Ben asked.

"I'm not sure, but it at least gives us a timeline and more background on Grant Albertson than we had before," Tori admitted. "Is there anything else in that file you think might be helpful?"

"No, not really," Piper replied, scanning the last few pages. "I think the only loose end we still have on him would be his relationship with the woman with the Dalmatian. Well, that and if his death involved his relationship with her or another reason we haven't figured out yet."

"I would have to agree," Ben confirmed.

"Same here," Tori replied, making a note on her notepad. "Okay, let's move on to Wade Hackett, victim number two."

"I have that file here," Ben advised as he flipped open the cover and began to read the information out loud. "Mr. Wade Hackett. He was born and raised in Shelbyville, Kentucky. At the time of his death, he was thirty years old, married and survived by his wife and one teenage daughter."

"And one very exotic mistress," Piper advised.

Flashing a crooked smile, Ben nodded and added, "And one very exotic mistress. He attended Shelby County High School and was a star on the track team."

"That makes sense since he was a jogger," Piper pointed out.

"He received a full academic scholarship to Brown University in Rhode Island for Mathematics and was also a member of the track team in college," Ben added.

"Brown University, that's one of the top ten," Tori noted, executing another search on her laptop.

"That's a sixty thousand a year tuition," Piper remarked. "I have a friend who went to college there but she wasn't lucky enough to have a scholarship. She's still paying off her college loans."

"Oh man," Tori muttered as she stared at her screen.

"What?" Ben asked, concerned.

"We might have the start of a pattern here. I found another article, this time an accident involving Wade Hackett, who was nineteen years old, at the time. He and a few friends from Brown were flying to Colorado for a winter break ski trip, and the plane malfunctioned. The pilot lost control of the plane over the Rocky Mountains. Everyone on board except for Wade Hackett was killed. He was the only survivor," Tori read.

"Are you serious? How big was the plane?" Ben asked.

"It was a small, single-engine Cessna and only had six people onboard, including the pilot, who happened to be one of the students. He had his pilot's license, and it was his father's plane," Tori replied.

"Wow," Piper exclaimed in surprise. "That's two family tragedies, each with only one survivor."

"And as Tori mentioned, it sounds like the start of a pattern," Ben agreed.

"What was his recovery story?" Piper asked.

"The copy of his medical report indicates Wade Hackett had two broken legs, a broken back, and a dislocated shoulder. He had to work through several months of extensive and I would imagine very painful physical therapy, just like Grant Albertson. That's an interesting coincidence," Ben observed.

"I don't believe in those," Tori muttered as she completed another browser search and read the responses. "What did it say about his mental state? Was he another sufferer of survivor's guilt?"

"Checking," Ben replied as he read through the next couple of pages. "Here we go. Yes, he did. He belonged to a support group at the hospital. From the dates noted in the file, he attended the group for several years."

"What was the last date they have noted for him?" Tori asked.

"October of 2010," Ben replied.

"Piper, does Grant Albertson's medical file say anything about him belonging to a support group?" Tori asked, curiously.

"Um, let's see," Piper replied, flipping back through Grant Albertson's file. "It says he was seeing a counselor named Dr. Bryce Reed, but nothing about a support group."

Making a note on her notepad, Tori asked, "Is there a number for Dr. Reed?"

"Five, zero, two, five, six, six, three, one, nine," Piper read out loud.

"What are you thinking, Red?" Ben asked.

Tori looked up to meet Ben's curious expression and asked, "Do you remember what Agent Hunter said about our third victim, Peyton Birch? He said he was a former Marine, who was the sole survivor of an IED explosion. All of the men in his unit were killed, except for him."

"So you're trying to find the connection since we have three victims who are all sole survivors of three tragic events," Ben nodded in understanding.

"Exactly," Tori advised.

"Then we need to find out more about Peyton Birch," Piper chimed in enthusiastically.

"Agreed," Tori replied, picking up her laptop and placing it on the sofa beside her. "But first, I need to take a break. My little angels are dancing on my bladder. Ben, will you help me up, please?"

"Absolutely," Ben replied, jumping up from his chair.

"Thanks!" Tori smiled.

Waiting until he heard the sound of the bathroom door closing, Ben turned to Piper and asked, "So how's she doing? Do you see anything off that I need to be aware of?"

"No, not at all," Piper replied. "Her aura has a healthy, vibrant green glow like normal."

"Okay, good," Ben replied.

"Yours, however, has some threads of brownish-yellow mixed into your normal blue color which means you're stressing yourself out too much," Piper advised.

Ben exhaled a deep breath and admitted, "You're right. I'm probably doing a lot more of that than I should. It's just so hard sometimes trying to remain calm and cool on the outside when I worry about her so much! Everyone expects a lot out of her all the time. I just hope it doesn't become more than she can handle."

"She'll tell us if it does," Piper reasoned.

"Will she?" Ben challenged. "I'm not so sure."

"Then we'll just have to remove as much of the work load off of her as we can, when we can," Piper advised, removing her cell phone from her pocket. She looked down at opened file in her lap and dialed a number.

"Who are you calling?" Ben asked.

"Dr. Reed, Grant Albertsons's therapist," Piper replied as she waited for the call to connect.

"Good idea. He's probably not in the office this time of night, though," Ben noted.

"Probably not, but I can leave him a message," Piper replied quickly as the doctor's answering machine picked up. "Hello, Doctor Reed. My name is Agent Piper Stirling from the FBI. I have a few questions I was hoping I could ask you about a former patient of yours. If you would please return my call, I would greatly appreciate it. My cell number is eight, zero, four, six, four, six, five, one, two, three. Thank you."

"Okay, that's much better!" Tori sighed as she returned. "What are you guys talking about?"

"I went ahead and left a message with Dr. Reed's answering service while you were in the bathroom. I'll follow up with him and see if he knows of a support group that Grant Albertson might have belonged to," Piper advised.

"Okay, great. Thanks, Piper!" Tori replied.

"And I sent Agent Hunter an email and caught him up to speed with what we've found out so far, so he can get us the medical records for Peyton Birch. Hopefully, we'll be able to match up some of the similarities we've already found with Mr. Albertson and Mr. Hackett to Mr. Birch," Ben replied.

"Awesome teamwork," Tori nodded happily. "Nice job! So let's see what we can find out about Mr. Birch."

"Well, we know he was a former Marine Corps Corporal and that he was the lone survivor of an IED blast that took out the rest of his unit," Piper recounted.

"Agreed," Tori nodded as she accessed Peyton Birch's file in the FBI database. "His military record also notes that wasn't the first attack he experienced. He did a tour in Afghanistan eight years ago. He drove a military vehicle into a barricade where insurgents were firing on his unit. Afterward, he was given a commendation for bravery."

"Agent Hunter just forwarded us Mr. Birch's medical records," Ben announced, reading an attachment to his email. "As we suspected, Peyton Birch had severe injuries from the IED blast that required physical therapy. It happened in May 2010. He lost his right leg and was deaf in his right ear. He had a prosthetic leg."

"I wonder what kind of mental state he had after all of that," Tori wondered as she accessed the Veterans Administration site.

"I would expect at the very least he would be grateful to be still alive," Piper admitted.

"I don't know, Piper," Ben shrugged. "Being awarded for bravery and then finding out you're the only one who survived an attack on your last assignment. That has to mess with a man's head."

"It did," Tori announced. "The VA shows Peyton Birch as being a part of a PTSD support group. Okay, we have three victims, all having a traumatic event in their past. All of whom required physical recovery afterward, and all three having survivor's guilt and being a part of either a support group or in counseling to help them cope."

"So what's our true connection here, the physical similarities or the mental ones?" Ben surmised.

"And how do they connect to our killer?" Piper reminded them.

"That's a good question, Piper," Tori paused, thinking back to her last two memory impressions of their shooter. "We know our killer was a former Marine so that only directly connects him to Peyton Birch. Our shooter climbed a seventy-foot tree to get to Wade Hackett, which means it would have taken a lot of strength and the use of both of his legs. Earlier today when I was having my vision of him about to shoot Peyton Birch, I felt both of his arms and hands, so he didn't have any physical limitations."

"Which would indicate that he may not have had to go through any physical therapy related to his incident," Piper noted.

"Yet, we still can't rule that out. Just because the guy didn't lose a limb, doesn't mean he didn't get shot or have an injury that still required some form of physical therapy," Ben pointed out.

"You're right, we can't rule that out," Piper agreed.

"Did Agent Hunter indicate whether they've found out anything new yet? Like maybe talked to the gentleman Mr. Birch was golfing with at the time or any other witnesses at the course that day that might have seen someone like our guy?" Tori inquired.

"Not yet," Ben advised. "He said they just left the police station and were on their way to check into their hotel. They have to wait for jurisdictional clearance by Director Gibbs before the Chief of Police will allow us to have access to their case information."

"Good old politics," Piper added sarcastically.

"Hmm, okay. They have to follow the rules too, so that's that. I guess that's as far as we can go until they've gotten that approval," Tori surmised.

"Well, he did confirm that Mr. Birch's personal effects were delivered to our office this afternoon. So we should go there first thing in the morning and see if you can pick up any visual clues from any of them," Ben suggested. "Piper, do you want to come with us?"

"Absolutely," Piper exclaimed. "If Tori will be doing a memory impression on a piece of evidence, I'll need to be there to monitor her."

"Okay, that sounds good to me," Tori replied, yawning.

"I better go before you turn into a pumpkin," Piper teased, as she began to pack up her things.

"I'm sorry! I wasn't implying you had to leave!" Tori apologized.

"No worries! It's getting late, and I can see your eyelids getting heavier by the minute. Besides, we're done for the night so this is good timing," Piper admitted.

"Are you sure you're okay to drive?" Tori worried.

"I'm good, thanks," Piper promised.

"Text me when you get home, okay?" Tori demanded.

"You're such a Mom!" Piper teased, leaning over to hug her friend. "I promise I will text you once I've secured my apartment, and I'm all locked in for the night."

"Thank you, sweetie," Tori replied, hugging Piper tightly.

"Goodnight, Piper," Ben added.

"Goodnight!" Piper smiled, closing the door behind her.

Chapter 20

Zander stared at his muddy boots lying on the floor beside the window, doing his best to fight the panic building inside of him. Seeing the dried mud and pine needles caked to the bottom of the soles in the daylight wasn't making the situation any less disturbing.

Shifting his gaze to the open rifle case on the bed beside him, he exhaled a deep breath of frustration as still no memory came back to him of removing it from his closet.

"......the murder appears to have been a single gunshot wound to the chest from a 22 caliber rifle..." he replayed in his head.

"Could I have done something like that?" he asked himself quietly. "Why would I have done something like that? And why can't I remember doing it!"

"...We were just out enjoying a nice Sunday afternoon together..." the man had said.

"What happened to Saturday?" he continued to agonize. "Maybe I slept through it. I did have another migraine. Maybe that's why I don't remember. I slept all the way through Saturday. That has to be it," he began to rationalize.

"*What's the last thing I remember*?" he thought back. Snapping his fingers, he replied, "Friday night! I filled the car up with gas, bought a six pack from the gas station and picked up a burger and fries on the way home afterward. That's right! I watched some TV and then went to bed. Now I remember! I must have slept through Saturday!"

"*When have you ever slept through an entire day, Alexander?*" the voice in his head challenged him.

Ignoring the voice he told himself, "Yep. That has to be what happened!"

Feeling better about his lost weekend, he glanced at the clock on the nightstand and saw that it was time for him to leave for work. Then his eyes averted back to the rifle and the boots. "I'll have to clean you guys up later," he told them both firmly as he rose from the bed. "I have to get to work."

Grabbing his phone, wallet, and car keys, he slid his feet into the pair of sneakers by the front door, locked the door behind him, and headed towards his car.

As he settled into the driver's seat of his car, he fastened his seatbelt and slid the key into the ignition. While the car sprang to life his eyes instinctively looked up to the dashboard panel to check for any warning lights. To his relief, there were none.

That is there were no warning lights on the dashboard display. The warning light in his head instantly went off and brought his eyes back to the gas gauge, which he had filled on Friday evening. The gas gauge that now showed the tank as empty.

"What the heck...," he muttered as the realization hit him. He hadn't slept through Saturday. And he had an empty tank of gas, a pair of muddy boots and a smoking gun to prove it.

"Oh, no," he whispered. "What have I done?"

Chapter 22

"Hi, guys!" Piper waved as she got out of her car.

"Good morning, sunshine!" Tori waved back, letting Goliath out of the back seat.

"Hey, Piper" Ben greeted.

"Come here, Goliath!" Piper encouraged as he galloped toward her across the parking lot. "How is my big, beautiful boy today?" she crooned as he made his way over to her.

"My, Piper," Tori heard Goliath happily announced when he saw her.

"Did you have a good night?" Piper asked, looking up at Tori, hopefully.

"Like a rock and dream free," Tori announced happily.

"Good! I was hoping you would," Piper smiled. Glancing down at Goliath's eager expression, she placed her hands on either side of his head and began gently rubbing his ears. "Oh, I just can't resist this face!"

"Goliath loves Piper," Tori heard him sigh.

Shouldering both laptop bags, Ben said, "Are we ready to get started?"

"Yep," Piper replied, giving Goliath one final rub. "Lead the way, big guy!"

"So did you hear from Riley last night?" Tori quietly asked Piper as they walked towards the building entrance.

Smiling secretively, Piper glanced at Ben, who was walking with Goliath a few steps ahead of them and replied, "Yes. He called me after he checked into his room and had dinner. I guess Logan mentioned that I dropped him off at the airport on the way to see you last night, so Riley was fine by the time I talked to him."

"Wow, so Logan played Cupid there without realizing it," Tori applauded.

"Sounds like it," Piper agreed.

"Do you think a part of him would cringe if he knew that?" Tori teased.

"Probably," Piper admitted. "Logan has a motive to just about everything he does. He doesn't often do things randomly like that."

"So do you think it really was random or could he have had a motive behind it?" Tori wondered.

"I thought about that too after I hung up with Riley, but I couldn't come up with a possible advantage for him doing that," Piper replied.

"Huh. Interesting," Tori mused. "I'll have to think about that too. I agree, that doesn't sound like our Logan. So otherwise, you and Riley are good?"

"Yep," Piper smiled. "We talked about what they did yesterday once they got into Crittenden, and then I caught him up on what the three of us worked through last night with the case files. We hung up in a good place."

"That's it?" Tori asked, glancing at Piper's face.

"What more should there have been?" Piper frowned in response.

"Oh, I don't know. Maybe something along the lines of, 'I miss you, Piper,' or 'when I get back in town, why don't we grab some dinner together, Piper,'," Tori dramatically emphasized.

Piper smirked and shook her head in amusement, "I already told you that's not going to happen."

"Okay then, why don't you make it happen?" Tori challenged. "You ask him out for dinner when he gets back like we talked about."

"You mean the whole ripping off the band-aid thing?" Piper asked hesitantly.

"Yep," Tori nodded. "That whole thing."

"Oh, I don't know if I can do that. What if he says no? I would feel stupid asking him on a date," Piper whispered, making sure Ben wasn't listening.

"Don't make it a date! Make it dinner or something casual like there's a new restaurant you want to try but you don't want to go alone or you have a buy one get another one free coupon or something like that. Take the pressure off of both of you and see where the conversation goes," Tori suggested.

"I guess I could do something like that," Piper reasoned.

"Just try it. He may surprise you," Tori encouraged. "I still think he's waiting for you to make the next move."

"It's worth a shot," Piper agreed.

As they stepped onto the sidewalk and approached the awning covering the sidewalk to the front door, Tori noticed Goliath hesitate and look around him. Then he slowly began walking forward again. A few seconds later, once they were all under the awning, he stopped again and began to whine.

Having seen him behave like this when she was in the conference room with Riley, Tori felt the hair rise on the back of her neck, and she instinctively looked around her.

A fraction of a second later, Goliath began barking frantically, and she heard the groan of metal bending. As she looked up, she saw the awning above them began to come down.

"Everyone, look out!" she exclaimed as she tried to jump back, but her feet got tangled in one another, and she lost her balance and fell. "Ouch!" she cried out.

"Ben!" Piper cried out as she dropped her laptop bag and grabbed onto the frame of the awning.

"I've got it! Help Tori," Ben shouted as he threw his and Tori's laptop bags to the ground so he could grab the other end of the frame.

Letting go of the frame, Piper heard Ben grunt as he felt the full force of the weight, and she turned to Tori. "Are you okay? Can you get up?"

"I think I might have twisted my ankle," Tori winced trying to put weight on her foot.

"I don't know how long I can hold this up, Piper," Ben warned, gritting his teeth. "You need to get her out of there!"

Thinking quickly, Piper ran around behind Tori, grabbed her under the arms and began to pull. "Ugh! I don't think I'm strong enough!"

"Goliath, call Remy!" Tori cried out, trying to push away with her good leg.

"REMY!" she immediately heard him bark.

Seconds later, she felt the air push forward from the force of his wings as Remy appeared. When he realized what was happening, he rushed forward and grabbed both Tori and Piper in his arms.

Quickly placing them onto the open sidewalk, he hurried over to where Ben was struggling and lifted the edge of the awning out of Ben's hands. As soon as everyone was clear, he dropped the awning down to the ground with a heavy thud.

"Are you okay?" he demanded, as he swiftly returned and crouched down beside Tori. "Are you hurt?"

"I'm okay. I think I twisted my ankle when I fell," she replied, gingerly running her fingers down her lower leg. "Thank you, Remy," she added, looking up into his panicked eyes.

As the panic in his eyes softened to affection, he gently touched her ankle, sending a warm radiating heat down her lower leg. "You're welcome," he smiled.

"Yes, thank you," Piper replied beside Tori, completely awestruck seeing Remy for the first time. "I promise I tried to move her; I just wasn't strong enough. You saved us both."

Tori gasped, not realizing that Remy had appeared in physical form to all of them. "They can see you?"

Turning to Piper, Remy bowed his shoulders forward slightly and replied, "It was my privilege, Piper, Guardian of the Chosen. It's a pleasure to meet you finally. You're a good friend to Tori."

"Likewise," she blushed, fascinated by the aura of pure white light surrounding him.

"He saved all of us," Ben advised, equally reverent in Remy's presence. "Thank you, Remy. I owe you my gratitude as well."

Rising to his feet, Remy turned his light gray eyes to Ben and smiled. "You're welcome, Ben. There are no obligations to return between us. Our mission is one in the same, to love her and to keep her safe."

Extending his hand, Ben smiled and said, "Agreed. It's an honor to meet you."

"The honor is mine," Remy replied, returning the handshake.

Tori smiled as her eyes filled with tears, grateful to see this moment between the two men.

"*Remy!*" Goliath barked happily, wagging his tail.

Turning to face him, Remy leaned forward and gently placed his hand on Goliath's head. "You did well, Goliath. I made the right choice, selecting you as one of her guardians."

"Yes you did," Tori agreed.

Turning back to Tori, Remy hesitated. "You're sure you're okay?"

"Yes," Tori nodded. "I'm fine."

"I would like to stay, but I need to find him. He's not going to get away with this. Not this time. He went too far this time," he warned angrily.

"I understand," Tori promised. "Please be careful."

Nodding in response, he paused long enough to get a sense of the air around him. Then his head turned to the right, and his eyes took on an ominous glare. A moment later, the space where he stood was empty.

"Wow," Piper breathed in amazement. "I can't believe that just happened. I just met a guardian angel."

"Yes you did," Tori smiled, enjoying the look of complete rapture on Piper's face.

"Should you go after him?" Ben suggested, warily. "You know, like you did the last time? Find out what's going on?"

Tori shook her head quickly and replied, "Uh uh. Did you see the look on Remy's face just now? He meant business. I'm not getting caught in between them right now."

"Did you see his wings? They were the most beautiful things I've ever seen. They completely radiated light!" Turning towards Tori, she exclaimed, "His whole body radiated pure white light!"

"I'm sorry sweetie I didn't see that part of it. Only you can see that. I'm sure it was beautiful," Tori admitted, shifting uncomfortably on the hard concrete.

Snapping to attention, Ben quickly came over to Tori and extended his hands to her, "Here, honey, let me help you up."

"Thanks, Ben," she agreed, reaching up to grasp his hands.

"Ready? One, two, three," he coaxed, gently pulling her up on her feet. "Brace yourself against me for a minute to see if you can put pressure on that ankle," he added as she regained her balance.

"My ankle is fine now," Tori admitted, putting her full weight on both feet. "I think Remy fixed it when he touched me!"

"Wow, he can do that too?" Piper exclaimed.

"I guess so," Tori shrugged. "Either way, my ankle doesn't hurt anymore."

"And everything else is okay? You didn't hurt yourself when you fell? The babies are okay?" Ben worried.

"We're all fine," she assured him, gently placing her palm against his cheek. "Thank you."

"Thank you, for what?" Ben asked, searching her eyes.

"For everything," she whispered, gently kissing him on the lips. "Thank you for trying to hold up the awning and allowing Remy to help, for being such a gentleman."

"You're welcome," he smiled, tenderly. "I love you."

"I love you too," she smiled.

"Did you see the look on Remy's face? What do you think he'll do when he finds Luc?" Piper interrupted excitedly, breaking the romantic mood. "Do you think he'll punch him in the face or toss him across the room with one of his wings? I bet their battles are epic! Maybe that's what's happening when we hear thunder and see lightning in the sky! Maybe it's Remy and Luc fighting with one another! What do you think? Do you think that's what happens? Who could we ask? Do you think Agent Sullivan would know?"

"There she goes," Ben chuckled as Piper's voice began to rise in pitch.

"We better stop her before she spins out of control," Tori giggled.

"I agree," he grinned, turning to look at Piper. "Since the show's over, how about we go inside and do what we came here to do? Would you mind grabbing the bags, Piper? I want to make sure Tori can walk without my help."

"Oh right! Sorry!" Piper replied, breaking free from her rant.

"Thanks, Piper!" Tori added as she and Ben began walking towards the door.

Stepping around the wreckage on the sidewalk, Piper quickly grabbed the bags and caught up with Tori and Ben. "Anyway, as I was saying, Remy and Luc's battles have to be epic! Have you ever seen one, Tori? What are they like? Are they flesh and blood? Have you ever seen one of them bleed…"

Chapter 22

"So what do you think?" Ben asked, watching Tori's face intently as she held the golf club.

Shaking her head slowly, she opened her eyes and replied, "Same as with the golf glove and the wallet - a big goose egg."

"Huh. I was sure the club would give you a memory impression considering he was holding it when he was shot," Piper frowned.

"Same here," Tori admitted, slipping the club back into the evidence container.

"Maybe it was a new club?" Ben suggested.

"Maybe, what else is in the box?" she added, motioning to the evidence box across the table.

"The last item we have, or items I guess I should say, are Peyton Birch's military dog tags," Ben advised, removing a clear plastic bag from the box.

"Was he wearing them when he was shot?" Piper hoped.

Glancing down at the copy of the police report, Ben nodded in confirmation, "Yes he was."

"Well then they should definitely have memories attached to them," Piper replied encouragingly.

"They may have more than we bargained for," Ben advised, looking worriedly at Tori. "Are you sure you're up for whatever you may see?"

"We don't really have much of a choice do we?" She shrugged.

Ben inclined his head in agreement and replied, "No, I guess not."

"Then I guess there's only one way to find out," Tori proclaimed, reaching for the bag.

"Okay," Ben sighed in resignation. "Here you go."

"Thank you," she replied, taking it from him. As soon as she made contact with the plastic, Tori's fingers began to tingle, and a gentle surge of energy began to flow through her. "Ladies and gentlemen, I believe we have a winner," she added softly.

Drawing in a deep breath, she opened the bag and tipped it downward, causing the chain to slide forward and pull the tags down into her hand. Instantly, the direct contact of the metal against her skin increased the flow of energy within her.

Pausing a moment to read the details inscribed on the tags, she gently traced the embossed lettering with her fingertips, envisioning the man behind the metal.

BIRCH
PEYTON J.
O POS
537-55-3221
USMC M
CHRISTIAN

"Well, he was a believer. That's a good thing," she noted, reading his religious preference on the last line. "Okay, here we go," she announced, closing her eyes.

The instantaneous surge of visions flooding into her head, coupled with the sound of an explosion, made her jump in surprise as she was thrust back in time to a small village bearing the scars of war and the harshness of humanity at its worst.

"Oh!" she exclaimed, unable to hide her surprise.

"Piper?" Ben asked quietly.

Watching the colors begin to swirl around her friend, Piper quietly replied, "So far mostly green with threads of violet and yellow. There's only a hint of black. They're all okay."

Tori squinted through thick billowing smoke polluting the air around her as it began to sting her eyes. Trying to look beyond the massive piles of rubble and twisted metal towering overhead, she noticed that many of the structures around her were gone. What remained were sections of blood-stained walls, riddled with bullet holes and gaping wounds from mortar blasts.

"The marks of death," she thought sadly.

"Can you help him?" A voice called out behind her.

Turning towards the sound, Tori squinted through the smoke and then her breath caught in her throat when she saw the bloodied and mangled bodies of soldiers lying on the ground a short distance away.

"Oh no!" she cried out in anguish.

"What? What do you see?" Ben asked Tori, glancing at Piper with concern.

"She's still okay," Piper whispered in reply.

"Bodies of soldiers," Tori replied as her eyes filled with tears. "They're on the ground everywhere around me."

"Are any of them alive?" he asked quietly.

"I don't know. They're so badly injured. I can't imagine anyone surviving something like this. There's blood everywhere," she whispered, walking forward slowly towards the bodies. As she gingerly stepped around the rubble, she looked down and saw a blood-stained boot with a foot and lower half of a man's leg still attached lying on the ground. Choking back a sob and the urge to vomit, she looked away and continued to move forward.

As she walked, the smoke began to drift away from her, and she could see the shimmering images of the spirits of the soldiers, standing at attention beside their bodies.

"Can you help him?" the spirit directly in front of her asked again.

"Can I help whom?" Tori asked him, cautiously.

"Corporal Birch," the man replied, pointing to one of the bodies lying on the ground a few feet from where they stood. "He's still alive, but he's in bad shape. Can you help him?"

Tori looked down at the man in question and saw he was missing his lower right leg. As she was about to respond, she heard the sound of men shouting behind her.

"There they are! Move in!"

Realizing she too was a spirit in this dimension, she watched as the approaching soldier's passed right through her, and rushed forward to check each body for vital signs.

"I've got one with a pulse! Over here," one man cried out to the medics.

"What about the others?" the soldier in charge demanded.

"They're all gone," the man replied. "This guy is the only one still alive."

"All right, get him stable and ready for transport!" the soldier ordered the medics. "The rest of you get our men into body bags and let's get them out of here!"

"What else do you see, Tori?" Ben asked quietly beside her.

"The rescue team is here. They're recovering the bodies. There was only one survivor, Peyton Birch," Tori announced to Ben and Piper as the smoke began to close in and the image began to fade. "The image is changing."

"Piper?" Ben checked again.

"There's a bit more blackness around her than before, but still she's in control," Piper advised.

"I'm fine," Tori declared as the new image began to appear of a brightly lit room with a highly polished floor.

"Where are you now?" she heard Ben ask.

"I'm not sure. It looks like some kind of a recreation room or a visitor's area at some kind of facility," Tori replied quietly, look around her.

"Describe it," Piper suggested.

"There're a lot of windows, and one side of the room has a bunch of tables and chairs set up near a shelf with a bunch of games. The other side of the room has an entertainment center with a big TV screen facing an old couch and a couple of recliner chairs," Tori replied.

"Are there any people in the room?" Ben prodded.

Tori nodded her head and replied, "There's a circle of metal folding chairs facing each other in the middle of the room. All of the chairs are occupied by men. One guy seems to be the facilitator of the group."

"It sounds like a support group meeting," Piper suggested.

"That's what I'm thinking too," Tori agreed.

"Do you see Peyton Birch?" Ben asked.

As Tori looked around the faces in the circle, she paused on one face that looked familiar to her but she couldn't place a name to the face. Moving on a few chairs down, she saw Peyton Birch. "He's here," she confirmed. "And he doesn't look very good."

"What do you mean?" Piper asked.

"He looks very tired and tortured," Tori noted. "This must have been shortly after his return to the states. His hair is disheveled, and it looks like he hasn't shaven in weeks. His clothes are wrinkled like he's been sleeping in them, and he keeps shifting in his chair like he's uncomfortable. I think it's his prosthetic leg. He hasn't gotten used to it yet."

"Is he talking?" Piper wondered.

"No, he's just listening," she replied as her eyes drifted back to the other man she noticed earlier.

"Honey, Zander is here," she suddenly recalled from her dream.

"Oh, that's him!" Tori blurted out.

"Who?" Ben replied.

"Zander! The man from my dream!" Tori exclaimed opening her eyes.

"Wait, what man? What dream?" he demanded.

Realizing she hadn't told anyone else about her dream yet, she winced apologetically and replied, "Oh, about that. Yeah, I kind of forgot to mention that one to you guys."

"You had a dream about a man who suddenly shows up in a vision from a piece of evidence tied to a murder, and you kinda forgot to tell us about it?" Ben argued.

Piper frowned at her and scolded, "You know better than that, Tori. Come on, you promised! You're the one who told us your dreams weren't just dreams, they were messages, and we needed to know about them so we could look for clues!"

"I know, I know, I'm sorry! Ganging up on me by the way isn't going to help!" Tori cried out in frustration. "This one was different. It was weird and fragmented and creepy. I couldn't make any sense out of it, and I guess I forgot to mention it."

"You forgot?" Piper challenged.

"Was that the afternoon I came home and found you crying at the sink?" Ben asked, gently touching her arm. "Ouch!" he exclaimed, drawing his hand back quickly. "You shocked me again!"

"I did? Oh, I'm so sorry! Why does that keep happening?" Tori apologized, reaching out her hand but then pulling it back to avoid touching him. "Are you okay?"

Rubbing his fingers gently, he laughed lightly and replied, "Yeah, I'm fine. It's just still a little weird."

"Why were you crying, Tor?" Piper worried. "What was the dream about that made you so upset?"

Setting the tags down on the table, Tori sighed and admitted, "Like I said it was weird and fragmented so don't expect it to make any sense. It started out with the nursery rhyme. The one we talked about that we painted on the walls in the nursery."

Piper nodded and said, "Right."

"That's where the nursery rhyme came from. Then I had a little visit with Luc," she added hesitantly which as expected, both Piper and Ben gave her an alarmed look. "That part didn't last very long. He was basically letting me know he knew about the twins and that all of heaven was abuzz with the announcement of the first Remiel boy."

"Tor," Ben exclaimed, shaking his head in disappointment. "That's not something to take lightly. No wonder he's getting bolder in his attacks. He doesn't want these children to be born. You do realize that, right? Having you as the proclaimed heir to the Remial prophecy is bad enough for him. Now you're about to give birth to the first Remial son. That has to be huge in a very biblical way! That accident earlier outside on the sidewalk – you could have been killed. Or even worse, that could have caused you to lose the babies!"

"But it didn't okay?" Tori defended. "And I won't lose the babies they're going to be fine!"

"How can you be so sure?" he argued, angrily.

"Because I met them! I talked to them!" Tori blurted out.

"Wait, what?" Piper interrupted.

"You talked to our kids?" Ben whispered, searching her eyes. "And you didn't think it important to tell me?"

Seeing the pained confusion on his face, Tori sighed and eased herself down into one of the chairs. "Please don't be angry with me, Ben. It was more than just talking to them."

"Tell me. Help me understand," he encouraged, sitting down in the chair beside her.

Exhaling a deep breath, Tori nodded. "Okay. It started out as the dream I've had before with the little red-haired girl riding Goliath like a pony. Remember?"

Ben nodded and replied, "Yes, I remember."

"Okay. So as I was helping the little girl down from Goliath's back, she turned to me and called me 'Mama' like she did before. Then she called out my attention to a little boy across the yard. He looked just like her except his hair was a little darker shade of auburn. He was playing in a water fountain. When he turned around, he smiled at me. But it wasn't just any smile, it was a very familiar, mischievous smile," Tori emphasized.

"I know that smile," Piper grinned.

Looking back and forth between the two women, Ben asked, "What smile?"

"Your smile," Tori advised, cautiously.

"It was RJ?" Ben exclaimed with wide eyes.

"Yes," Tori confirmed.

"Wow," Ben breathed, leaning back in the chair. "You met RJ."

"Yeah," Tori agreed.

"Okay, I'll admit that's a little cool and weird to be able to talk to your unborn children and all, but why did that keep you from telling me?" Ben challenged.

Wondering if it would be too much too soon, to share all of the details, Tori hesitated a moment but then decided Ben needed to be prepared for anything.

"Um, well that's the thing. RJ wasn't just playing in the water from the fountain, he was playing with the water in the fountain," Tori replied.

"So?" Ben shrugged. "Kids like to play with water. That's not a shocker, Tor."

"He's right. Water balloons, sprinklers, slip-and-slides…" Piper added.

Realizing she hadn't made her point, Tori tried again. "So, maybe playing with the water isn't the right description," she admitted, thinking about it further, "Okay, try this. Instead of him playing with the water, try he was controlling the water in the fountain."

Now totally confused, Ben frowned at her and asked, "Controlling as in?"

"Rip it off like a band-aid, Tor," she suddenly heard in her head.

"He was freezing the water in mid air with his hands, and then unfreezing it again back to water," she blurted out.

"Whaa…" Piper breathed.

Staring at her with eyes as big as satellite dishes, Ben's mouth dropped open, and he froze in shock.

Biting her lip nervously, Tori waited, allowing the visual to sink in.

"He was what?" Ben insisted, recovering quickly.

"Freezing and unfreezing water with his hands," Tori repeated cautiously.

"He was controlling the elements," Piper began to reason out loud. "He's going to be gifted too!"

"Huh? What are you talking about?" Ben asked, turning to look at Piper.

"That makes total sense!" She exclaimed, excitedly. "RJ is the yellow in the aura colors!"

"Oh, here we go with the colors," Ben began to argue.

"Hey!" Piper cried out, defensively.

"Now hold on, we all need to keep an open mind about all of this," Tori mediated. "What do you mean, Piper?"

"Thank you, Tori," Piper praised, glaring at Ben in the process. "As I was saying, RJ must be the band of yellow I keep seeing mixed in your aura."

"Why do you think RJ is the yellow?" Tori wondered.

"Yellow is the color of emerging psychic and spiritual awareness and abilities. If RJ is going to have the gift of controlling the elements, then it makes sense that the yellow belongs to him."

"So what, he's going to be some kind of magician?" Ben scowled.

"No! If what Tori saw was a premonition of what Gemma and RJ are going to be like, then RJ is going to be a completely new kind of guardian! Oh, now I really can't wait to meet this little boy!" Piper declared, happily.

"Let's not get ahead of ourselves, it's possible that none of this may happen," Tori tried to reason.

"And it's just as possible that it will! Has Gemma shown you any of her abilities yet?" Piper demanded.

"No, not that I remember," Tori admitted.

"We don't know for sure any of this is real, you know," Ben interrupted. "It could still all just be part of Tori's dream, and things that could be, not what they will be."

"True, which would be nice considering what I saw in the rest of my dream," Tori agreed.

"What do you mean?" Ben asked.

"That's when it got really creepy," Tori declared.

Chapter 23

"So you think the young man named Zander, in the military uniform from your dream, is the same guy you saw in the vision of Peyton Birch's support group meeting?" Piper replied as she rose from her chair and began walking around the table towards the whiteboard.

Carefully stepping over Goliath, who was stretched out and asleep on the floor, she picked up a dry erase marker from the tray and added the notes on the whiteboard beneath Riley's bullet points.

"Yes. I'm sure of it," Tori nodded firmly.

"Okay, so we have an elderly man sitting in a rocking chair on a porch. The same man wearing a uniform, years earlier on the same porch, but in better condition, and another man, who we believe to be the man's son. You said it looked like he was coming home from somewhere, wearing his uniform. And then an unknown body falling from the clouds, plummeting towards the earth," Ben re-read the notes out loud.

"Correct," Tori agreed.

"That's it? That was the end of your dream?" he asked.

"Yep," Tori lied. "That was it."

"Okay, I have to agree with Tori on this one," Piper admitted. "That part of her dream really is weird and creepy, especially the body falling from the sky."

"We'll get to that later. First off, let's go with what we think we know then and how it relates to our case. We know Peyton was former military as was this guy Zander and they were in the same support group. So we have a connection and a commonality. The PTSD," Ben reasoned.

"The next logical step would be to decide if Zander is our shooter or another victim," Piper added.

"Let's go with shooter," Tori advised.

Giving her a puzzled look, Ben challenged, "Why? What makes you say shooter?"

"I don't know. It's just a feeling I have," Tori admitted.

"Shooter it is," Piper agreed, writing the name 'Zander' under the column for a list of possible suspects.

Reading the notation, she turned to Tori and Ben and asked, "Is it safe to assume Zander is a shortened version of Alexander? I should probably note that as well, right?"

"I would agree that's a safe assumption," Tori agreed, entering a search string into a web browser on her laptop.

"I agree. How common do you think the name Alexander is?" Ben asked.

"One step ahead of you, sweetie," Tori winked at him as she waited for her search results to pull back. "Um, according to this baby names registry site, it's the fourteenth most common boy's name that parents name their sons," she announced.

"Yeah, that's not going to help us," Ben admitted.

"Nope," Tori sighed, leaning back in her chair.

"How else can we narrow it down?" Ben wondered out loud.

While each of them quietly wrestled with trying to consider another option, the room was silent, other than the gentle sound of Goliath's breathing as he slept.

"Do we have the authority to override doctor-patient confidentiality?" Piper asked, breaking the silence.

"I believe we do, where circumstances involve a possible crime like murder," Ben replied. "Why? What are you thinking?"

"I want to know if there was someone named Zander in either Grant Albertson's or Wade Hackett's groups," Piper declared, looking at the whiteboard. "We have a lot of loose ends here. I don't like loose ends."

"Me either," Tori agreed. "Did Dr. Reed call you back yet?"

"No, not yet," Piper admitted. "I'll keep trying."

"I'll contact King's Daughter Hospital in Ashland regarding Wade Hackett's group at the hospital," Ben offered. "I would think they should still have records from 2010."

"They should," Tori nodded. Looking back at the board she asked, "So what else do we have that we can dig into?"

"Let's talk about the old man on the porch," Ben suggested. "You said he was wearing a uniform. Did it look like the same kind of uniform? Like maybe both the older man and Zander were both Marines?"

"They were a little different but not by much," Tori admitted. "I would say they were both Marine Corps uniforms."

"Good. Father and son were both Marines," Piper nodded, making a note on the board.

"How old would you estimate the man you saw in Peyton's support group was, Tor?" Ben asked.

Closing her eyes to call back the man's face in her mind, Tori replied, "I would say between twenty-five and thirty-five years old."

"And how old did he look when you saw him getting out of the taxicab?" Ben prodded.

Thinking back, Tori replied, "Younger than that but not by much. I would guess early twenties."

Pausing to do a little math in his head, Ben suggested, "Okay, let's estimate our timeline. Peyton Birch lost his leg in May 2010. The last record of him attending his support group was October 2013. According to Tori, this Zander guy was in his support group sometime during those three years. So if he was between twenty-five and thirty-five years old then, do you agree it would be safe to assume he was in his second tour of duty since they generally last four years?"

"I would agree with that," Tori nodded.

"Me too," Piper agreed.

"Let's just say eight years then for an even number for now which would put Zander in boot-camp around 2005, give or take a couple years either way," Ben replied.

"And what are we doing with this information?" Piper asked, adding the timeline to the board.

Snapping her fingers, Tori's face suddenly recognized Ben's plan. "I see where you're going with this! That's brilliant!"

"Thank you!" Ben beamed, proudly.

"What's brilliant? Tell me!" Piper demanded.

"I'll write the program now and set the search parameters. It shouldn't take me too long. Ben, why don't you explain what we're going to try," Tori suggested while she began busily typing on her laptop.

"Okay," Ben agreed, turning to Piper. "We're going to search the Marine Corps military records between the years of 2001 through 2008, and look for all men with the first name of Alexander. Then we'll cross reference that list with matches whose fathers also served in the Marine Corps which will shorten our list to a more manageable number. Then we can start eliminating matches from that list based on ethnic background, whether they sustained any injuries or were discharged before completing their tours. Anything that will parse down the matches to ones we feel we need to focus on. Then finally, we can retrieve the pictures of those who remain, which Tori should be able to then identify as the Alexander we're looking for."

"Oh, that is brilliant!" Piper exclaimed excitedly. "I'm impressed, Ben!"

"Thanks, Piper!" Ben grinned.

"So how long will it take until we can get started?" Piper asked.

"I'm checking my code now to make sure it will work, and then I'll release it and set it loose," Tori replied, her eyes fixed to her laptop screen.

"What does that mean?" Piper frowned, looking at Ben for an explanation. "What is she setting loose?"

"That means she's going to insert a stealth program into the US military database, and it will start digging until it finds what she's asked it to," Ben whispered.

"Why are you whispering?" Piper whispered back.

"Because technically what I'm doing is illegal," Tori whispered.

Piper stared at Tori for a moment, hoping she was joking, but Tori didn't laugh. "Which means I'm now an accomplice, right?"

"Pretty much," Tori grinned, slyly.

Nodding her head in understanding, Piper sarcastically replied, "Great, thanks for that!"

"You're welcome!" Tori grinned.

Turning to Ben, Piper advised, "Yep. I was right. You are going to have to bring your children to the women's prison, Ben. Apparently they'll be there to visit their mother AND their Aunt Piper."

"Well technically he'll be in prison too at that point so I guess Grandma Sarah and Grandpa Tanner will be the ones bringing the kids to see all of us," Ben teased.

"Hmm, you're right," Tori admitted. "How do you think Piper will look in an orange jumpsuit?"

"I'm not sure. It might clash with her red hair," Ben mused, surveying Piper's spiked red hair.

"You know, sometimes you're both jerks," Piper argued, trying not to laugh.

"I know, right?" Ben grinned.

Chapter 24

"Thank you again for arranging this meeting with your friend, sir." Tori acknowledged as they drove through town.

"You're welcome, Agent Cooper," Agent Hunter replied. "Just remember, Whit's condition is severe, and he's heavily medicated. There's no guarantee what kind of a day he'll be having. We won't know for sure how things will go until we talk to him."

"Understood," she agreed. "I'm very appreciative of his willingness to meet with me. I think it will be helpful for me to have a better understanding of what our killer may be experiencing."

"Well then let's hope today is a good day," he admitted, slowing the car as he made the final turn into the subdivision.

As they approached the house, Tori saw a small girl in a flowered pink top and denim shorts, playing hopscotch on the driveway. Each time the little girl jumped, bright, colorful beads bounced in the air from the artfully braided cornrows around her head.

"That must be Fionna," she smiled, watching the little girl.

"Yes, that's her," Agent Hunter smiled as he parked the car on the street in front of the house.

Hearing the sound of the keys being removed from the ignition, Goliath woke from his sleep and lifted his head from the back seat to look around outside. When he saw the little girl, his tail immediately began to wag.

Patting him gently on his head, Tori said, "Are you ready to meet someone new, Goliath?"

"Play with little girl?" she heard him ask.

"If you would like to, sure," Tori agreed.

As they exited the vehicle, the little girl's face immediately registered recognition, and her face broke into a huge grin. Shouting towards the open door behind her, she ran towards them. "He's here; he's here! Grandma, Uncle Gabe is here!"

"Uncle Gabe? That's so cute!" Tori grinned, opening the back door for Goliath.

"Hello, Uncle Gabe!" the little girl announced as she threw herself into his arms.

"Hello, Peanut," Agent Hunter smiled, giving her a warm hug. "Look at how big you're getting!"

Pulling back to look at his face, she frowned and gently scolded him. "You missed my dance recital."

"I know, I'm sorry, sweetie," Agent Hunter replied, embarrassed. "I had to work."

"You're always working!" she complained. Glancing over at Tori, the little girl studied her face and then smiled. "You're pretty. Who are you?"

"Thank you! My name is Agent Cooper, but you can call me Tori," Tori replied extending her hand to the little girl. "It's very nice to meet you, Fionna. Agent Hunter has told me a lot about you."

Extending her hand, she shook Tori's hand and politely replied, "Nice to meet you, Tori. Is that your dog?"

"Yes, it is. His name is Goliath," Tori replied.

"Like the giant?" Fionna giggled.

"Exactly like the giant!" Tori smiled.

"Fionna, why don't you let Agent Hunter and his friend come inside, honey," a woman's voice called out from the front porch.

Tori looked over and saw an elderly dark-skinned woman, standing in the doorway on the porch, wearing an apron coated with a light dusting of flour. She held a dish towel in her hands and was attempting to wipe the flour from her fingers. Her once jet black hair, now streaked with thick threads of silver, was combed back and tightly secured in a bun on the back of her head. The contours of her gentle face held deep wrinkles, revealing the passage of time and a struggled walk in life.

"Okay, Grandma!" the girl happily replied as she began to slide out of Agent Hunter's arms.

Quickly setting her feet firmly on the ground, Agent Hunter stood upright and began walking towards the porch. "Hello, CeCe," he greeted warmly.

"Good to see you, Gabe. Why don't you two come inside," she invited.

Fionna, who was now standing beside her grandmother, waited patiently for Agent Hunter, Tori and Goliath to make their way up the driveway. "Grandma, this is Tori. She works with Uncle Gabe. And this is her dog, Goliath."

"It's nice to meet you, Mrs. Jones," Tori greeted the woman, extending her hand politely.

Starting to extend her hand in return, the woman laughed gently when she remembered the coating of flour dried on her fingers. "Please call me CeCe. It's very nice to meet you, Tori. I would shake your hand, but I'm afraid they're a bit dirty right now. I was just making dough for bread."

"I understand completely. I make bread all the time. Did we catch you at a bad time? I know how important timing is when making the dough," Tori worried.

CeCe smiled and said, "I just finished kneading it as you pulled up so now it just has to rise, your timing couldn't have been more perfect!"

"Are you going to have a baby?" Fionna suddenly interrupted, placing her hand gently on Tori's stomach.

"Oh!" Tori gasped, taken slightly off guard.

"Fionna!" CeCe snapped, sternly. "That's rude, stop that!"

Immediately the little girl drew her hand back, and she frowned, sullenly. "I'm sorry."

"No, sweetie, that's okay," Tori reassured the little girl. "You just took me by surprise a little; that's all. And yes, I am going to have a baby. Well, actually I'm going to have two!"

The little girl's eyes widened as she gazed down at the size of Tori's stomach. "Two? How do they both fit in there? Do they push each other around? Can you feel them moving?"

"Fionna," CeCe warned, quietly.

"No, it's okay," Tori laughed, understanding CeCe's concern. Meeting the little girls curious eyes, Tori added, "If it's okay with your grandmother, maybe later when the babies are moving around, you can touch my stomach and will be able to feel them."

Jumping up and down, Fionna looked up at her grandmother, pleadingly and asked, "Can I, Grandma? Can I please?"

"May I," CeCe corrected the little girl firmly. "And yes you may as long as Tori offered."

"Thank you," Fionna's faced beamed as she smiled back at Tori happily.

"Why don't we go inside," CeCe suggested, stepping aside in the doorway so the others could enter the house. "Fionna, honey, go play in the backyard with Goliath, so I can watch you from the living room."

"Okay, Grandma! Come on, Goliath," Fionna beckoned as she skipped through the kitchen to the door leading out to the backyard. Pausing momentarily, she turned back to Tori before going outside. "Don't forget. When they start moving, come and get me, okay?"

Tori chuckled lightly and replied, "I promise."

Once Fionna and Goliath were gone, Agent Hunter turned to CeCe who was now washing her hands. "How are you?" he quietly asked. "Has anything changed since the last time we talked?"

As she dried her hands, CeCe exhaled a deep breath and replied, "He's had a few bad days this past week. His dreams are getting more troubled, so he's not sleeping as well. Today seems to be a better day. I checked on him a little while ago, and he was sleeping soundly. He must have worn himself out." Pausing to look at Tori, she

225

added, "Have you had any experience being around people with PTSD, Tori?"

Not knowing how much Agent Hunter had shared with CeCe before their arrival, Tori replied, "Very little, actually. But we may have a suspect in our current case who suffers from the condition which is why I really appreciate yours and Mr. Jones's willingness to talk to me."

Nodding her head, CeCe replied, "Like I told Gabe on the phone, I can't make you any promises as to how willing he'll be. PTSD sufferers often live inside their own mind. They don't see the world the same way we do. I just want to make sure you're prepared for what may or may not happen."

"I promise I'll try not to upset him," Tori vowed sincerely.

"Why don't we sit in the living room and talk while we wait for Whit to wake up," CeCe suggested, motioning to the doorway on the other end of the kitchen. "Gabe, I'll let you show Tori the way. I'll bring some iced tea in a few minutes."

"That would be nice, thank you, CeCe," Agent Hunter nodded, indicating to Tori that she should go before him.

"Yes, thank you," Tori agreed.

As they entered the living area, Tori looked around, appreciating the tasteful décor. Deep caramel colored walls and thick plush tan carpet gave the room a warm, welcoming atmosphere and a wall of windows overlooking a spacious backyard, provided just the right amount of natural light. She smiled when she saw Fionna and Goliath playing outside. The little girl was running through the grass, laughing as she looked behind her while Goliath galloped a short distance behind.

"He's going to sleep well on the drive home," she laughed, inwardly.

Turning her attention to the interior of the room, she noticed a large sectional sofa, carefully arranged to allow a clear view of the backyard, a beautiful stone fireplace on the right side of the room, and an entertainment cabinet with a flat screen television on the left side of the room. Beside the sofa, there was a small end table, placed between two recliner chairs across from the fireplace, angled towards the television.

Noticing a cart with a BPAP machine in the corner of the room, Tori walked over to take a closer look, immediately recognizing a small baby monitor placed beside a row of tiny glass bottles, filled with what Tori assumed were Whit's medications.

Recognizing Tori's confused expression, Agent Hunter quietly advised, "CeCe is a registered nurse. She administers all of Whit's medication and monitors his condition herself."

"That's a lot to manage, taking care of her husband and her grand-daughter," Tori noted, quietly. "What happened to their daughter?"

"She's dead," CeCe's voice cut through the silence like a knife.

Turning around quickly, Tori saw CeCe standing beside the coffee table, holding a tray of glasses filled with iced tea.

"Oh, I'm so sorry," Tori blurted out, embarrassed. "I didn't mean to...,"

Setting the tray down gently on the table, CeCe walked over to the mantle and picked up a picture frame that had various sized seashells glued along pieces of driftwood that had been assembled into a rectangular shape to hold a picture. Gazing lovingly at it for a moment, she handed the frame to Tori and said, "This is Kayleigh. She was our daughter, Fionna's mother. She made this frame for me."

All too familiar with death and how it changes a family, Tori looked at the image of the smiling, beautiful young woman with flawless cocoa colored skin, and dark brown eyes. Memories of the woman when she was a child flowed through Tori's mind as she held the frame.

"I'm so sorry for your loss. She was beautiful," Tori murmured, meeting CeCe eyes. "She had your smile."

"Thank you," CeCe replied, smiling sadly. She took the picture back and looked upon her daughter's face one more time before placing the frame back on the mantle. "Please sit down."

Sitting beside Tori on the couch, CeCe turned to her and said, "My daughter was a drug addict. She took her life when Fionna was three years old, and I've been raising her on my own since then."

"I didn't mean to pry," Tori assured CeCe, reaching out to touch her hand, comfortingly.

As their hands made contact, Tori gasped at the slight jolt of electricity that ran through her while visions of CeCe as a young woman and a young man in a uniform, held the hands of a little girl between them. They were laughing as they lifted the girl by her hands, swinging her back and forth in the air.

Drawing her hand away, Tori's vision cleared, and she saw CeCe looking at her, curiously.

Clearing her throat gently, Tori averted her eyes and reached over for a glass of tea.

"You have the sight," CeCe announced, matter-of-factly.

Pausing mid-sip, Tori set the glass back down and glanced at Agent Hunter, unsure how to respond.

Reading into the look, CeCe's eyes flicked over to Agent Hunter, who sat motionless without expression.

"And you already knew that," CeCe deduced, turning back to Tori. "Tell me what you saw," she implored, quietly. "Please?"

"Your daughter loved you very much," Tori quietly assured the woman beside her. "Regardless of what her life became in the end, I felt how much she loved you."

Searching Tori's eyes carefully, CeCe asked, "How can you know that with just that one touch? You never even met her."

Realizing Agent Hunter was allowing her to determine how much to share, Tori reached out and placed her hand back on CeCe's, reconnecting to the images from the woman beside her.

Instantly, the replay of the couple with the little girl returned as Tori saw the evolution of the family that once was before they became what they were today. When the visions stopped, Tori once again pulled her hand away, and she felt hot tears streaming down her cheeks.

Unable to stop herself, she flung her arms around CeCe's neck and pulled her into a tight embrace. "How have you remained so strong after everything you've been through? You have the bravest heart I have ever felt," she proclaimed, fiercely.

Shocked by Tori's unexpected embrace, CeCe hesitated for a moment. Then she realized it had been far too long since anyone understood what her life had been like. Returning the embrace, she allowed the tears that were brimming in her eyes to fall, and whispered, "It is only by the grace of God that I am where I am today. If this is the life He has chosen for me; then I have to trust that He has a reason for it. That's what keeps me going. That's what makes me brave."

Pulling free from the embrace, she clasped Tori's hands tightly and stared intently into her eyes. "Now tell me what you saw!"

Blinking away the tears, Tori debated how much she should tell CeCe, but she knew if it were her, she would want to know everything. "It started when your husband came back from his last tour, after the incident in Iraq when he and his troop were attacked."

Out of the corner of her eye, she saw Agent Hunter shift in his chair.

"Go on," CeCe urged her quietly, ignoring him.

"When Whit came home, and Kayleigh first saw him, she was scared of him. She didn't recognize him because of all the scars on his hands and his face. His voice was no longer soft and soothing; it was harsh and gritty. He didn't have the same light in his eyes he had before he left. There was darkness in his eyes that terrified her," Tori advised, carefully watching CeCe's face.

CeCe nodded, solemnly and whispered, "What else?"

"The drugs and the alcohol began when she was about sixteen?" Tori asked.

CeCe nodded again and whispered, "Yes."

"It was a form of escape for her," Tori continued. "It started out as marijuana because that's all she could afford, but then she met a boy who gave her cocaine. It was a high she had never felt before. It made her forget everything," Tori paused, thinking back and added, "His name was Derek."

Taking a deep breath, CeCe nodded, exhaled slowly and admitted, "I know who that was. What else?"

Glancing over at Agent Hunter, she saw his eyes fixed on hers, yet they revealed nothing.

"There's the poker face I've come to know so well," she thought to herself.

Looking back at CeCe, Tori said, "Derek got her a job at a place called The Freeze, right? It was an ice cream shop?"

"Yes," CeCe admitted. "It was her first summer job."

"Once she was earning her own money, Kayleigh had money to buy her own drugs. That's when she decided to try meth. That's when her addiction began wasn't it?" Tori asked.

CeCe nodded again and confirmed, "I didn't know about it until her junior year in high school. She was at a party, and the police raided the house. She was arrested and charged with possession."

Turning to look at Agent Hunter, Tori announced, "Which is when Uncle Gabe stepped in and put Kayleigh in rehab, isn't it?"

Registering surprise for the first time, Agent Hunter inclined his head in admission. "Obviously that wasn't enough."

"What happened wasn't your fault, Gabe! You know that! We've never blamed you for what happened," CeCe demanded, fiercely. "Not once! You've been such a good friend to me and Whit all these years! You did what you could."

"It doesn't seem to matter now, does it?" he argued, his eyes filled with pain. "I couldn't save her."

"None of us could," CeCe whispered.

"She's right," Tori advised, quietly. "Kayleigh knew you were trying to help her. She was trying to help herself. She found out she was pregnant while she was in rehab. She tried so hard to fight the urges. I felt it! She really tried. She struggled through her entire pregnancy because she wanted to make sure Fionna would be healthy."

"What happened after that? What did we do wrong that caused her to take her own life?" CeCe begged.

Shaking her head slowly, Tori admitted, "I don't know what happened. That's all I saw. That's all I felt. I don't think what happened was intentional. I didn't get the feeling that she wanted to end her life."

"You think it was an accident?" CeCe whispered, hopefully.

"Yes, I do," Tori reassured. "She loved her father, she loved Fionna but most importantly, she loved you. She wasn't trying to leave you."

"Thank you," CeCe whispered, patting Tori's hand gently.

"You're welcome," Tori smiled back at her.

"So is this what you do for Gabe's team? You use your gift to help find the people he's looking for?" CeCe wondered.

"Agent Cooper has many gifts, all of which make her an invaluable member on my team," Agent Hunter interrupted, subtly giving Tori permission to tell CeCe what she wanted to know.

"Really?" her eyebrows raised in surprise. "What other gifts do you have? Have you had them all your life?"

"Well, I think I've had them all my life but I only discovered my abilities a few years ago," Tori admitted.

"What do you mean?" CeCe frowned in confusion.

"It's kind of a long story so I'll try to explain without going into too much detail," Tori advised as she paused to summarize her thoughts clearly.

"My maternal heritage is part of a prophecy, dating back to the days when the Archangels who fought with God over the control of heaven, were cast down to earth. One of those angels, named Remiel, found favor with a human female, and they bore a child from their union. Through the ages, all of those children have been female, and all of them had the ability to communicate with the spirits of humans who have been killed at the hand of another human," Tori began.

"You're able to talk to the dead?" CeCe breathed, awestruck.

"I am," Tori nodded. "Whenever possible, they tell me how they died and we, Agent Hunter's team and I, find the people who killed them and bring them to justice. Then I help the spirits find peace by crossing them over into heaven."

"I would imagine you also help their families, as well," CeCe surmised. "Do you share your gift with them too?"

Tori shook her head and advised, "Not usually, no. As I mentioned, the women in my family have always had the gift. Sometimes, people who have known about our gift have abused it for their own gain, while others have become frightened and thought my ancestors were witches. My mother tried to deny her gift, and she never shared it with me. She was afraid of it. I've chosen not to. However, I have to be careful with whom I share my story."

"Agent Cooper can also pick up resonant images and feelings from touching objects that are part of a crime scene," Agent Hunter advised, hoping CeCe would understand.

"Which is why you're here," she deduced correctly. "You've seen something related to your suspect you believe has a past like Whit?"

"Something along those lines, yes," Tori confirmed. "I can feel who he is, and I've seen what he's done. He doesn't feel like other killer's I've felt before. This man is angry and confused about what he's feeling. His thoughts are fragmented and chaotic, not planned and vindictive as one would expect. He has a past and has experienced things

235

that make me think he has PTSD. That's why I wanted to talk to Whit."

Suddenly the light band on the baby monitor lit up, and they could hear a raspy cough through the speaker.

"Well, it looks like Whit is up from his nap. Let's hope he can give you some of those answers," CeCe replied. "Before I get him, you need to know a few things. He doesn't like to be touched, and he will only let me hand him things. He doesn't trust people he doesn't know. Also, depending on his mood, he may be a little abrupt so please don't take offense. It won't be because of anything you've done."

"I understand," Tori agreed.

Rising quickly from the couch, CeCe announced, "Okay. Give me a few minutes and I'll bring him out."

Chapter 25

Having already seen what Whit looked like through CeCe's memories earlier, Tori prepared herself for what she saw. Still, it almost made her instinctively want to reach out to him in sympathy.

He was wearing a long-sleeved shirt, yet she could see patches of pink and white leathered skin forming a mosaic pattern on his face and upper neck from skin grafts applied to replace the previously destroyed tissue. The blanket on his lap hid his hands, which she already knew were missing several fingers that had been too damaged to save or reattach after the explosion.

As CeCe pushed his wheelchair into the room, his eyes immediately sought Tori out first. Returning the intensity of his gaze with a warm smile, she waited until CeCe made the introductions.

"Whit, this is the lady I was telling you about. This is Agent Tori Cooper. She's works with Gabriel," CeCe announced.

"It's very nice to meet you, sir," Tori politely greeted him, deliberately keeping her hands folded on her lap.

Acknowledging her gesture, he gave a brief nod and in a voice that sounded like sand-paper replied, "Nice to meet you, Agent Cooper." Turning his head to look at Agent Hunter, he added, "Good to see you, Gabe."

"It's good to see you too, Whit," Agent Hunter smiled, warmly. "Do you want me to help you into your chair and get you settled?"

Whit gave a brief nod and replied, "Sure, you can give CeCe a break. I'm sure she could use one."

"Oh, don't be silly. I don't need a break from you," CeCe crooned affectionately as she allowed Agent Hunter to steer the wheelchair towards one of the recliners. "Thank you, Gabe."

"My pleasure," Agent Hunter replied, quietly.

While Agent Hunter and CeCe helped Whit into the recliner, Tori noticed that he continued to steal curious glances in her direction. She assumed it was due to him trying to figure out what she was going to ask him. She also noticed Whit didn't seem to have any objections to Agent Hunter helping CeCe, which she took as a good sign. Finally, when they were done, Whit sat back in the chair and exhaled a deep sigh.

"Are you okay?" CeCe asked, worriedly. "Can I get you anything?"

"I'm okay," he assured her, gruffly. Turning his eyes back to Tori, he bluntly asked. "So CeCe tells me you have some questions to ask me?"

Before Tori could answer, CeCe quickly intervened and replied, "Oh we have time to get to that. Gabe, why don't you tell us what you and Miranda have been up to since we last talked to you? How is Willow? She's getting close to graduation, isn't she?"

"She's in her last year now," Agent Hunter confirmed.

"Remember, Whit? Gabe's daughter Willow is at the University of Maryland, getting her Ph.D. in Criminal Justice," CeCe reminded her husband, gently.

"Of course I remember! I'm not senile!" Whit grumpily replied. "Why you would encourage your daughter to pursue a career putting her life in danger every day the way you do is beyond me."

"She chose this path herself. Even after I told her what my job is like, she decided this is what she wants," Agent Hunter gently advised.

"Well I think it's an honorable pursuit," CeCe nodded firmly. "It takes a special kind of person to help others."

"Hogwash," Whit grumbled, scowling sourly at his wife.

"You used to have some of those same beliefs back in the day as I recall," Agent Hunter replied, dryly.

"Yeah well, that was before we found out what life was really like," Whit mumbled quietly, returning his focus on Tori. "What about you, Agent Cooper? What do you believe? What kind of a world do you believe you're bringing your child into?"

Feeling the spotlight suddenly thrust upon her, Tori drew in a deep breath and exhaled slowly as she decided which direction would be the wisest to take.

"Well, so far, from what I've seen and experienced, I believe that everyone has the power to do good and the power to do evil. Life is all about choices. If one chooses to live an honorable life, focusing their energy in helping others, then they should be prepared to make some difficult decisions and to be disliked by others. If someone chooses to live a dishonorable life, they have to be prepared to pay for the consequences of their actions," Tori declared.

"And what about those people who chose to live an honorable life helping others who are punished for their choices?" Whit challenged. "What do you think about them?"

Taking the bait, Tori bravely replied, "Is that what you feel, sir? Do you feel you're being punished for the choices you made?"

Whit's eyes widened in surprise at her frank response, and he sat back in his chair laughing heartily. Looking over at Agent Hunter and seeing a surprised look on his face as well, Whit replied, "Oh, I think I'm going to like you, Agent Cooper. You don't let anyone get away with anything do you? Gabe, you've got your hands full with this one!"

"*In more ways than you realize,*" Tori thought, sarcastically.

"Is that really what you think?" CeCe murmured quietly, staring at Whit. "Do you think what happened to you is a form of punishment?"

The smile quickly left Whit's face as he turned to CeCe and admitted, "Maybe. I don't know. What difference does it make? None of that matters now."

"It matters to me," CeCe whispered, fiercely. "You're a good man, Whitley Jones. You've never done anything to make the good Lord punish you for anything."

"It matters to me too," Tori replied. "I think men like you and Agent Hunter are the bravest men I've ever met. Fighting for your country and putting your lives in danger to protect others is truly honorable. Thank you for making the sacrifices that you made while you were in service."

"You're welcome," Whit nodded, slightly uncomfortable of her praise after his earlier comment.

"Do you remember what it felt like in the beginning?" Tori asked curiously. "When you first enlisted, and you found out you were being deployed? What was it like?"

Whit's eyes drifted off as he thought back and he grinned as a memory came back to him. "We were fearless. We thought we were indestructible. They teach you that during boot-camp. They tell you that you are part of a military machine and that you're indestructible. Would you agree, Gabe?"

"Yes. Yes they do," Agent Hunter quietly agreed.

"Then they hand you your gear, load you up on a plane and send you off to fight the monsters," Whit murmured, lost in another memory. "Do you remember the Fall of Saigon, Gabe?"

"I do," Agent Hunter replied.

"All of it?" Whit asked.

"No," Agent Hunter admitted. "Too many horrible things happened during that time. Things I don't want to remember."

"Me either," Whit whispered, fearfully. "But that doesn't stop the monsters from coming! The monsters split us up, you and me. They broke us apart from our unit. We were corralled like cattle going in for the slaughter. Then we saw the flash of light and everything exploded. Everything around us just exploded into a bright white light."

Surprised at how quickly the conversation turned, Tori interrupted, forcing Whit to bring his panicked eyes back to hers. "Whit? I don't want to know about that day, okay? I don't want you to go there, today. Let's talk about today. Tell me what today is like for you."

Whit's eyes traveled over to CeCe, and the fear in his eyes immediately disappeared. In its place, she saw affection, trust and safety.

"Today is good," he whispered. "There are no monsters today."

Tori glanced at CeCe, indicating confusion at Whit's response. Hoping to help give Tori an explanation, CeCe nodded and asked, "So you slept well today, Whit? There were no monsters in your dreams today?"

"No, I didn't' see any monsters today. I must have picked a good hiding place today. The monsters couldn't find me," Whit murmured, his eyes drifting off again as his mind chased another memory.

CeCe waited a moment, recognizing the expression on his face, and then she glanced at the clock on the mantle. "Would you like a cookie, Whit?" she asked in a louder tone than before. When he didn't respond, she turned to Tori and said, "I'm sorry, he won't be able to talk to you any more today."

"What? What happened?" Tori exclaimed, now very confused.

CeCe smiled and patted Tori's hand gently. "I tried to warn you earlier. He has his good days and his bad days but sometimes even on a good day, he can turn inward."

"Turn inward? What does that mean?" Tori asked.

"It's like a cocoon for lack of a better term," CeCe began to explain. "When Whit turns inward, it's his minds way of protecting itself from any further trauma. Let me try and give you a little bit of background. People who experience PTSD generally fall into three types of groups, each who experience different symptoms resulting from their trauma. The first group involves reliving the trauma in some way such as becoming upset when confronted with a traumatic reminder. The second group will either stay away from places or people that remind them of their trauma."

"So my asking Whit about what it was like, triggered a reminder that caused his brain to protect him and stop talking to us? I didn't mean to do that!" Tori replied.

CeCe gave Tori a sympathetic smile and assured, "It wasn't your questions, Tori, I promise. It takes so little to trigger a memory for Whit, there's no predicting what it could be. Wouldn't you agree, Gabe?"

"Yes, that's true," Agent Hunter confirmed.

"In fact, just the other day, Whit and Fionna were sitting on the patio enjoying their lunch and Fionna asked Whit what color blue he thought the sky was. Just the thought of the color of the sky made him remember something and that was the last time he spoke that day," CeCe replied.

"Oh, poor Fionna," Tori murmured, looking out the window at the little girl happily trying to teach Goliath to catch a Frisbee in his mouth. "Do moments like that upset her?"

"No, she's used to his mood changes and understands as much as she can for a child her age. It's all she's ever known, so it doesn't seem strange to her," CeCe replied.

"Very much like his appearance I would assume," Tori noted. "She's not afraid of the scars like Kayleigh was because the way Whit looks now is how he's always looked to her."

"Exactly," CeCe smiled.

"So what can you tell me about the third group of PTSD survivors? You mentioned there were three types of people who suffered from PTSD," Tori asked.

"I haven't met anyone in Whit's therapy groups who I would consider displaying classic symptoms of the third group, however, what I've read indicates people in the third group seem to be a bit more social than the other two groups. They have jobs and families. They display symptoms of being startled easily when caught off guard or they have dramatic mood swings with or without provocation. Some even experience brief periods of memory lapses where they either lose track of time or don't recall conversations they've had. I've read that certain medications can help to some degree, but again, I don't have any personal experience with anyone like that," CeCe replied.

"Nor have I. However I did a bit of research before coming here and was surprised to learn that PTSD is considered to be both a biological condition as well as a psychological one," Tori revealed.

"What about that surprised you?" CeCe asked, curiously.

"I guess I always just assumed it was purely psychological," Tori admitted. "I understand the depression, substance abuse and impairment of functionality in society. I guess what surprised me was what actually goes on in the brain. The hypothalamus, the limbic system, and the neocortex control many of our regulatory functions like sleeping, but they also monitor and assess what is new, dangerous, or gratifying to us. The limbic system maintains and directs our emotions and behavior necessary for self-preservation and survival. Someone classified as having the biological condition may display behavior like hyper-vigilance that would keep the person on alert most of the time and would more likely respond with fight – or – flight reactions."

"Is that what you think is going on with your suspect? Do you think he falls under the third category?" CeCe asked.

"I'm not sure yet, but I'm starting to think yes, based upon what I saw with Whit today," Tori replied.

"So today was helpful even though you didn't get a chance to talk to Whit very long?" CeCe asked.

"Oh absolutely! Thank you so much for going to all this trouble for us. Being here was very helpful," Tori assured her.

CeCe smiled and replied, "Good. And you're welcome any time. Both of you," she added glancing over at Agent Hunter, who she noticed was watching Whit thoughtfully. "You've been quiet today, Gabe. Is there something on your mind?"

Meeting her eyes, he replied, "He turned quickly today. Much quicker than I've seen before."

"It's been a while since you've seen him," CeCe replied, bluntly. "This is his normal these days."

"Is it becoming more than you can handle? Please don't lie to me," he asked.

CeCe turned to look at Whit's face for a moment and then looked back at Gabe. Shaking her head she replied, "We're okay for now. I'm not ready to consider placing him in a long-term care facility if that's what you're asking. He still has more moments of lucidity than he does moments like this."

Nodding in acknowledgment, he asked, "Promise me that when it gets to be too much for you and you need help, you'll let me know? I'm never too far away to help you whenever you need it. You, Whit and Fionna are family to Miranda and me. You know that, right?"

Smiling warmly at him, CeCe replied, "Yes, we know."

Chapter 26

"Honey, please sit down and have some breakfast with me. You're acting all nervous and fidgety today. Is everything okay?" Tanner gently scolded.

Setting a plate of fruit on the table, Sarah glanced at Aubrey, who was standing beside Tanner's chair, and replied, "Everything is fine! I'm almost done. I just need to get one more thing."

"More? This is more food than we normally have. Are we having company?" Tanner exclaimed, noting the abundance of food in front of him.

"N-no, it's just us," Sarah replied anxiously, returning with a sheet of paper and a pen in her hand. As she sat down in her chair, she gently placed the paper in front of Tanner and laid the pen beside it.

"What's this for?" he asked, curiously.

"Um, well," Sarah paused, looking up at Aubrey expectantly.

"Go ahead, Mom, I'm ready," Aubrey encouraged.

"Um, okay," Sarah paused again, searching Tanner's face.

"Sweetheart, what is it? Is something wrong?" Tanner asked, getting worried.

"No, nothing is wrong. It's actually very exciting. I'm just not exactly sure how to start," Sarah admitted, looking back up at Aubrey.

"You know you can tell me anything," Tanner quietly reminded her.

"I know I can, darling. It's not that. It's, um, well, you see it's um…," Sarah trailed off, worriedly.

Understanding her mother's hesitation, Aubrey smiled and replied, "Don't worry, Mom. I'll take it from here."

Focusing all of her attention on the pen, it slowly rose from the table and poised itself over the sheet of paper. As it did, Tanner caught the movement out of the corner of his eye.

"What the….what's going on?" He exclaimed, jumping back in his chair with wild eyes.

"Just relax, honey," Sarah replied, placing her hand on his. "Aubrey wants to show you something."

"Aubrey is doing this?" he breathed, as he watched the pen begin to move over the page. "But how can she physically touch something? Move something? How is that possible?"

"I don't exactly know. She first showed me this the other night. She said she noticed she was able to move small objects shortly after Meda and Karla left," Sarah replied.

Meeting her eyes, Tanner frowned and asked, "Why would them leaving give Bree this kind of ability? Do you think the two are connected?"

"I don't know," Sarah shrugged. "It's as much a mystery to me as it is to you. But knowing how everything that's been happening lately has a connection to one another, I would assume that they probably are."

When Tanner looked back down at the sheet of paper, he gasped when he saw the message his daughter wrote for him.

I love you, Daddy. ☺

He stared at the message in disbelief as tears filled his eyes, blurring his vision. Wiping his eyes with the back of his hand, he choked out, "I love you too, baby girl."

"Ask him what he thinks of my surprise!" Aubrey eagerly demanded.

Sarah smiled and repeated, "She wants to know what you think of her surprise?"

"I think it's the most wonderful surprise in the whole world, baby. I can't think of anything else that would be more wonderful than reading those words from you," Tanner smiled.

He laughed as the pen began moving again and he recognized the symbol she added beneath her message.

Watching him carefully, Sarah asked, "So how are you doing? Are you okay with all of this so far?"

He laughed and replied, "Am I okay? Are you kidding? I'm more than okay! This is amazing, truly amazing! I've wished I could see Bree and talk to her the way you've been able to since she came back to us. Now maybe she and I can do some of that together. You know, like we used to when she was still alive!"

"Tell Daddy I hope we can do that too," Aubrey replied.

"She says she hopes you both can do that too," Sarah repeated. "In fact, I came up with something that I would like us all to try, if you would be willing to give it a shot. Aubrey has already agreed she would like to try it."

"Okay, what is it?" Tanner asked curiously.

Giving Aubrey a quick nod, Sarah explained as Aubrey disappeared and re-appeared in the kitchen. "Remember the little copper bell Tori and Ben had on the door to their office on the sidewalk side of the building? So they would know if someone came inside their office during the day?"

"Yes," Tanner acknowledged.

"Well, since you weren't really using it, I brought the bell home and put it up on the wall in the kitchen by the desk next to a new whiteboard I bought. So now, when Aubrey has something she wants to tell you, she can let you know," Sarah replied.

When Sarah stopped talking, Aubrey focused her thoughts on the string leading from the little copper bell, and a moment later, the bell tipped and clapper hit the rim with a rich, resonating tone.

Tanner smiled slowly when he heard the chime and admitted, "Okay I have to say it, this is pretty cool!"

Smiling back at him, Sarah exclaimed, "Well go take a look!"

"Oh, right!" Tanner chuckled, quickly rising from his chair and heading towards the kitchen. He laughed again when he saw the message on the whiteboard.

Hi Daddy!!

"Hi, baby girl," Tanner replied, happily. "This is truly amazing, honey."

"Can I do the door now, Mom?" Aubrey pleaded, excitedly.

Sarah smiled, enjoying the excitement on Aubrey's and Tanner's faces. Turning to Tanner, she advised, "Bree has a few other things she would like to show you. Are you ready?"

Tanner's face lit up in expectation, and he quickly replied, "Ready when you are, sweetie!"

Chapter 27

Glancing around his apartment to make sure he had everything packed that he would need, Zander picked up the last duffel bag and his rifle case and carried them out to the car. Carefully repositioning everything, so the rifle case was buried in the back of the trunk, he locked the car and went back inside.

Then he pulled on a pair of latex gloves, and methodically went through the apartment, spraying all surfaces with a solution of bleach and water, wiping away as many of his fingerprints and traces of DNA as he could.

When he was done, he put the rags and the spray bottle in a plastic bag, along with the cut up pieces of the credit cards he could no longer use, and placed the bag by the door. Making a final pass through each room, he left his cell phone on the kitchen counter, picked up the bag of garbage and locked the door behind him, severing all ties to his former life.

Not that he expected anyone to miss him right away. Hopefully, he had done everything he could to make everything look like normal until he knew whether anyone was looking for him.

He'd given his notice at the Wal-Mart where he worked, cashed his last paycheck and withdrew all the money from his checking account. From now on, everything would have to be paid for in cash.

He even paid his rent a month in advance, just in case, telling the girl in the office he was going to visit his sick mother. The puppy dog eyes she gave him afterward, telling him what good son he was, made him feel sick to his stomach. If she only knew the kind of man he was.

He had done enough research over the past several days to know that somehow, he was responsible for the deaths of at least three men, even though he didn't remember doing it. He had recognized their names and faces as soon as he saw the news stories describing the details of their murders.

Feeling the onset of another migraine, he cursed himself silently for not opening the windows in the apartment while he cleaned up.

"Stupid bleach," he complained as he tossed the garbage bag on to the floor mat in front of the passenger seat. "You should have known better than to be in an enclosed area with that smell."

Starting the car, he rolled down his window and tried to ignore the stabbing pain behind his eyeballs as he pulled out onto the street.

The biggest question in his mind was why? Why would he kill anyone, much less those men? They were all men he knew. Men he had talked to, men who had shared their most traumatic moments of their lives with him, and he with them. What was wrong with his brain that it couldn't remember something so brutal and awful? Were there any others he didn't know about yet? What if there were more? What kind of a monster was he?

"That's why Rhea left you," the voice in his head whispered. *"She couldn't live with a monster like you."*

"Shut up," he growled, as he drove. "That's not why she left."

"Then what made her leave?" the voice teased.

"I said shut up!" he shouted angrily at his reflection in the rear view mirror.

Realizing he was acting irrationally, he ignored the voice in his head and mentally went through the checklist again. The last thing he needed to do was to make the car disappear. Fortunately, it was Saturday night, so he knew exactly where to go.

Turning into the parking lot of the local multiplex theater, he slowly drove down each aisle, scanning the license plates on all the vehicles, until he found a set of numbers very close to those matching his. Thankfully the vehicle in question was parked in a darkened area of the lot. He pulled his car into a vacant spot, looked around the surrounding vehicles for anyone who might see him, and then quickly exchanged the license plates.

Hoping the owner of the other car wouldn't notice the difference right away, he exited the parking lot and headed for the highway out of town.

"Where are you going?" the voice asked him.

"That's a good question. Where am I going?" Zander thought to himself. *"Should I go home? I could check in with Mom and Dad. See how they're doing."*

"No, they may already be watching them," he replied to himself out loud. "It's too risky."

"I know a place you can go," the voice taunted again. *"There's someone I want you to meet. Why don't you let me drive for a while?"*

Feeling the pain in his head intensify, Zander felt himself slipping away as he obediently relinquished control. "Fine," he murmured. "You drive for a while. I'm tired of making all the decisions."

Chapter 28

"I feel like I've been here for hours. What am I supposed to be looking for?" Tori thought wearily as she continued walking through the thick blanket of fog. Sensing her discontent, she felt a gentle kick from one of the twins, partially awakening her from her dream. Moaning softly, she mumbled, "Go to sleep, baby," and turned over on her other side.

As her breathing deepened and her subconscious floated back down to her dream state, her ears picked up the slightest sound of a woman singing. Following the sound, Tori slowly walked towards it, straining her ears to listen.

As she got closer, she found herself surprised when although she didn't know the song, she already knew the lyrics.

"Children from the light, see into the night, fear and darkness creeping. Bring them 'round, safe and sound, the fearless who are sleeping," the woman sang.

Within moments, the fetal kicking ceased as the twins responded to the soothing sound of the woman's voice.

"That's odd," Tori thought to herself.

Still unsure of the direction she was going, she continued to walk forward slowly, feeling her way through the mist until a blurred image of a woman came into view. As Tori got closer, she could see that it was a young woman, not much younger than she was, about the same height as her, with a flawless, creamy complexion, long dark hair and brightly glimmering crystal blue-green eyes. She wore a long white sleeveless dress that gently draped down her slender frame, barely touching the tops of her bare feet.

Ending the last line of the verse, the woman stopped singing, turned to Tori and smiled warmly at her.

"Hello, Tori," the woman greeted.

"Hello," Tori replied. "Are you who I was supposed to meet here tonight?"

"I am," the woman nodded.

"Who are you?" Tori wondered.

"My name is Elsbet. I am the spirit of the amulet," she replied, calmly.

"What?" Tori gasped in surprise. *"Wow. I seriously did not see that one coming,"* she immediately thought.

"I am the spirit of the Remiel amulet," Elsbet repeated, pointing to the stone on Tori's necklace.

"Hold on," Tori demanded, lifting the amulet from her neck and cradling it in the palm of her hand. "You're the spirit inside of my amulet? This amulet? Are you the reason the amulet glows? Why it responds to my touch? That's all you?"

"That's all me," Elsbet replied, patiently. "Your amulet used to be my amulet."

"Why haven't you revealed yourself until now?" Tori asked, curiously. "Why should I believe you?"

"I was waiting. I needed to be sure," Elsbet replied.

"Be sure of what?" Tori asked.

"That you were worthy," Elsbet admitted.

Tori blinked in surprise and replied, "Worthy? You needed to make sure I was worthy? Is that really your call to make?"

Elsbet laughed lightly and nodded in approval, "You're brave, and you have a strong mind. That's good. I can see why he's so taken with you."

"You can see why who's so taken with me?" Tori demanded, fearing Elsbet meant Luc.

"Remiel," Elsbet replied.

"Remy? What are you talking about?" Tori argued.

"You challenge him. You force him to see things in ways he hasn't thought about before. You're good for him," Elsbet advised.

"You can see him?" Tori asked.

Elsbet smiled and replied, "Yes, I've been watching him. I've been watching you both."

"You have?" Tori exclaimed. "Why?"

"I had to be sure you were strong enough to handle the power and responsibility that comes with the prophecy. I was the last of Remiel's daughters to possess both the statue and the amulet and look what happened to me! Once you claimed ownership of the statue and the amulet, you unlocked your rightful place as the chosen one. I needed to be sure you would make wiser choices than I did so you didn't end up here trapped like me!" Elsbet exclaimed.

"Trapped? Why are you trapped inside the stone?" Tori asked.

"It was my punishment for my betrayal," Elsbet admitted.

"Your betrayal?" Tori asked, puzzled.

"For allowing Lucifer to tempt me into using our gift to punish the fallen and not to redeem them as we have been called to do," Elsbet admitted.

Tori frowned and replied, "I don't understand. Remy's never said anything about you being punished for your decision. Who put your spirit in the amulet?"

"I don't know," Elsbet admitted. "Once the elders in my village declared me guilty, my punishment was death. That is my earthly punishment. Afterward, I ended up here. I've wandered for decades through the mist, alone, not knowing where I was or why I was here. My isolation forced me think about what I had done. I had hoped that it meant one day I would be forgiven, but I'm still here, so I guess that will never happen."

"But you know as soon as you ask for forgiveness, it's given to you, right? If you believe you haven't been forgiven, that's because you haven't forgiven yourself. God forgives those to come to him in true repentance," Tori insisted.

Noticing Tori's confused expression, she added, "Did you understand what I was showing you that day? When I took you to the place I died? When I took you to the meadow?"

"That was you?" Tori blinked in surprise.

"Yes. That was me," Elsbet confirmed. "Did you understand? I need to know that you understood what you saw."

Tori nodded and replied, "I think so. You were showing me what happened to you because of your decision and what would happen to me if I made the same choice."

"Yes," Elsbet replied. "That was only part of it though. Because of what I did, I caused a rift between Remiel and Lucifer. They will always be at war because of my decision."

"I'm not sure I understand," Tori admitted.

"Lucifer claimed the victory that day turning one of Remiel's daughters against him. That's why the statue and the amulet were divided, to keep it from happening again. What happened between them was my fault! Remiel was allowed to leave the heavenly host so he could redeem Lucifer and the other fallen angels. The anger he feels in his heart because of what happened to me is clouding his heart. No matter what happens with Lucifer, Remiel won't be able to return to his place with God until he removes that darkness from his heart! Only you can do that! But you have to remain pure of heart and not allow Lucifer to tempt you into making the wrong choice!" Elsbet insisted.

"Why did you choose the way you did? How was Luc able to turn you away from God and from Remy like that?" Tori wondered.

Elsbet dropped her eyes, guiltily and said, "You wouldn't understand."

"Try me," Tori encouraged. "If I'm the only one who can help Remy, I need to know what could have made you turn away from him the way you did."

"Lucifer is very persistent and very skillful in the ways of deception, Tori. Never underestimate him, and don't fool yourself into thinking there's any redemption for him.

263

Salvation is not something he's looking for. He'll lie to you and tell you anything you'll want to hear."

"Is that what he did to you? Did he lie to you and tell you he wanted salvation?" Tori asked.

"I'm not sure I can explain what happened to me. I didn't realize it until it was too late. Just promise me that you won't let him fool you the way he fooled me," Elsbet warned.

"I promise, I won't let him," Tori declared, defiantly.

Elsbet shook her head and looked at Tori doubtfully. "He's already working every angle he can to figure you out. I can see him watching you, studying you. He's fascinated by you and infuriated by you at the same time. He's never met anyone with a will as strong as yours, and he'll stop at nothing to break you."

"I said I won't let him," Tori declared, again.

"Remiel won't always be there to save you," Elsbet advised, mournfully.

"He misses you, by the way," Tori offered, quietly.

"He does?" Elsbet whispered, bringing her eyes back to Tori. "Is he still angry with me?"

"I don't know about that. He doesn't seem to want to talk about it when I bring it up. The look in his eyes changes when he talks about you. In a good way," Tori nodded.

"I've missed him too," Elsbet admitted, sadly, looking away. "We were close, once. Before I...," her voice trailed off, lost in the memory.

Breaking from her trance, she looked up and met Tori's eyes, curiously. "He's different with you."

"What do you mean different?" Tori eyed her warily.

"There's a closeness between you and Remiel. It's deeper than anything we ever had," Elsbet advised.

"I'm still not following you," Tori shrugged.

"I think he loves you," Elsbet replied, bluntly.

"He loves all of his daughters!" Tori replied indignantly.

"Agreed," Elsbet conceded, "But you're different. He watches you when you're not aware he's there. He worries about you. That's why he brought you, Goliath, to protect you when he's not with you. I think he's also IN love with you."

Tori scowled and shook her head vehemently. "No, I disagree! We're close, yes, and I'll admit that there's a mutual feeling of love for one another, but not in a romantic way. We're related! Remy is more like my great, great, great, grandfather! I think you're wrong! Besides, I'm married! AND I'm pregnant with another man's children!"

"Remiel is tender and more loving with you than I've seen him behave with any of his other children, even more so than he was with me. This is true love for him, and true love has no boundaries," Elsbet declared firmly. "It has no limits; it has no barriers. Nothing and no one can stop it."

Tori stared at Elsbet in complete surprise. "Wow! You're like your own little greeting card wrapped up in a fluffy white cloud, aren't you?"

"I'm a what?" Elsbet frowned, missing the humor.

"A fluffy...never mind," Tori sighed. Suddenly remembering the lullaby, she asked. "Hey, what was that song you were singing earlier? How did you know about the lullaby? The one you were singing? What does it mean?"

"How do you know about the lullaby?" Elsbet replied in surprise.

"I had a dream a few weeks ago, and the twins were repeating it over and over again," Tori replied, gently running her hands over her stomach. "Well they were repeating the lyrics, you put it to music."

"They talk to you too?" Elsbet marveled, looking down at Tori's belly. "I thought only Remiel and I could do that!"

"Wait, you talk to them?" Tori exclaimed.

Elsbet nodded and replied, "I sing to them at night, so they don't wake you."

"That's so sweet," Tori exclaimed, touched. "I didn't realize you were doing that. Thank you! What do the words mean?"

"It's an ancient folk tale our family has passed down through the generations, telling the story about the daughter's of Remiel," Elsbet advised.

"So we're all children from the light?" Tori asked, curiously. "It's not just the twins?"

"Yes, we all are, as in the light of the world," Elsbet smiled.

"What will that mean for my son then? Will his role in the prophecy be different from my daughter?" Tori worried.

Elsbet shrugged and replied, "I don't know. RJ is the first male child to be born in the descended line. There is no precedent on record as to what his role will be."

"Oh," Tori breathed, disappointed. "I was kind of hoping you would tell me this had happened before so I would know what I needed to prepare for."

Sensing her concern, Elsbet added, "I truly wish I could. However, I do believe that the Lord does not do anything without a purpose. If RJ is to be the first Remiel son, then RJ was created for a reason. We'll just have to trust Him and believe that He has a wonderful plan for your son."

"I sure hope so. The last thing I want to think about is Luc deciding it's time he needs an heir to his throne and think RJ would be the ideal candidate," Tori sighed. Looking around her, she asked, "Where are we anyway? This isn't heaven is it?"

Elsbet shook her head and replied, "No, only believers who have passed on or have been guided by one of us, have passage into heaven. This is another plane of existence between earth and heaven. It's where we exist in the interim."

"We? I thought you said you've been wandering alone for decades through this mist recounting your sins. Is someone else here with you?" Tori asked, curiously.

Deciding Tori had passed her test Elsbet smiled and motioned Tori to follow her. "Come with me. I think it's time you met the others."

Chapter 29

Tori closely followed Elsbet, fearing she would lose her in the mist, but she need not have worried. They only walked a short distance until suddenly blurred images of other women wearing long white gowns began to appear all around her. When she turned to Elsbet to ask who the women were, she jumped in surprise when she recognized the women beside her.

"Karla!" Tori cried out. "Is it really you?"

"Yes, it's really me!" Karla laughed as she rushed forward to pull Tori into a warm embrace. "Oh, it's so good to see you again!"

"Oh, this is amazing! I can actually touch you!" Tori wept, unable to hold back the joy she felt. Pulling back to look at her friend more closely she exclaimed, "I can't believe it! I can actually see you, touch you! You look so beautiful!"

"Me? Look at you! You're pregnant! So much has happened since I left!" Karla smiled, glancing down at Tori's stomach. "You're so close to giving birth! We are all so excited to meet them!"

"So I've heard!" Tori smiled. Looking around them, she added, "Where's Meda?"

"She's not here, Tori," Karla replied.

"Not here? What are you talking about? Why? What happened to her?" Tori cried out, as her voice revealed the panic rising within her. "I-I-I did everything right that night! I said the words; I envisioned her path! She should have arrived here with you!"

"Breathe, Tori!" Karla assured her friend calmly. "They're both fine. They crossed over, just like you intended."

Taking a deep breath, Tori nodded and replied, "Okay, I'm breathing. See? I'm okay. Why aren't you with Meda and Tobias? What is this place? Why are you here?" Tori demanded.

Noticing the confusion on Tori's face, Karla turned to Elsbet and said, "This is a lot for her to take in. Are you sure now is the time? Shouldn't we ease her into this slowly?"

"Time is something we don't have a lot of right now, Karla. You know that. Look how close she is to giving birth!" Elsbet insisted.

Glaring at Elsbet, Tori challenged, "I thought you said you were trapped here! Who are all these other women? "Why is Karla here and not with her mother?"

"When I first arrived here, I was alone. I was the first of the Remiel daughter's to have been killed while still human. The other daughter's who died of natural causes fulfilled their part of the prophecy. That's why they're not here. They're in heaven with God."

Following so far, Tori nodded and asked, "So that's why you said you wandered for decades alone?"

"Yes," Elsbet admitted. "During the next few hundred years, other's began to show up. As they each shared their stories with one another, it became evident that they were brought here because their lives had been taken before they had a chance to fulfill their role in the prophecy."

"But how did you know for sure that was the reason?" Tori argued. "You said you could no longer talk to Remy once you were here. Does God talk to you here?"

Karla shook her head and exchanged another quick look with Elsbet. "Not exactly, no. He doesn't talk to us, but there've been times, one of us will get a sense of something that we should do. Then when we do it, we find out more about what we're capable of."

Tori frowned and admitted, "Okay, now you've lost me."

One of the other women stepped forward, gently placing her hand on Elsbet's shoulder. "My name is Kaia. I was the second to arrive here. When Elsbet and I shook hands, the contact of our hands touching, revealed our stories with one another. We understood that we were both daughter's of Remiel and that we were sisters. Together, we could also see our other sister's still alive on earth. We didn't have much power in the beginning, we could send warnings and thoughts to our earthly sisters through their dreams, but we couldn't save them when we saw they were in danger. We could only wait for them to arrive here and help them come to terms with their existence here with us."

"Over the years, as more of us have come here, our powers have grown," another of the women advised.

"So the thoughts and warnings you were sending to them, are those the visions I've seen?" Tori asked, curiously.

"Some of them, yes," Karla nodded. "Collectively, we channel our power into the amulet but the amulet chooses what it wants you to see."

Tori frowned, glancing down at the amulet suspended from the cord around her neck and argued, "So you're telling me the amulet is alive? That it has its own power to either hide or reveal things to me?"

"In a manner of speaking, yes," Karla admitted. "Neither we nor it can tell you everything we know. You need to learn and evolve like we do so you can figure some of it out on your own."

"Why? Why can't you tell me everything now?" Tori demanded, now very confused.

"Because of the power of choice," Kaia replied, firmly.

"If we tell you, you no longer have the ability to choose what is right or wrong," Karla confessed.

"What?" Tori argued, shaking her head.

Elsbet stepped forward and motioned to the amulet. "May I show you?"

Tori hesitated and looked at Karla for direction. "Karla?"

Understanding her hesitation, Karla nodded and said, "It's okay. It will help you understand."

Turning back to Elsbet, Tori nodded and agreed, "Okay."

Elsbet slowly reached out and picked up the amulet, which instantly burst into a spectrum of light at her touch.

"Wow," Tori breathed, averting her eyes. "It does that when Remy touches it too!"

"Place your hand on top of mine," Elsbet instructed to Tori.

As she did, Tori looked up and noticed the other women were now standing in a tight circle around them, their hands all clasped with one another. As Karla took Tori's other hand, completing the circle, a series of images began flooding into her mind, images of each of the women around her as they lived and died on earth, as well as their time here with the others.

Suddenly a blinding flash of light surrounded them and everything seemed to slow down as if the surrounding mist instantly turned to honey. Glancing upward, Tori saw the image of a human form, slowly falling from the sky, like the one she had seen in her last dream. This time, however, she could see it was the form of a man and that he had a pair of beautiful white wings. But the wings were broken, and he could not fly.

Then a second flash of blinding light forced her to look away. When she opened her eyes, she was standing on a sidewalk in front of a brick building across from a large city park. Feeling someone watching her, she turned her head towards the trees and her vision seemed to accelerate forward as she zeroed in on the barrel of a rifle several hundred feet away, pointed directly at her. Her sight continued to zoom in until she was staring at the face of the man behind the trigger.

"I know that face!" her mind instantly told her.

Before she could even register the fear the image revealed to her, a third flash of light blinded her. Squinting at the image in front of her, she saw herself lying on a table, unconscious, covered in blood. A bright light hovered over the table but the immediate area around the table was cloaked in darkness. Somewhere in that darkness, she heard the sound of a baby crying.

"No!" she cried out, as she let go of Karla's hand and opened her eyes.

"Tor? Honey, are you okay?" Ben asked worriedly beside her.

Still feeling the warmth from Karla's hand, Tori looked around her and recognized the familiar images of their bedroom. "She's gone," she murmured, looking down at her hand.

"Who's gone, honey?" he asked quietly.

Searching out his eyes in the darkness, she choked out a sob as the tears stared to flow. "Karla! She was right here! I can still feel the warmth of her hand in mine, and now she's gone!"

"Shhh...., come here, baby," he soothed, pulling her into his arms. Rocking her gently back and forth, he slowly rubbed her back and waited until her sobbing slowed and she was able to talk again.

"Do you want to tell me about it?" he offered, still holding her against him.

"She was here," Tori whispered against his chest.

"Is she okay?" he asked, patiently.

"I think so," Tori replied, pushing away to sit up and face him. Wiping the tears from beneath her eyes with the sleeve of her shirt, she looked over and saw Goliath sleeping, undisturbed. "It was a dream. I know she wasn't really here."

"That doesn't make it any less real to you," Ben smiled and exhaled the breath he felt like he'd been holding, glad that her sense of reason was coming back as she began to think through the details of her dream.

"I guess," she whispered.

"Notebook or tablet?" he asked, knowing she needed to record all of the details before any of them began to fade from her memory.

"Tablet, please. I don't feel like writing right now," she admitted, pushing her hair away from her face.

Leaning over to turn on the light, he retrieved her tablet from the nightstand, selected the audio memo application and placed the tablet on the bed between them.

"Ready when you are," he urged her gently, pressing the record button.

"Okay," Tori sighed, collecting her thoughts. "The dream started out okay, I guess. I was walking through a dense fog for a long time and remember feeling tired which is strange because I don't usually feel tired in my dreams. Then I heard a woman singing, so I followed the voice until I found her. She was singing the lyrics to the lullaby verse we painted on the walls in the nursery."

"That seems quite coincidental," Ben noted, with raised eyebrows.

"I agree. As it turns out that verse is a lullaby she and her family used to sing to their children. It's the story of the daughter's of Remiel. According to her, we're all children from the light," Tori advised.

"Who?" Ben asked, puzzled.

"What?" Tori asked.

"You said, according to her. Who are you talking about, Karla?" Ben repeated.

"Oh, sorry! No, I meant Elsbet!" Tori replied.

"Elsbet! As in the last descendant possessing the statue and the amulet?" Ben asked, surprised.

"The very one," Tori nodded. "Elsbet is the spirit inside my amulet," Tori revealed, holding the amulet up between them. As if in greeting, the amulet gently glowed, casting a blue-green shadow of Tori's silhouette against the wall behind the bed.

"Why is her spirit inside the amulet?" Ben puzzled, staring at the pulsating light.

"She said it was her punishment for her betrayal. She's been in this kind of flux state since the day she died," Tori replied.

"What do you mean by flux state?" Ben frowned.

"Remember how in the past I've mentioned being in a place that felt like a big white room but I wasn't sure it was really a room because I never see the ceiling or any walls?" Tori prompted.

"Yeah," Ben nodded.

"Well, this place is just like that. It's this big empty place, and she's in it. Well, it was empty in the beginning before the other's started to show up," Tori noted.

"Others? I thought you said it was just Elsbet and Karla. And where does Karla fit into this? I thought you crossed her over with Meda and Tobias. Were they there too?" Ben asked, now completely lost.

"No, according to Karla, Meda and Tobias crossed over as we've all assumed they did. Only the daughter's who've been murdered go to the place where Elsbet is. Since Meda's death was from natural causes, she fulfilled her calling, and she's in heaven with Tobias," Tori replied.

"Well, that's good! I would hate to have either Meda or her husband end up alone after all those years waiting to be with one another," Ben admitted.

"I agree. Not so with Karla and the others. The power from the amulet started out with just Elsbet, but over the centuries as more of Remy's daughters were killed, they began to show up. As they made contact with one another, they were able to channel their power together so now their combined power is what fuels the amulet through Elsbet. She's still ultimately the spirit of the amulet, but her power comes from the others as well," Tori replied.

"And they exist harmoniously?" Ben wondered. "None of them seem to mind being where they are? What about Karla? Did she seem happy?"

Tori smiled, thinking back and replied, "Yes. I think she was. There were about twenty of them there, and they all seemed happy."

"Then what made you so scared when you woke up?" Ben asked, cautiously.

Exhaling a deep breath, Tori closed her eyes for a moment, reliving the last few moments of her dream. "Karla said something about the amulet being a living thing and that it ultimately chooses what it reveals to me. Even though Elsbet said she's the spirit of the amulet, it sounded like the amulet has a soul or something like that."

"Okay, that makes no sense to me at all," Ben admitted.

Nodding her head, Tori replied, "It didn't to me either. When I said that, Elsbet decided to show me instead. We all joined hands and when Elsbet and I both touched the amulet together, and I saw images of things that I'm not sure I really fully understood."

"Tell me what you saw," Ben urged, supportively.

"At first, I saw flashes of the other women. It was like watching a movie of what they looked like while they were still alive on earth and images of how they died. Some of the images were more violent than others but before I could really process what I was seeing, the image changed, and I saw the form of the human falling from the sky like in my last dream. Except this time, I could see it was a man and that he had wings," Tori noted.

"He had wings!" Ben exclaimed in surprise. "Was it Remy?"

"I couldn't tell," Tori admitted. "It could have been Remy, Luc or any of the other fallen angels that were cast out of heaven."

"It may not have been a vision from the past. What if it was a vision of the future?" Ben suggested.

"You're right, I have no idea," Tori mused. "But again, before I could really process that vision, it changed again. This time, I was standing on a sidewalk in front of a building across from a park. I had a sensation that someone was watching me so I turned my head and all of a sudden it was like my sight rushed forward like I was looking through binoculars and I was looking at the barrel of a rifle."

"I don't like the sound of that," Ben growled. "Where was the barrel pointed?"

"Directly at me," Tori grimaced. "Not sure about that either. What's weird is as I looked beyond the end of the barrel, I saw the face of the man holding the gun."

"Let me guess, it was our guy," Ben surmised.

Tori nodded and drew in a deep breath. Exhaling deeply, she added, "There's more."

"Go on," he sighed.

"The last vision I saw was me lying on an operating table. There was blood everywhere, and my eyes were closed. I couldn't tell if I was still alive or not. Then I heard the sound of a baby crying, which scared me. That's when I cried out and woke up," Tori said, quietly. "What if I just saw my death, Ben? What if the baby crying was Gemma or RJ and I don't survive?"

"Let's not speculate on any of what you saw right now. Okay? You said it yourself. Not all of your visions are of things that actually happen. Sometimes they're of things that could happen, depending on the choices that you make. Or based upon what you just learned, what the amulet chooses to reveal to you. So for right now, let's send your audio file to the rest of the team, and try to get some rest. I'm sure once Agent Hunter and the others review what you send them; Agent Hunter will call a meeting, and we can all talk this through together. Okay?" Ben suggested.

Tori nodded and agreed, "Okay. But I'm not sure I'll be able to sleep anymore tonight."

"To be honest, after what you just told me, I'm not sure I'll be able to either," Ben admitted.

Glancing at the clock, Tori paused as an idea came to her. "Are you hungry at all?"

"Sure, I could eat," Ben chuckled, wiggling his eyebrows at her.

Laughing at his expression, she replied, "Shocker!"

"I know, right?" he laughed. "What do you have in mind?"

"I have a craving for mushroom fettuccine with tarragon and goat cheese sauce," she admitted. "Is that weird?"

"Nope," Ben smiled, wiping the tears from her cheeks. "Do you want to make it or may I make it for you?"

"Let's make it together," she agreed. "A little cooking therapy might be just what I need right now."

"It's a deal," he replied, pulling back the covers and getting out of bed.

"I need to use the restroom before we do so I'll meet you in the kitchen," Tori admitted as she eased herself out of the bed.

"Okay, I'll start pulling out the ingredients and meet you there!" Ben replied.

~~~~~~~~~~

Thirty minutes later, Tori stood in front of the stove, stirring goat cheese, Parmesan cheese and milk in a saucepan into a rich, creamy sauce while Goliath sat vigilantly by her feet; his nose pointed in the direction of the stove.

"No Goliath, you already had your treat. This is for me and Ben," Tori gently scolded. "I think the sauce is done. How's the pasta?"

"It's perfect!" Ben announced, testing one of the noodles. "I'm ready to drain it and then it's all yours."

"Scoop out about a cup of the pasta water before you do, please so I can blend that with the sauce," Tori instructed, turning off the burner.

"As you wish," he replied, taking a measuring cup out of the cupboard and scooping out a cupful.

Once the pasta was drained, he emptied it into a large bowl and placed the bowl beside Tori. "Here you go."

"Thanks," Tori replied, whisking the pasta water into the goat-cheese mixture. Once she had the consistency she was looking for, she poured the sauce on top of the pasta, added a handful of fresh chopped tarragon, and tossed the noodles into the sauce until everything was mixed together.

"Here are the chives," Ben offered, handing her a small bowl.

"Perfect!" she smiled, sprinkling the chives on top of the pasta. "Voila! It's ready!"

"Thank goodness, that smells amazing! I'm really hungry now after smelling that the past half-hour," Ben replied.

Grabbing two plates from the cupboard, Tori spooned a large portion of the pasta onto each one, sprinkled a generous amount of shredded Parmesan on top and handed the plates to Ben. "I'll grab the silverware and meet you at the table!"

"Deal," he replied, eyeing the pasta hungrily.

After they settled into their chairs, Tori swirled a large mound of pasta around her fork and took a bite. "Yum," she groaned as she chewed. "Oh, that is so good!"

Following her lead, Ben took a large bite and grunted in satisfaction. "Oh, have I told you how much I appreciate your food? This is so good!"

"Thanks," Tori mumbled as she chewed.

He looked over at her contented face, pleased to see her looking relaxed and happy. "So is this helping?" he asked.

"Cooking therapy always helps," she smiled. "And the company makes it even better. Thank you, Ben."

"For you, anytime," he smiled.

Chapter 30

"Hey, sweetie, how are you doing?" Piper asked, pulling Tori into a tight hug as she, Ben and Goliath entered the conference room.

"I'm okay," Tori replied, embracing her friend.

"Are you sure? That was some dream you had," Piper worried, pulling back to search Tori's face.

"Yeah, I've had better," Tori admitted. "But I'm fine."

"Good morning everyone," Ben greeted, glancing around the table as he set his backpack down into one of the empty chairs. "Hey, Agent Sullivan, I didn't know you would be joining us today. It's good to see you!"

"Hello, Agent Vincent!" Agent Sullivan replied. "It's good to see you as well. Agent Hunter forwarded Agent Cooper's email to me and asked me to join everyone today, considering the subject matter." Turning to Tori, he regarded her with fatherly concern and asked, "Are you sure you're feeling up to diving into the specifics of your dream? It seems as if there were quite a few details that were pretty unsettling."

Tori shrugged and admitted, "Better to talk about my demons than lock them up inside of me, right? It's not as much fun keeping it all to myself."

Narrowing his eyes at her, Agent Sullivan replied, "You are taking all this seriously, right? There were several poignant details in your dream that you need to consider carefully. And everyone here in this room cares about you, and what happens to you. You know that?"

Tori eyed Agent Sullivan warily and asked, "Why are you asking me that, Agent Sullivan? What did you take from that dream that I haven't considered yet?"

"Why don't we all take a seat and start from the beginning?" he replied, motioning her to an empty chair.

"Okay," Tori replied, easing herself down into one of the chairs. As she did, Goliath protectively positioned himself directly next to her. "Who wants to go first?"

Instinctively, everyone remained quiet and conceded the floor to Agent Sullivan, who quickly jumped in. "Why don't we talk about your conversation with Elsbet first?"

"All right, any part of the conversation in particular?" Tori asked, calmly.

"Well, let's start with the nursery rhyme since that's where you first met her. You said you were walking for what felt like a long time before you heard her singing. Do you remember what you were thinking right before you heard her?" he asked.

Tori thought back for a moment and replied, "I remember feeling tired. I was beginning to think that my being there was pointless, and I was wasting my time."

"And then you heard her singing," Agent Sullivan prompted.

"No, actually, then I felt a kick from one of the twins and it started to wake me up. Then I heard the singing," Tori admitted.

"Interesting," Agent Sullivan replied, considering an idea.

"What?" Tori asked, curiously.

"It sounds to me like Elsbet singing was to calm the twins so they didn't wake you up, so you could stay in the dream longer," he replied.

Considering his theory, Tori said, "That seems plausible considering the kicking stopped shortly after that. Even I found her singing to be soothing and peaceful. It was a very pretty tune."

"Do you remember it?" Piper asked.

"No, that's the strange part. I don't," Tori confessed.

"What happened next?" Agent Sullivan prodded.

"Next we introduced ourselves, even though she already knew who I was," Tori replied when suddenly a memory came back to her. "Come to think of it, there was something else I forgot until now. When I asked her why she waited so long to reveal herself to me, she told me she wanted to make sure I was worthy."

"Worthy?" Piper frowned.

"Does she have the right to determine whether you're worthy or not?" Riley interrupted.

"That's what I said!" Tori exclaimed, dramatically.

"And what did she say when you asked her?" Reagan asked.

Tori exhaled a deep sigh and replied, "She said she needed to be sure that I wasn't going to be weak like she once was. She said I needed to be strong enough to prevent Luc from tempting me into making the same decision she did."

Turning to Agent Sullivan, she added, "She did make a point of telling me that Luc is not at all interested in his salvation, so your earlier thought was correct, Agent Sullivan. He's happy being the dark prince of the earth. He has no desire to go back to heaven."

"So did she admit that she believed you were strong enough?" Agent Hunter asked.

"I guess she must have considering she took me to meet the others afterward," Tori surmised.

"Or maybe she had no other choice," Agent Sullivan suggested, quietly.

"Hey!" Tori objected, feeling hurt.

"No, that's not what I meant!" Agent Sullivan quickly assured. "What I meant was considering what you saw in the rest of your dream, maybe the impending birth of the twins forced her hand into contacting you sooner than she had planned."

"What do you mean by that, sir?" Ben asked, leaning forward in his chair.

"Agent Cooper is only a few weeks away from her due date as far as we can tell. Perhaps it was urgent for Elsbet and the others to make contact with Tori, to prepare her for what they already know," Agent Sullivan suggested.

"But Elsbet and Karla made it very clear that they couldn't tell me what they knew, they could only show me visions of what could happen, based upon the choices that I make," Tori argued.

"I still can't believe you spoke to her," Reagan noted quietly.

When no one else said anything, Tori looked around the table at the faces of Agent Neviah's former team, each of them dealing with the shock of learning the fate of their former teammate.

"She seemed happy where she was if it's any consolation," Tori offered to the group. "It seemed like she was in the right place with the others."

"Even though it meant she wasn't with Meda and Tobias?" Reagan worried.

"Yes," Tori smiled. "She understands that Meda lived out her purpose as intended and that being apart from her parents for now was what was supposed to have happened. She's surrounded by other women who understand exactly who she is. For the first time in her life, she's not an only child anymore. She has sisters!"

"I want to go back to Agent Sullivan's comment earlier," Ben interrupted. "What did you mean about Elsbet's hand being forced to confront Tori now?"

Agent Sullivan rose from his chair and began pacing the length of carpet along the table as he theorized. "Elsbet admitted that even though she's the spirit of the amulet, the power of the amulet comes from the combined energy from the other daughters of Remiel, who have died at the hand of another human. So in the simplest of terms, consider murdered daughters equal power, daughters living out their lives naturally do not."

"I'm with you so far," Ben agreed.

"Same here," Tori added.

"Agent Cooper's death would obviously be a bad thing on many levels. Not only would the universe no longer have a chosen one guarding the amulet and the statue, but her death would also give the amulet even greater power, even though there wouldn't be a rightful heir to claim it," Agent Sullivan suggested.

"But there would be two rightful future heirs with the twins," Piper argued.

"Correct, however again, Lucifer wouldn't want Gemma to die unnaturally because her power would also fuel the power of the amulet, so keeping her alive is in his best interest," Agent Sullivan paused, emphasizing his point.

"But then what would that mean for RJ?" Tori worried.

"Exactly!" Agent Sullivan exclaimed.

"He's a wild card," Logan candidly remarked.

"Yes. He's a wild card," Agent Sullivan confirmed.

"I'm not following you," Ben admitted in frustration.

Pausing long enough to create an analogy in his head, Agent Sullivan turned to Ben and asked, "Do you play poker, Agent Vincent?"

"Sometimes," Ben admitted.

"Not very well," Logan muttered sarcastically.

"Hey!" Ben began to argue.

"Regardless, you're familiar with the game?" Agent Sullivan interrupted.

"Yes," Ben agreed, scowling at Logan.

"Okay good. So then you know the wild card cannot stand for any card you choose, but is considered an ace unless you use it to play a flush or a straight. For example, if you have five-six-seven-eight-joker, you can play the joker as a nine to make a straight. If, however, you have five-five-six-seven-joker, you have to play the Joker as an ace, it cannot be a five," Agent Sullivan explained.

"Yes, I understand that," Ben agreed. "But you're talking about a game of cards and taking risks by playing the odds. I'm talking about a human life! More specifically, you're talking about my son's life!"

"Who better to play the odds by risking a human life than the devil?" Agent Sullivan asked bluntly.

"Either way, Luc has nothing to lose," Piper noted, seeing where Agent Sullivan was going. "It all comes down to power and who has more of it. Nobody knows how much power RJ will have, if any."

"Precisely!" Agent Sullivan applauded.

"What do you mean, Piper?" Tori frowned.

"If RJ dies and has power, that's only one of the twins fueling the amulet. But being the first male, his power may not be the same as the other daughters, so he may negatively affect the collective power. If RJ doesn't have any power, he's mortal but still able to procreate, thus creating more potential daughters of Remiel, who do have power. If Luc kills RJ, he wins the hand," Piper surmised.

"Yes," Agent Sullivan agreed.

"So you're saying that Luc is planning to use RJ as a bargaining chip?" Tori accused angrily.

Agent Sullivan shook his head and replied, "I don't know what he's going to do. None of us do. I'm suggesting there's a possibility that he could. You even said everything is about choice. And none of us can predict what anyone would do until the moment we're forced to choose. At some point in both of their lives, Gemma and RJ are going to have to choose the paths they take. Apart or together, either they'll stand or they'll fall. Neither you nor Remy will be able to do anything about it."

"Speaking of falling, who do you think Tori saw falling from the sky, Agent Sullivan?" Piper wondered. "Do you think the man with the wings was Remy or Luc?"

"That part is a mystery to me as well," Agent Sullivan admitted. "I don't have any insight as to what that part of her dream could have meant."

"Me either, but that's the second time I've seen it, so it has to have some significance," Tori noted.

"Agreed," Agent Sullivan nodded.

"Not that I don't think all of this is good discussion," Riley interrupted. "However, I would like to talk about the vision of Tori seeing herself as our killer's target. I think that's the most pressing piece of her dream we should be focusing our attention on right now. Especially since the vision Tori saw immediately afterward seemed to imply she was injured."

"Or dead," Tori shuddered, gently stroking her stomach.

"Oh, please don't say that," Regan murmured sadly. "I don't want to even consider that possibility."

"None of us do," Agent Hunter agreed.

"If Tori saw herself as a target, that would imply that at some point, our killer gains some level of knowledge about her. We need to come up with a list of possible scenarios where that happens," Riley advised, approaching the whiteboard. Adding a new bullet point, he said, "The first one that comes to mind is the result of her search program. It's possible that our killer has some level of technical expertise, and he figures out she's the one behind the program."

"I agree, we need to take that into consideration," Agent Hunter nodded.

"Speaking of which, how is that search going?" Agent Sullivan asked, curiously.

"The first search result came back with over five thousand possible matches, which was way too many. So after my dream last night where I saw our killers face, I tweaked my code a bit, added a couple additional search filters and kicked it off again. When we left the house earlier, it was still running, which is good. That means its taking out more of the probable mismatches," Tori replied.

"Ugh, that is good. Having to sift through five thousand hits would have taken forever!" Reagan groaned.

"So what does our mystery man look like? How good of a look did you get?" Piper asked.

"Are you seriously asking if our killer is hot?" Logan accused.

"Don't be dense!" Piper exclaimed, glaring at Logan. Thinking about it more, she turned to Tori and added, "Wait, was he?"

"Piper!" Tori laughed, giving Piper a quick nod indicating she was on the right track.

"Like Thor hot or Wolverine hot?" Piper whispered across the table.

"Thor hot," Tori whispered back.

"Oh!" Piper breathed, appreciatively.

"Are you two done?" Ben interrupted.

"What?" Piper asked innocently. "We're going to have to ID this guy eventually. We'll need to know what he looks like in order to do that. After all, Tori is the one who has said she doesn't feel like this guy is a cold-blooded killer and that he may be confused about what he's doing. Maybe he's really one of the good guys and what he's doing isn't by his choice."

"It's pretty hard not to remember killing someone, Piper," Logan argued.

"Actually, Agent Stirling brings up a good point. Let's add a supernatural possibility to your list, Agent Hughes," Agent Sullivan declared. "Since in the past, we've seen Lucifer use other people to do his bidding, we need to consider that our killer may be under his influence."

Riley added the bullet point to the board and said, "I would agree with that possibility."

"I concur," Agent Hunter agreed.

"See?" Piper defended herself.

"You backed into that little victory, just so you know," Logan noted.

Suddenly, the sound of a loud growl erupted in the room. Instinctively they all turned to look at Goliath, who was still sitting beside Tori, attentively listening to the conversation.

"Sorry, that was me," Tori winced, embarrassed. "Ben and I kind of had a middle of the night fridge raid, so we skipped breakfast earlier this morning."

"Do you want to break for lunch?" Agent Hunter asked.

"No, I'll be fine, we should keep going," Tori replied.

"Tor, if you're hungry, you should eat," Ben advised.

"I wouldn't mind running out to get drinks and sandwiches and bring them back here," Reagan offered. "The deli around the corner has our usual order on file. All I have to do is make the call and pick it up. It will only take me fifteen minutes."

"I could eat," Ben admitted.

"Same," Piper agreed.

"Actually, that does sound good," Tori confessed.

"Go ahead and make the call. Thank you, Agent Nichols," Agent Hunter replied.

"It's no problem, sir!" Reagan happily replied.

"Ooh! Would you add an extra order of pickles to my sandwich, please?" Tori begged, apologetically.

"Seriously?" Regan chuckled.

"I know, a pregnant woman asking for pickles. That's so cliché," Tori laughed, rolling her eyes.

Regan nodded and replied, "Considering that's the first time you've asked for something I would consider as a typical pregnant woman's craving, I absolutely have to oblige! Extra pickles on the number five sandwich for Tori."

"Thank you!" Tori smiled happily.

"You're welcome," Reagan replied, pulling her cell phone from her pocket. "Okay everyone, I'll be back soon."

As Reagan left, Riley looked at Tori and asked, "Did you feel any emotions or get any impressions from the man with the rifle, during your dream?"

Tori shook her head and admitted, "Honestly, no, none. But that whole scene played out so fast, even in slow motion it was fleeting. I do remember how familiar it felt. Like it was something I do every day."

"And you didn't hear the sound of the gun fire, right?" Piper asked.

"No why? Is that important?" Tori wondered.

"Maybe, maybe not. Have you ever had one of those dreams where you're falling but you wake up before you hit the ground?" Piper asked.

"Yes," Tori nodded.

"Some psychologists say that when you fall in your dreams, it suggests that you may have lost control over a situation in your life," Piper replied. "Hitting the ground is supposed to mean that you're dead but who can really say for sure unless someone comes back from the dead and says that they've died?"

Thinking that through, Tori inclined her head in agreement and asked, "Okay I see where you're going. Well, the first part anyway. Not the dead part. What about dreams of being shot?"

"Dreams about being shot represent a form of self-punishment that you may be subconsciously imposing on yourself," Piper suggested.

"What am I subconsciously punishing myself for?" Tori frowned.

"Earlier in your dream, you mentioned that you were upset because Karla wasn't with Meda and Tobias. Maybe you were feeling guilty because you felt responsible for their separation. That your guidance the night of Meda's death didn't work the way you thought it did," Piper replied.

"I guess that's possible, but I don't think that's the case in this situation. I feel certain that seeing our shooter's face means that I'm a future target," Tori decided.

"I would have to agree," Riley advised. "There are far too many other pieces from previous dreams and visions indicating Tori's involvement in our killer's story, more than just self-imposed guilt."

"I agree as well. Let's keep talking through that theory and see what else we can come up with. At least until Agent Nichols comes back with lunch," Agent Hunter instructed.

Chapter 31

Regan stuffed a handful of paper covered straws and napkins into her jacket pocket, and casually glanced at the faces of the other customers while she waited for the cashier to call her name. Her eyes skipped by one individual briefly, but then she quickly looked back to take a second look.

"Now there's a Thor if I've ever seen one," she thought to herself, appreciatively. *"He has beautiful eyes!"*

Sensing her gaze, the man looked directly at her and gave her a friendly smile.

Embarrassed at being caught staring, Reagan smiled back and quickly averted her eyes back to the counter.

"Dang it, you guys!" Reagan silently cursed Tori and Piper. *"Now you've got me doing it!"*

"Nichols?" the cashier called out loudly to the people waiting.

"Here!" Reagan replied, raising her hand.

Smiling in greeting, the cashier handed Reagan a large handled bag and a drink carrier with all of the drinks. "Here you go. Eight sandwiches, eight drinks and one beef bone for Goliath."

"Thank you, Jackson," Reagan replied, taking the items from him. "Oh, did you remember the extra pickles on the number five?"

Scowling, apologetically, the man replied, "Oh, shoot! I didn't. I'm so sorry. Give me one second, I'll be right back."

"Thanks, I appreciate that!" Reagan smiled.

A minute later, the man returned with a small plastic container and said, "Here you go. Sorry about that. Do you want me to put it in the bag with the sandwiches?"

"No, that's okay. Just put it on top of one of the drinks, it should be okay," Reagan replied. "Thanks again."

"You're welcome. Enjoy!" he replied, giving her a small wave.

Making her way to the door, Reagan realized it swung inward, and both of her hands were full. As she began to maneuver the drink carrier to her other hand, she heard a deep, throaty male voice behind her.

"Here, let me get that for you."

She looked behind her and instantly recognized the face belonging to the voice. *"Great, of course, it would be Thor offering to open the door for me. Even his voice is sexy."*

"Thanks," she smiled, uncomfortably.

As he leaned towards her to grab the door handle, she was caught off guard and started to lean away, causing the drink carrier to tip sideways and the container of pickles to slide off.

"Oh!" she exclaimed as she saw the container start to fall.

"I've got it!" he replied, catching it in one hand while opening the door with his other hand.

"Nice catch!" she smiled, impressed with his quick reflexes.

"Thanks! Maybe having this on top of the drinks isn't such a great idea," he winked, mischievously.

"Yeah, you're right. Would you mind putting in the bag with the sandwiches? I'm sorry my hands are full," Reagan pleaded, apologetically.

"That's a better idea," he grinned, reaching into the bag to set the container on top of one of the boxes. "There you go!"

"Thanks, I really appreciate your help!" Regan smiled, stepping through the opened doorway.

"No problem! Have a nice day," he replied with a quick wave, letting the door close behind her.

"You too!" she called out before the door shut. *"What a nice guy!"* she thought happily as she walked down the sidewalk towards the office.

~~~~~~~~~~~

"Hey, guys and gals, lunch is served!" Reagan announced, holding up the bag and drinks as she entered the room.

"Oh hey, let me help you with that," Ben quickly replied, getting up from his chair to take the drinks from her.

"Thanks, Ben! Man, there are nice guys coming to my rescue everywhere today!" she replied as he freed up her right hand.

"Really? Do tell," Piper remarked, with a curious look.

Reagan laughed at Piper's expression and replied, "It was just a nice guy at the deli who helped me with the door as I was leaving. It was no big deal."

"They put the charges on our account, right?" Agent Hunter asked.

"All taken care of," Regan nodded. "Everything is marked with your names, including a bone for Goliath. Oh, here are the straws and napkins," she added, pulling them from her jacket pocket. "I think we're all set. I'm going to wash my hands really quick. I must have touched something sticky because my hands feel gross."

"No worries. Ben and I can hand everything out. Thanks, Reagan," Piper said, as she began taking the boxed lunches from the bag.

"Yes, thanks, for picking up lunch, Reagan," Tori said.

"You're welcome! Don't wait for me, seriously. I know how hungry everyone is. I'll be right back!" Reagan smiled, leaving the room.

"Here, let me help pass some of those out," Riley offered, taking several boxes from Piper.

"Thanks, Riley," she smiled.

As the aromas of the food began to fill the air, Goliath's nose followed the smell to the bag and his tail began to wag.

"Goliath bone?" he asked Tori, his eyes filled with anticipation.

Tori chuckled, and said, "Piper, would you mind giving Goliath his bone before he starts to drool all over the table?"

Seeing the pitiful look on Goliath's face, Piper crooned, "Oh, poor, Goliath! Hold on, sweet boy." Immediately succumbing to his wishes, she began pushing the boxes aside until she found the bone wrapped up in butcher's paper. "Here you go, buddy," she soothed, pulling the wrapping free and handing him the bone.

"Thank you!" Tori heard him happily reply as he gently took the bone from her and trotted off to the corner of the room.

"He said thank you," Tori advised, politely.

"You're welcome, Goliath," Piper called out across the room.

"Oh, this is so good," Tori murmured, leaning back in her chair as she chewed. "Why is it sandwiches always taste better when someone else makes them?"

"Agreed," Ben replied, mid-chew. "I swear I've tried to make this exact sandwich at home, but it never tastes like this."

"Same thing with salads," Piper noted. "There's no mystery to making a salad, but they always taste better in a restaurant."

"Yeah, why is that?" Logan frowned.

"I can give you the psychological explanation for that question, if you really want to know the answer," Agent Sullivan offered. "There've been many studies on that very question."

"Seriously? There've been studies on why my sandwich tastes better when someone else makes it?" Logan demanded.

"Yes," Agent Sullivan shrugged.

"Well then I have to know the answer," Logan insisted eagerly.

"All right," Agent Sullivan replied, setting down his sandwich. "Extended exposure to a stimulus, in this case, the sandwich decreases the psychological and behavioral responses. By that, I mean our desire to eat it."

"So you're saying overexposure to something makes it less desirable," Riley surmised.

"Exactly," Agent Sullivan replied. "It's human nature." Turning to Logan, he asked, "You're a beer drinker, right Agent Chase?"

"Yes," Logan confirmed.

"Which sip of that beer tastes better, the first one or the last?" Agent Sullivan prodded.

"The first," Logan admitted.

"What? I leave for five minutes, and we're talking about beer?" Regan laughed as she returned and sat down in her chair.

"We were all agreeing that a sandwich tastes better when someone else makes it," Piper advised. "Agent Sullivan was giving us the psychological reason."

"Well gosh, that pretty much applies to anything when you think about it," Regan noted as she unwrapped her sandwich. "Why do you think married couples who have been married a long time stop having sex?" she asked, taking a bite.

"And the conversation just got weird," Logan muttered.

"Seriously, grow up! It's human nature!" Reagan insisted. "Ask anyone who has been married a long time. It happens!"

Realizing he was the one in the room married the longest Agent Hunter saw a few glances slide over in his direction. "Don't even think about it," he noted, dryly.

Rolling her eyes, Reagan said, "Okay, then. Let's go back to the food reference." Turning to Tori, she asked, "Tori, the extra pickles you asked for earlier. They were given to you in a plastic container so you couldn't smell them until you opened them. Once you did, you felt your salivary glands start to give you that tingle of anticipation behind your jaw, right?"

Glancing down at her now empty sandwich wrapper, Tori frowned and looked back up at Reagan, doubtfully. "Actually, I didn't get a container with extra pickles. They must have forgotten them."

"No, they didn't! I specifically had to ask for them because at first they did forget! Where's the little plastic container that was in the bag with the sandwiches?" Reagan insisted, getting up from her chair.

"I don't remember seeing a little plastic container," Piper argued.

Reaching for the bag, Reagan looked inside and declared, victoriously, "Here it is! See, they didn't forget them! Here you go," she added, sliding the container across the table to Tori. "I almost dropped them but this really nice guy who helped me with the door caught the container before it hit the floor."

"Thanks, Reagan," Tori smiled as she picked up the container. "Oh!" She suddenly gasped as a surge of electricity flowed through her. Unable to move, the smile froze on her face as her eyes began to glaze over.

"Tor, what is it? What's wrong?" Ben exclaimed, jumping up from his chair. He placed his hand on her shoulder, and instantly a shock went through him, sending him backward onto the floor. "Ouch!"

"Oh my gosh!" Reagan exclaimed as she quickly walked around the table towards him.

"Are you okay?" Piper rushed forward, helping him up.

"Yeah, I'm fine," he grunted as he stood. "She shocked me again."

As the commotion brought everyone out of their chairs, Reagan looked over at Tori's face. "Ah, guys?"

Noticing the transfixed expression on Tori's face as well, Agent Hunter asked, "Piper, do you see anything?"

Studying the aura around Tori, Piper shook her head and admitted, "Actually no. Her color is fine."

Goliath quickly pushed through everyone and came to Tori's side. *"Get Remy?"* he asked her.

"No," Tori murmured, as she drew a deep breath and her eyes regained their focus. "I'm okay."

"What just happened?" Ben quietly asked, tentatively touching her shoulder again, testing for another shock.

Breaking free from her trance, she looked up to meet his eyes, and announced, "He's here."

"Who's here?" he asked, confused.

"Our killer," she replied, holding up the container towards Reagan, "is your nice guy from the deli."

"What? Are you kidding me?" Regan agonized. "Of all the people I could have come into contact with, that was him?"

"We need to act fast," Agent Hunter demanded. "He can't have gone too far since Agent Nichols returned. Can you give us a physical description of him, so we know who to look for?"

Pausing to visualize her mystery man again, Regan exhaled a deep, frustrated breath and advised, "Let's say six foot two, about one hundred and eighty pounds and well muscled. Even through his shirt I could see the guy was built." Realizing she said that last part out loud, she gave a pained expression and kept going. "Anyway, uh, he had long dark blonde hair pulled back in a pony tail, light blue eyes, and a slight covering of facial hair on his face. I would say it's been a few days since he's shaved."

"I would agree, it looked like that to me too," Tori confirmed.

"What was he wearing? Is there anything unique that would make him stand out in a crowd?" Riley asked.

"Uh, nothing that comes to mind. Denim jeans; a tan and brown flannel shirt and hiking boots," Reagan admitted.

"Okay, listen up everyone," Agent Hunter announced. Pointing to Reagan and Tori, he instructed, "Agent Nichols, you take Agent Cooper back to the deli and talk to the cashier as well as any customers who remember seeing our guy and the direction he went when he left. Find out if he paid cash or if he used a credit card. And see if they have a surveillance camera set up in their shop. If we're lucky, maybe we can get an image of our guy and start running it through our facial recognition software."

"Got it," they both replied.

"Agent Vincent, you and Agent Chase pair up and start canvassing the area west of the Deli. Agent Sullivan and Agent Stirling will work the area on the east side of town. Agent Hughes and I will take the woods on the back side of the park," Agent Hunter advised.

"Yes, sir," everyone confirmed.

"Keep your cell phones on you at all times and under no circumstances does anyone approach our guy if you find him. If you do, call me, and I'll pull the team into your location. During that time, you observe only, do not engage. It's the middle of the day which means there are a lot of civilians out there walking around as well. This may be our only chance to catch him off guard, so it's important we keep a low profile. Does everyone understand?" Agent Hunter instructed.

"Yes sir," everyone immediately agreed.

"Does anyone have any questions?" Agent Hunter asked.

"Should Goliath go with Tori?" Goliath asked Tori.

"Yes, Goliath, you come with me," she whispered back to him.

"All right, let's move out!" Agent Hunter commanded, ushering everyone out the door.

~~~~~~~~~~~

As everyone made their way out of the building and began to split up into their designated teams, Tori abruptly stopped walking when she realized where they were.

"Oh no," she exclaimed, looking around her.

"What?" Ben asked, alarmed at her expression.

"This is the spot. This is the building, the sidewalk where I was standing," she insisted urgently.

~~~~~~~~~~~

"Do you see her?" Satan whispered in his ear.

"Yes," Zander murmured.

"Remember what I told you. I don't want you to kill her, just injure her," the demon warned.

"I remember," he replied, watching the woman in the crosshairs of his scope. He remained motionless, admiring the way the sun reflected off her auburn hair when suddenly she turned and looked straight at him. His breath caught in his throat, all at once feeling exposed. "She sees me," he cautioned.

"No, she senses you," Lucifer advised. "This one is different. She knows things that she cannot see. Don't lose your focus! I picked you for a reason. Don't disappoint me."

"I won't, sir," Zander replied, taking aim.

~~~~~~~~~~~

Reliving the moment from her dream, everything seemed to slow down as Tori felt the hair rise on the back of her neck, knowing he was watching her. Turning her head slowly towards the direction of the woods, she recognized the spot in the trees where he was hidden.

"He's right there!" she thought to herself, just a fraction of a second before she heard the sound of the shot being fired.

When he realized what was about to happen, Goliath instantly lunged forward, to push Tori out of the bullet's path and promised, *"Goliath will save you!"*

Hearing his proclamation, Tori turned and gasped in surprise when she saw the look of fierce determination in his eyes as Goliath raced towards her. "Goliath, no!" she screamed frantically.

Bracing for impact, she raised her hands upwards and as his paws made contact with her, their eyes met.

"Create a shield!" she heard a voice command urgently. *"Tori complete the connection!"*

Grabbing onto Goliath's front legs, she felt a wave of electricity flow from her fingertips, creating a bond between them. As she did, a burst of light instantly exploded from the amulet, forming an iridescent bubble around them.

Unfortunately, the shield was only strong enough to slightly decrease the momentum of the bullet, and it shattered like shards of glass and disappeared as the projectile penetrated the outer barrier.

Then the bullet struck.

Still staring into Goliath's big beautiful golden eyes, Tori saw the look of fierce determination on his face transform into alarming surprise, followed by incredible pain. As that golden light began to fade, his eyes glazed over, and his paws began to slide from her shoulders.

"NO!" she screamed, as he fell to the ground at her feet. Trying to support his massive weight as he fell, she cried out, "Oh, God, please, No! Remy, where are you?"

Responding to her call, Remy appeared to her and then looked around at the scene before him. "What happened? Are you okay?"

"It's Goliath," she pleaded through her tears. "You need to help him!"

"TORI!" Ben cried out in alarm, rushing toward her, not realizing she was talking to Remy and not to him. "Someone call 9-1-1! Tori's been hit!"

"No, I'm fine! It's Goliath! He's been shot. We need to get him to a vet," she insisted. Suddenly feeling a sharp pain in her chest, she cried out, "Ah!" Then she noticed the blood-stain rapidly spreading out from a hole in her dress.

"No, baby, you've both been shot," he replied, trying to get her to let go of Goliath. Turning to look at Piper, he demanded, "Piper, call 9-1-1, NOW!"

"I'm already on it," Piper exclaimed frantically, having already keyed in the numbers on her phone. "Hello, I need an ambulance at the front entrance of the FBI building on Commerce. An agent has been shot."

"We need to get Goliath to a vet!" Tori insisted again, kneeling beside Goliath to check for a pulse. "Goliath, baby, can you hear me?" When Goliath failed to respond, she looked up toward Remy and screamed, "You need to do something!"

Still thinking she was talking to him, Ben replied, "He risked his life to save yours, Tori. You need to let me get you to a hospital."

"Why won't you help him?" she begged.

Knowing he wasn't allowed to intervene, Remy hesitated and insisted, "You know I can't do that!"

"Agent Vincent, get Agent Cooper to the hospital," Agent Hunter insisted, as he sprang into action. "Agent Chase, Agent Hughes, you come with me. The shot came from the direction of those trees. Let's go!"

"Yes, sir!" Logan and Riley both replied, running after him.

"I don't feel a pulse! Ben, you've got to get someone to help Goliath! Please!" Tori cried out, feeling lightheaded from the smell of her blood.

"Agent Sullivan and I will take care of Goliath, Tori," Reagan assured her calmly, fighting back the tears in her eyes, fearing he might already be dead.

"Yes! I'll get my car. We'll take care of him," Agent Sullivan promised, giving her a worried smile before hurrying down the sidewalk.

"Don't let him die," Tori slurred as she lost consciousness and began to fall over.

"TORI!" Ben cried out as he caught her in his arms. Easing her down to the sidewalk, he noticed a dark, wet stain along the bottom of Tori's dress. "What is that?"

"Oh no! Not now!" Reagan groaned.

"What? What is it?" Ben demanded, frantically.

"That's amniotic fluid!" Reagan exclaimed. "Tori's water just broke!"

Chapter 32

"It didn't work!" Karla cried out, watching the scene play out on the sidewalk below them. "It was supposed to protect her!"

"We didn't know what the shield would do, Karla," Elsbet calmly replied. "It's the first time we've tried extending our power beyond the amulet."

"If the whole reason we're here is to keep her safe, how do we do that?" Karla demanded. "And why isn't he helping her? He gave Goliath to her to protect her and now he's not even trying to save him for doing it! Why?"

"I don't know," Elsbet admitted, helplessly. "Maybe he saw this day coming, and Goliath did what he was meant to do."

"Well if Remy saw this day coming, he should have prevented it from happening!" Karla insisted.

"You know he can't do that," Elsbet reminded her.

"Whatever! We have to try something else! There has to be something else we can do!" Karla insisted.

"Like what? What else is there?" Elsbet frowned.

"I don't know! But if we're going to call ourselves her guardians, we're going to have to try harder than this!" Karla argued.

Chapter 33

"I wonder if he's smart enough to know Dad's not the one throwing his ball to him," Aubrey thought humorously as she sent the tennis ball across the yard again.

While she waited for Corkey to chase after it and bring it back to Tanner's chair, she looked over her father's shoulder to see what he was reading.

"Ugh, the financial section," she muttered, derisively. "That's not interesting at all. He could at least have spread out the entertainment section or the comics for me!"

As Corkey returned, he dropped the ball and wagged his tail at Tanner. Just as Aubrey was about to send the ball back out again, she suddenly felt a terrible sense of dread come over her, followed by an image of her sister, lying on the ground. "Something's wrong," she worried out loud. "Something's happened!"

Knowing her mother was out shopping, she knew she had to get Tanner's attention. Acting quickly, she left the yard and materialized in front of the whiteboard in the kitchen and wrote out a quick note.

Something's wrong! It's Tori!! Call Mom!

Focusing all of her energy on the string attached to the bell, she pulled string down, forcing the bell to tip and the clapper to hit the rim. Repeating the process again, she kept ringing the bell until finally she heard Tanner's voice.

"Okay, okay! Give me a minute! I heard you the first time, sweetheart. What is it?" Tanner exclaimed as he entered the kitchen.

Anxiously waiting, she watched the surprise register on his face as he read her note. As he did, he immediately reached for his phone. "Okay, baby, I'm calling Mom now."

"Please hurry, Daddy," Aubrey whispered, knowing he couldn't hear her but wishing he could.

When the call connected, she heard her mother's voice through the phone, "I haven't even been gone an hour yet. Don't tell me you both miss me already," Sarah laughed lightly.

"Honey, have you heard from Tori today?" Tanner quickly asked.

"No, I haven't," Sarah paused, hearing the urgency in his voice. "Why? What's going on?"

"Bree just wrote a note on the board. She thinks something's happened to Tori," Tanner replied. "I'm going to call Ben. Maybe you should call Piper and see if anything has happened, just to be sure."

"I'll do that right now and call you back," Sarah replied, ending the call.

Chapter 34

"How is she?" Ben demanded loudly over the sound of the ambulance siren.

"Sir, we're trying to get her vitals stable until we get to the hospital. Please sit back in your seat at fasten your seat belt," the paramedic instructed, patiently.

Frustrated, Ben sat back down in his seat and turned to Piper, sitting beside him. "They won't tell me anything."

"They're doing their job right now which is taking care of your wife, not to give you regular updates," Piper tried to reason with him.

"Look how pale she is. She's lost a lot of blood," Ben worried, chewing his bottom lip anxiously.

"We're almost there," Piper reassured him, quietly.

"How does her color look?" he whispered in her ear so the paramedics wouldn't hear him.

Hoping he was too preoccupied to ask her, she sighed and whispered back, "It's very faint. She's holding on."

He looked at her intently, realizing what she meant and asked, "So you're only seeing her aura, not the twins?"

Piper shook her head and replied, "I don't see anything but hers right now, but that doesn't mean they're not okay. For all we know they could be sleeping."

Ben frowned at her failed attempt to reason with him and replied, "We both know after what just happened, neither one of them would be sleeping."

"Okay, fine, but again, just because I can't see their auras anymore, doesn't mean they're not okay. We need to think positive!" Piper insisted.

Suddenly the ambulance's siren stopped, and they felt the vehicle begin to slow down. As it did, the paramedics immediately began preparing all the equipment and IV's for mobility. When they came to a complete stop, the back doors flew open, and a team of medical staff dressed in surgical scrubs converged upon the opening, and everyone began calling out instructions to one another.

Mesmerized by the apparent pre-rehearsed choreography before them, Piper and Ben sat wide-eyed and motionless as the gurney Tori lay on was quickly brought down to the ground and whisked away. Unbeknownst to either of them, Remy followed her.

Feeling his phone vibrate in his pocket, Ben retrieved it and looked at the name on the display. "It's Tanner. I can't talk to him right now. I need to go with Tori."

Feeling a vibration from her phone as well, Piper pulled her phone from her pocket and advised, "Its Sarah. Them both calling us at the same time can't be a coincidence. They know something's wrong. You go, be with your wife. I'll take the call. Sarah can fill Tanner in afterward."

"Thanks, Piper. I don't know if I can talk without losing what little grip I have right now," he admitted with tear filled eyes.

"I know. I'm scared too," she nodded, fighting back her own tears. "Now go! I've got this."

"Thanks," he replied, pocketing his phone.

As Ben jumped down from the back of the ambulance and rushed inside the building to find Tori, Piper took a deep breath and engaged the call. "Hi Sarah," she greeted, calmly.

"Has something happened to Tori?" Sarah insisted urgently. "Aubrey seems to think something's wrong. Is it true?"

"Tori's been shot, Sarah," Piper replied.

"She's been shot!" Sarah cried out, frantically. "Who shot her? Is she okay? Why didn't someone call me?"

Stepping down out of the ambulance, Piper walked towards a bench along the sidewalk and sat down. "We believe it was our suspect. Agent Hunter, Logan, and Riley are in pursuit. I don't know if they found him or not. It was a clean shot through her shoulder. She's unconscious right now, so we don't know the extent of her injuries. We literally just arrived at the hospital. I promise I was going to call you once we got here. Ben's inside now trying to find out more about her condition."

"Oh, sweet Lord," Sarah whispered. "What about the babies?"

Taking another deep breath, Piper replied, "The trauma from the gunshot caused her water to break, Sarah. She's in labor. We have to act quickly and set our plan in motion a bit earlier than we expected. Since Agent Hunter is out of pocket right now, go ahead and make the call. I'll text you the address where we are."

"Okay," Sarah replied, rushing towards her car. "I'll call as soon as we hang up. I'm on my way back home now to pack our bags. I'll call you when we're on the way to the airport, so you know when to expect us."

"Got it," Piper agreed, preparing to hang up.

"Piper," Sarah paused.

"Yes?" she replied.

"Is he there with you?" Sarah asked. "Does he know?"

Having wondered the same thing herself the past half hour, Piper looked around for any sign of Remy and shook her head slowly. "I haven't seen him, Sarah. I don't know if he's aware of what's happened or not."

"Okay," Sarah sighed. "We could really use a little heavenly help right about now."

"Agreed," Piper admitted.

"Well, in the meantime, we'll have to go with our plan then. I'll call you later." Sarah advised.

"Okay. Bye," Piper replied, ending the call.

Chapter 35

"All right you dirt bag," Logan thought angrily as he stealthily crept forward through the branches of the pine trees. *"All I need is one clear shot, and you're mine. I don't care if you do look like the God of Thunder; you won't look so good anymore when your body is lying on the cold metal table in the morgue."*

On the other end of the cluster of trees, his partner was having similar thoughts.

"It's been a while since I've had to fire my weapon, but I wouldn't hesitate for a second if given the opportunity," Riley grieved silently for his teammate. *"She has to be okay. Lord, please let her be okay."*

As the three men converged upon the location they discovered earlier where they believed the shooter fired, Agent Hunter quietly asked, "Did you find anything?"

"No," Logan frowned, looking down at the patch of ground by their feet. "No bullet casings, cigarette butts or anything else to nail this guy. This partial boot impression is the only thing out here. He was very careful not to leave any evidence behind."

"He was too careful," Riley agreed.

"So you're not thinking our guy is civilian anymore, are you?" Agent Hunter asked.

"No, I don't. I think we're looking for someone with a military background. I've called our forensics team and let them know we need a cast of the impression so we can log it as evidence," Riley advised.

"Thank you, Agent Hughes," Agent Hunter nodded.

"This guy is a ghost," Logan complained, frustrated they had nothing to go on. He looked through the trees across the grass, and added, "He was completely concealed in these trees. The parking lot back there has an access road leading directly away from the scene, and no one saw a thing. This vantage point is a direct shot to the sidewalk where she was standing. She never had a chance to avoid getting hit."

"Agreed," Riley noted, dryly. "He surveyed the area and knew exactly where he needed to be to avoid being seen. Thank God for Goliath. If he hadn't acted as quickly as he did, she might be dead right now."

"That stupid, wonderful dog," Logan muttered. "I've never known a dog to have such courage and complete devotion to another human the way he does."

"Nor I," Agent Hunter agreed, solemnly.

Logan turned to Riley and asked, "Any word from Reagan or Agent Sullivan yet?"

"No, nothing," Riley replied.

"If we're going to help either one of them at all, then we need to find our shooter. He's definitely stealthy; I'll give him that," Agent Hunter agreed. "But he's still human, and humans make mistakes. Let's keep looking. There has to be something else out here."

Chapter 36

Ben paced the floor of the waiting room for the thousandth time, becoming more and more frustrated as the minutes ticked by. He rubbed his eyes, wearily, looked up at the clock on the wall and sighed heavily. It had been over an hour since they took Tori into surgery and after a brief consult with Ben, the doctors had given Tori a drug to slow down her labor in hopes of giving them a bit more time to treat the bullet wound.

"Please, God," he silently prayed. *"If I'm not being too selfish in asking, please don't take them from me. I love all of them so much. But if you have to choose, please at least let Tori survive. I don't think I could live without her."*

"Hey," Piper quietly interrupted him as she returned with two cups of coffee in her hands. "I thought you could use this. Double shot of espresso, light cream, two sugars."

"Thanks, Piper," Ben replied, taking the cup from her.

"Still nothing?" she asked, noticing the deep hue of blue sorrow surrounding him.

"No, not yet," he murmured. "Have you heard from Sarah?"

Piper nodded and advised, "Yes. They'll be here in about an hour."

"That's good," he replied.

"Ah, Ben, there's something I need to tell you," Piper paused, hoping the timing of her news would be good.

He searched her eyes, warily and asked, "What is it? Is something wrong?"

"No, it's actually something good. It's just the timing isn't quite what we all expected," she admitted.

"Just tell me, Piper," Ben sighed. "I really don't want to play any games right now."

"Okay, fine. First of all don't get mad. We all had the best of intentions regarding what I'm about to tell you. We just felt this was a better option than the one you and Tori planned," Piper proposed.

"We?" Ben frowned, narrowing his eyes.

"Me, Sarah and Agent Hunter," Piper replied.

Exhaling a deep breath, he asked, "What did you do?"

"We decided Dr. Matthews wasn't really the best choice for delivering the twins, so we've made other arrangements. We found someone we believe to be more suitable, given the circumstances," Piper replied.

"You did what?" Ben exclaimed, angrily. "Now is not the time to bring in someone new, Piper! Especially not under these circumstances! We need someone who is already familiar with Tori's condition and what will need to be done! I can't believe you all went behind our backs and did something like this!"

"So much for him not getting mad," Piper noted, inwardly. "Ben, Dr. Matthews has no idea what she's dealing with. This is not your typical pregnancy, and those babies are not your typical children. You heard her yourself when you went in for the sonogram. She couldn't even figure out how far along Tori was! And she has no idea about the psychic connection Tori and the twins have. What if something supernatural happens during delivery and Dr. Matthews were to freak out and do something that could harm one of them? Are you willing to take that risk?"

"It's not like we really had much of a choice, Piper! Our insurance company doesn't have a category filter for doctors who deal in the supernatural to choose from!" Ben exclaimed.

"I wonder if they looked," Piper thought to herself, curiously. Waiting long enough to make sure he was done ranting, she said, "You haven't even asked me who we picked."

"How would I know who you picked? Dr. Matthews is the only doctor Tori knows," Ben argued.

Shaking her head slowly, Piper replied, "No she's not. There's one other doctor Tori knows. Someone she trusts completely, and even more importantly, someone who is already familiar with her supernatural abilities."

Ben frowned, trying to think who she could mean and finally asked, "Who?"

"From what I hear, everybody calls him Max," Piper grinned, wryly.

"Max as in Dr. Maxwell Allen from Greeley?" Ben exclaimed in surprise.

Pleased to see the happy surprise on Ben's face, Piper winked and replied, "The one and only!"

"How in the world did you manage to arrange that?" Ben asked.

"Honestly, it wasn't me. It was Agent Hunter's idea," Piper admitted.

"Max. That's actually a really good idea. Where is he? When will he be here? Is he arriving with Sarah and Tanner?" Ben demanded.

"No, Sarah, Tanner, and Aubrey are all flying in from Cheyenne. Max is already here. In fact, he's in surgery with Tori and the medical team now," Piper replied.

"He's in surgery with Tori now? How did he get here so fast? When did all this secret planning go down?" Ben asked.

Walking over to one of the chairs, Piper sat down and said, "After you and Tori went to see Dr. Matthews, Sarah and I talked and decided that we weren't comfortable with her level of expertise, considering the circumstances. So we decided to talk to talk to Agent Hunter about it and fortunately for us, Miranda, his wife who understands the situation, also mentioned that maybe the doctor Tori was seeing wasn't the best choice. So we all got together and talked about it more and decided Max was the perfect choice. Agent Hunter indicated Max and Tori developed a friendship when you met him in Greeley a few years ago."

"Yes, we did, but Max retired after his daughter had her baby," Ben argued, sitting down in the chair beside her. "He and his wife wanted to spend more time with their granddaughter, so he gave up his practice."

"True, however, did you know that his daughter's husband was recently relocated to DC, so they're living here now?" Piper asked.

"No, I didn't! Did Max and his wife move here too?" Ben wondered.

"No, they still live in Greeley. Agent Hunter called him and explained the situation to him. So since we only had a few weeks until the babies were born, Max and his wife decided to visit their daughter so Max could be available when the time came. Fortunately for us, the timing worked out," Piper replied.

Placing his hand on hers, he gave a gentle squeeze and smiled, appreciatively. "Yes, it did. Thank you, Piper.

You're a good friend. I would never have come up with that idea myself. It's a great idea."

"You're welcome, Ben. You and Tori are my family. I love you guys. I would do anything for you," Piper promised.

"We love you too, Pip," Ben replied. Leaning back in his chair, he rested his head against the wall and gave a sigh of relief. *"Thank you, God,"* he prayed.

Chapter 37

"Tori, can you hear me?" Remy whispered quietly. "You need to wake up."

"*Remy?*" Tori thought, sleepily.

"How much longer until she wakes up," Tori heard Ben ask from somewhere nearby.

"It should be any time now," a familiar voice replied. "Her vitals are much stronger now, so we've stopped the medication that was slowing down the labor. She should start feeling the effects wearing off soon. Remember, don't push her. Let her memories come back slowly. It may not all come back to her right away."

"*I know that voice,*" Tori realized. "*How do I know that voice?*"

"What are we going to tell her if she asks?" she heard Piper ask.

"You mean when she asks," Ben corrected.

"Ask about what, the babies? Did something happen to them?" Tori's mind began to ask.

Feeling some of the fuzziness in her head begin to clear, she saw a dim light beginning to glow through her closed eye lids. As she lay there, the light grew stronger, and she began to recognize some of the sounds around her.

A steady beep of a machine...

A creak as someone shifted their weight in a chair...

Then she heard the familiar sound of a fetal heart monitor and the thrumming of a tiny heartbeat. First she only heard one heart-beat then she heard the second one.

"They're okay, Tori," she heard Elsbet assure her, quietly.

Taking in a deep, peaceful breath, she lay unmoving listening to the sound of her children's heartbeats, until suddenly she felt a sharp cramp in her stomach.

"Mmmmm...," she moaned quietly.

"She's waking up!" Piper whispered, excitedly. "Ben, come here! Tori, can you hear me?"

Hearing the creak of the chair again, a few seconds later, she heard Ben's voice quietly whisper, "Hey, sweetie. Open your eyes, baby."

Tori's eyes fluttered open, and she saw Ben smiling down at her, his face filled with a mixture of concern and joy.

"Hi," he whispered, happily, kissing her on the forehead.

"Hi," she croaked. "Where am I?"

"You're in the hospital," Ben replied.

"Where's Remy?" she mumbled. "He was just talking to me."

"We haven't seen him, baby," Ben advised.

Unbeknownst to any of them, Remy was there, by her side, unseen. "I'm right here," he whispered, in anguish, worried that she was angry with him for not helping Goliath earlier.

Turning her head to the side, Tori looked around for Remy, but he wasn't anywhere in the room. Instead, she saw Piper standing on the other side of the bed, smiling at her. "Hey. How are you feeling?"

Tori winced as another cramp traveled across her abdomen and whispered, "My stomach hurts. Can I have some water?"

"Of course!" Piper exclaimed, reaching beside her for a small cup with a straw in it. "Here you go, sweetie," she murmured, positioning the straw by Tori's lips.

Taking a long sip, Tori swallowed carefully and replied, "Thank you." She laid her head back against the pillow and turned to look back at Ben. "What happened?"

Frowning slightly, he replied, "You were shot, Tori. Do you remember?"

"I was shot," she repeated quietly, searching her memory. She looked down at her chest and through a small gape in her hospital gown she saw a patch of gauze just below her collar bone, secured to her skin with surgical tape.

"*You were both shot,*" her memory reminded her as the images began to come back to her.

Then suddenly, it all came back to her.

"Goliath!" she gasped, looking back at Ben. "Where is he? Is he okay?"

Ben hesitated slightly, and replied, "We don't know, yet. We're waiting to hear."

"You don't know? Why don't you know?" she cried out in alarm, trying to sit up. "Ah," she groaned, as a much stronger cramp gripped her.

"Tor, sit back. Try to relax," Ben urged, gently.

"Relax? How can I relax when Goliath could be dead!" she exclaimed.

"The last we heard, he was in surgery, Tori," Piper assured her. "Reagan and Agent Sullivan are with him at the animal hospital. They promised they would let us know when they had news."

"Well, how bad is it?" Tori insisted, feeling the panic begin to build inside of her. "Do you know anything about his condition?"

"We don't know, but I promise we'll let you know as soon as we hear from them okay? Now lie back sweetie, your heart rate is starting to rise, and you need to relax," Piper assured her, trying to gently push her back against the bed.

Clenching her teeth as another cramp shot through her, Tori furrowed her brow and asked, "Ah! Why does my stomach hurt so much? I only remember being shot one time in the chest. What's going on?"

"Your stomach is hurting because you're having contractions. You're in labor, sweetie," Piper replied, carefully.

"I'm in what? What do you mean, I'm in labor?" Tori exclaimed fearfully. "It's too soon! They need to stop it! Can't they stop it?"

"Your water broke right after you were shot, honey," Ben confirmed. "The doctor slowed the labor down with medication while you were in surgery so they could remove the bullet, but they can't stop it. You're going to have to deliver the babies right now."

"Right now, are you serious? Where's Doctor Matthew's? I want to talk to her! There has to be something we can do to hold off a little longer!" Tori demanded.

"Ah, Dr. Matthew's isn't coming," Piper replied, hesitantly, exchanging a look with Ben.

Noticing the look, Tori frowned and narrowed her eyes at Piper. "What do you mean, Dr. Matthew's isn't coming? Of course, she's coming she's going to deliver the babies. What's going on?"

Piper stared at Ben, hoping he would explain, but instead he shrugged, indicating she needed to be the one to break the news.

"Okay, fine, I'll do it," Piper rolled her eyes at him, dramatically. Turning back to Tori she said, "After we realized there may be a supernatural element with the twins, your mom, Agent Hunter and I talked and agreed that maybe Dr. Matthews wasn't our best option."

"What do you mean our best option?" Tori challenged as she breathed through another contraction. "Dr. Matthews was my choice, not yours!"

"True, however, we felt there was someone else more qualified, who understood the circumstances better. Someone you trusted who would be discreet and had the right level of experience," Piper advised.

Tori scowled at Piper, doubtfully and asked, "Really. And who would that be exactly? Dr. Matthews is the only doctor who has had any involvement with this pregnancy and the only doctor I know."

"She's not the only doctor you know," Piper replied, trying her best to suppress a grin. Turning to address the doctor talking to a nurse on the other side of the room, she called out, "Excuse me, Doctor?"

Immediately the man turned, and briskly walked over to join them. "We've been over this already, Piper. Call me Max! Everyone calls me Max," he advised, good-naturedly.

"Max!" Tori exclaimed in surprise. "My goodness, what are you doing here?"

"Hello, Tori," he replied, warmly. Patting her hand gently, he said, "You gave us all quite a scare there for a bit, my dear. How are you feeling?"

"You're my doctor?" she asked, incredulously.

"I am if you'll have me," he promised.

"Of course I'll have you! Nothing would make me happier!" Wincing as the pain from another contraction washed over her; Tori pleaded, "Well, there is one thing that would make me happier right now. I don't suppose you're going to be able to give me an epidural, are you?"

"No, I'm sorry, my dear, I can't do that. It's too risky considering your condition. Not to mention the possible side effects the drug could cause to either you or the babies if mixed with the drug we used to slow your labor earlier," Max advised.

"So you seriously can't do anything to stop my labor? Isn't it too soon for the twins to be delivered" Tori worried.

"From what I can tell, you're pretty close to full-term already so they should be fine. Their vitals are strong, and there's a lot of movement so we're ready when you are," Max assured.

"I really wish you could give me something for the pain," Tori conceded, reluctantly. "I guess we're going to have to do it the old-fashioned way."

"I'll do my best to help minimize your discomfort as much as possible, my dear," Max smiled.

"Thanks," Tori panted, as her stomach seized up again.

"How far apart are they now?" Max asked Piper.

"They're about a minute apart. She's pretty close," Piper replied.

"You've been timing my contractions while we've been talking?" Tori accused.

"Hey, you're not the only one who can multi-task!" Piper defended herself, proudly.

Biting her lip as she waited out the contraction, Tori winced and growled, "That one was less than a minute."

Glancing at the clock on the wall, Piper's eyes widened, and she agreed, "She's right. They're pretty much back to back right now."

"Well then I guess we need to take a look," Max announced. Walking over to the foot of the bed, he lifted up the end of the sheet, took a quick look and immediately sprang into action. "Oh! It would appear that one of your children is in a bit of a hurry to meet you, my dear! He or she is already crowning!"

Turning to the nurse, he instructed, "Nurse, please prepare our patient for delivery and call for two more nurses to assist."

"Yes, doctor," the nurse replied, rushing away to make the call.

"Wait, we're doing this right now?" Tori cried out, frantically.

"I'm afraid so," Max smiled. "Don't worry! I've delivered more babies throughout my entire career than half of the doctors in this hospital combined! Trust me. I know what I'm doing."

"Okay, I do trust you, Max," Tori replied. Turning to Ben, she reached out to grab his hand and said, "I guess we're doing this now."

Taking her hand firmly in his, he smiled at her and replied, "Don't worry, sweetie. You're in the best hands possible."

As the reality of what was happening set in, Tori suddenly realized someone was missing. "Wait! What about my mom and dad! Do they know what's going on?"

"They're on their way, Tor," Piper assured her friend. "I called Sarah, and she, Aubrey and your dad are on a flight on their way here right now. They should be here soon."

"Oh okay, good," Tori breathed in relief. "Thank you, Piper."

"You're welcome," Piper smiled. "Is it okay if I stay?"

"Of course it is!" Tori exclaimed. "I'm going to need both you and Ben here!"

Still wondering where Remy was, Piper nodded and replied, "Good because I didn't want to leave."

"Ah!" Tori cried out suddenly as a much stronger contraction washed over her. "Max, I feel a lot of pressure down between my legs. Is that normal?"

"Yes, that's one of the twins making their way down the birth canal," Max advised, calmly. "I'm going to need you to push down the next time you feel a contraction okay? Can you do that for me?"

"I think so," Tori panted, feeling another contraction coming. "Like right now!" she grunted, pushing firmly.

"That's good," Max encouraged her. "Keep pushing just like that."

Chapter 38

Wringing out the washcloth in the bowl on the table beside her, Sarah glanced at numbers on the blood pressure monitor, concerned that Tori's pressure was getting too high. Turning back to her daughter, she folded the cloth into an elongated strip and laid it across Tori's forehead. "Here you go, sweetie."

"Thanks, Mom," Tori panted, wearily as she began pushing through another contraction. "Grrr....!"

Suddenly, Aubrey materialized through the wall leading out to the hallway. "Dad just talked to Reagan. Goliath made it through surgery, just fine. He's going to be okay," she announced happily.

"Thank you, God," Tori whispered, lying back against the bed to catch her breath before the next contraction.

"*Thank you, Father,*" Remy prayed silently beside her, still hidden from view.

"Uh, Mom, Tori's bleeding," Aubrey pointed out.

"That's normal, honey," Sarah advised firmly. "When you have a vaginal birth, sometimes there's tearing as the baby is delivered and you bleed."

"No, I know that! I mean she's bleeding from her bullet wound!" Aubrey exclaimed.

Now seeing the bright red stain seeping through Tori's gown, Sarah pulled the fabric aside and gasped in surprise. "Max! Tori's wound is bleeding!"

"I was afraid that might happen," he admitted, quickly leaving his post at the end of the bed to take a look. "Tori's pushing is applying pressure on the incision."

"Well, what can we do?" Sarah frantically replied.

"Unfortunately, applying pressure against the pressure is our only option," he readily replied. "Nurse, I need you to come over here and keep a steady pressure on this gauze until we deliver these babies."

"Yes, doctor," the nurse closest to him replied, quickly coming over to assist.

"This is taking too long! What about a C-section?" Ben asked. "Can't you take the babies out so Tori won't have to push anymore?"

"Not without risking her life in the process, no," Max replied. "We can't give her any medication and one of the twins is already fully descended into the birth canal. We need to deliver them naturally."

"MAX!" Tori suddenly screamed, feeling a searing pain between her legs. "AHHH...!"

Rushing back down to the foot of the bed, Max, looked down and happily exclaimed, "The head is out, Tori! I'm going to gently take hold of the baby's shoulders and ease the rest of the body out. When I tell you to push, I need to push hard and don't stop until I tell you. Okay?"

"Okay," Tori breathed, wearily. "I'm getting tired, Max, but I'll try."

"I know you are, my dear," Max soothed. Noticing the nurse switch out a section of gauze with a thoroughly blood-soaked patch, he urged, "Just a little while longer."

"Okay," Tori whispered, preparing herself.

"Here we go," Max advised. "Push now!"

"GRRRRR......," Tori growled, pushing down as hard as she could.

Moments later, the sound of a baby crying filled the room.

"There you are, sweet little Gemma," Max greeting the infant as he gently wiped the blood and fluid away from her face.

"Gemma," Tori breathed, as she lifted her head to look at her daughter. "I want to see her!"

"One moment," Max replied firmly. "Let me cut the cord and I'll bring her to you." Glancing up at the clock, he turned his head to the nurse standing beside him and advised, "Nurse, please note the time of birth for Gemma as eleven fifty-seven PM."

"Yes, doctor," the nurse replied.

When he was done, he stood up from the stool and walked around the bed to lay Gemma on Tori's chest. "Here she is," he smiled, tenderly.

Tori blinked away fresh tears that were blurring her vision, and looked down at the dark matted auburn curls on the top of Gemma's head. "Hi, Gemma," she whispered happily, gently tracing Gemma's face with her finger.

Hearing her mother's voice, Gemma raised her head and her bright green eyes locked with Tori's. Time seemed to freeze at that moment as they stared into one another's eyes for the first time. "Oh, she's so beautiful," Tori breathed, enraptured.

Smiling at the sound of her mother's voice, Gemma reached up her tiny hand and grabbed onto one of Tori's fingers. As she did, Piper noticed the faint green aura around Tori begin to glow more brightly, as it braided itself into Gemma's deep band of violet surrounding her.

"*Hi, Mama!*" Tori heard clearly in her head.

"Oh!" Tori gasped unexpectedly. "I can hear her!"

Suddenly feeling light-headed, Tori's eyelids began to close, and the alarm on her blood pressure monitor began going off as her pressure dropped.

"Max!" Ben cried out, fearfully.

"Ben, take the baby please," Max ordered briskly. "Nurse, keep a steady pressure on that shoulder. We need to deliver the other baby now!"

As Ben gently pulled Gemma away from Tori, she let go of Tori's finger and the band of color between them dissolved. Distressed at being pulled away from her mother, the expression on Gemma's face darkened and she immediately reached out for Tori and began to cry.

Heartbroken by the obvious stress she could see on Gemma's face, Piper glanced over at Tori and saw the faint green glow around her began to disappear. "Wait!" she exclaimed. "You need to keep them together! There's a bond between them already! Tori's aura is fading without Gemma! Put her back down!"

"Piper, we don't have time to deal with your aura readings right now!" Ben replied angrily.

"She's right!" Remy suddenly announced, appearing in front of everyone. "They need to stay together, Ben! Do it now!"

Ben hesitated only a moment, realizing he needed to obey Remy's command. Placing Gemma gently back down on Tori's chest, she immediately reached down and grabbed Tori's finger, re-establishing the bond with her mother.

"Is that….?" Max began to ask, staring at Remy when his voice was suddenly cut off from the alarm on RJ's fetal monitor.

"The baby's heart rate is dropping, doctor," the nurse warned. "We're running out of time!"

"We're going to lose them both!" another nurse exclaimed.

"Oh, no we're not!" Max shouted, quickly checking the monitor. Grabbing a bottle of Betadine solution, Max splashed the liquid over Tori's lower abdomen and instructed the nurse beside him, "Nurse, get me a syringe filled with two milligrams of Ketamine and inject it into the mother's IV."

"Wait! What are you going to do?" Sarah exclaimed frantically.

"I'm going to deliver this baby!" Max declared, looking up at her through the lenses of his glasses.

"You said you couldn't do a C-section! You said it was too dangerous!" Sarah challenged.

"We don't have time to wait! The Ketamine will work within a few minutes and she won't feel the pain of the incision. It's our only chance in delivering the baby alive and saving Tori at the same time," Max reasoned.

Sarah turned to Remy with frantic eyes and pleaded, "What should we do?"

"Somebody do something!" Ben pleaded, watching Tori's blood pressure continue to drop.

Chapter 39

Karla watched as the scene unfolded below, terrified for her friend. "Can't we do something?" she cried out fearfully to her sisters around her. "We have to save her! She's one of us!"

Then Karla noticed the women were already taking action, forming the circle. Karla hesitated, not sure what to do but then Elsbet came up beside her and said, "It's time you learned how to use your gift, Karla."

"But how can I help her now? I'm a spirit, I have no power here," Karla argued.

"You have more power here, than you ever had on earth," Elsbet smiled. "Let me show you."

With that, she took Karla's hand and led her to the edge of the circle. As she did, the women parted, making room for Karla and Elsbet. Karla clasped hands with the woman beside her, and as soon as the circle was connected, she felt a surge of energy flow through her.

"OH!" she exclaimed in surprise, turning to look at Elsbet.

Elsbet smiled and calmly replied, "This is your legacy Karla, daughter of Remiel. From now until the end of time, we channel our energy to the reigning daughter on earth in possession of the statue and the amulet, so she has the power she needs to fight the darkness."

"What do you mean? How?" asked Karla.

"I'll explain later. Right now, we don't have time. We need to help Tori," Elsbet warned. "Are you ready?"

"Yes, of course!" Karla exclaimed. "What should I do?"

"Close your eyes and picture the amulet in your mind," Elsbet instructed, closing her eyes.

Karla immediately obeyed by closing her eyes, concentrating on the gem.

"Do you see it clearly in your mind?" Elsbet asked.

"Yes, I do!" Karla cried out.

"Good! Now focus all of your energy towards it," Elsbet instructed. "Clear your mind and think of nothing else, just the amulet."

"All right!" Karla replied. *"Come on, Tori! Hang in there,"* she thought fiercely.

"I'm trying, but I can't stay awake. I'm so tired," Tori thought sleepily as she heard the rhythmic beeping of the alarm on the baby monitor lulling her to sleep. *"I can't do this, I'm not strong enough,"* she told herself.

"Yes you are!" she heard a voice argue.

"No, you're not," Lucifer taunted quietly in her head. "Ignore her, just go to sleep, Tori. When you wake up, everything will be as it should be."

"No!" Tori fought. "I don't want to listen to you, Luc."

"Of course you do, my dear. Listen to how soothing my voice is. It's like ocean waves gently washing over you. Go to sleep," he soothed.

"Yes, smooth and peaceful like the ocean," she began to agree.

"Stop! Don't listen to him! You need to wake up, Tori," a familiar voice called out to her sternly.

"What?" Tori murmured, semi-consciously.

"Victoria Analise Cooper, you wake up this instant! Your babies need you! We need you!" the voice in her head demanded.

Then Tori heard Ben cry out, "Somebody, do something!"

"Somebody, do something," she repeated in her head.

Recognizing the sound of panic in Ben's voice, Tori struggled to open her eyes. As she did, she saw Gemma's face, inches from hers, her eyes carefully watching Tori.

Locking eyes with her tiny daughter, Tori quietly whispered, "Help me."

Understanding her mother's plea, Gemma tightened her grip on Tori's finger, reached her other hand down to the glowing amulet on Tori's chest and circled her tiny fingers around it. As she did, the amulet suddenly burst into a rainbow of colors and the infants emerald green eyes began to glow.

Feeling a sudden surge of power within her, Tori took a deep breath, gave one final push and then collapsed back against the table. Moments later, she heard the wailing cries of her newborn son.

Chapter 40

"So this is what true happiness feels like," Tori thought blissfully, watching her babies sleeping contentedly in her arms. She closed her eyes and silently prayed, *"Thank you, God, for allowing us all to live and for loving me the way You do."*

"Do you need a break?" Ben asked quietly, as he sat down in the chair beside her bed.

"No, not yet," Tori smiled, opening her eyes to look at him.

"You are so beautiful, motherhood suits you," he marveled.

"Thank you," she replied, feeling her cheeks flush from embarrassment.

"I don't know how you do it, Tor," Ben shrugged. "After everything you just went through, you should be wiped out. Instead, you look absolutely amazing."

Tori smiled and replied, "It's probably all the adrenaline in my blood right now. Believe me it's going to hit me eventually so don't go too far."

"Are you kidding? I can't imagine anywhere else I would want to be right now than right here with you," Ben vowed.

"Where's everybody else?" she asked, noticing they were alone in the room.

"Your parents went to check into their hotel. They'll be back in about an hour. Everyone else is outside in the hallway, giving us some privacy," he replied.

"Well, they can come in now! They don't have to wait outside in the hallway!" Tori exclaimed.

"Just a few more minutes, he pleaded.

"Okay," she agreed, smiling at him.

"Oh, a word of warning, according to your mom, Bree wants to show off more of her new abilities again later," Ben advised.

"Is that so? What does she want to do this time?" Tori smiled, having enjoyed her sister's display levitating flowers from the floral arrangements in her room earlier.

"She's decided she wants to try holding one of the babies," he advised with raised eyebrows.

"Well, we'll have to see about that another time. I'm not quite ready for that yet," Tori admitted, ruefully.

"Nor I," Ben admitted. "I'm still a little wigged out with her new found powers. Seeing Gemma or RJ floating in the air is something I'm going to have to prepare myself for."

Tori laughed, lightly and replied, "We're all going to have to get used to a lot of new things now that they're here."

"Agreed," Ben nodded.

"Everything's about to change for us," she warned quietly. "Are you sure you're ready?"

"I may not have any special supernatural abilities as you and the twins, but yeah, I'm ready," Ben admitted.

"Just because you don't have any supernatural abilities doesn't mean you're not special, Ben," Tori declared. "You're their father. And you have some wonderful qualities that you'll be able to share with them and teach them."

"Thanks," he smiled, appreciatively, watching Gemma's face while she slept. "So you really heard her talk to you earlier?"

"I did," Tori confirmed.

"I don't know how to process that," he admitted, meeting her eyes.

"We'll figure it out together," she promised.

"Hey, how are our Gemini Twins doing?" Piper asked cheerily as she entered the room

"The Gemini Twins?" Tori asked.

"Gemma and RJ!" Piper exclaimed.

"Why are you calling them that?" Tori puzzled.

"That's their zodiac sign! They're both Gemini like me!" Piper announced proudly. "See how well that ended up working out?"

"Oh, right! I forgot about that," Tori admitted.

"You're going to have to work out the special birthday party details; you know that right?" Piper advised.

Confused again, Tori frowned at Piper and asked, "What do you mean?"

"Big sister was born right before midnight on June fifth, and little RJ was born at five after midnight on June sixth. That means their birthdays are a day apart! You're going to have to work out the birthday party details when they get older!" Piper replied.

"Let's not rush too far ahead, Piper," Ben teased. "How about we enjoy the moment right now considering what Tori just went through."

"Right, of course, you don't have to think about that stuff today!" she agreed.

"Hi, Tori," Reagan greeted, tentatively as she entered the room. "Is it okay if we come in?"

"Of course," Tori replied, happily. "I've been waiting for you guys!"

Poking her head back outside the door, Reagan announced, "She said we can come in!"

Tori's smile broadened as Agent Hunter, Agent Sullivan, Riley and Logan all filtered in quietly, each holding an assortment of balloons, flowers, and stuff animals.

"Hey, guys!" Tori greeted.

"Wow! You look great! You can't even tell you just gave birth! Aw, look at how beautiful they both are!" Reagan declared, setting a vase of flowers down on the table.

"They are beautiful!" Agent Sullivan agreed, placing a potted plant on the table beside Reagan's arrangement. "Congratulations to you both!"

"Thank you," Tori and Ben replied in unison.

"Hey guys," Logan greeted, setting a bottle of bourbon and a box of cigars down on the table. "Those are for you and me later," he winked at Ben.

"Thanks, buddy!" Ben chuckled.

"How are you feeling, Agent Cooper?" Agent Hunter asked.

"I feel wonderful, thanks!" Tori replied.

"Hi," Riley greeting awkwardly, his arms full of stuffed animals.

Tori looked at Riley and snorted a laugh. "What do you have there?"

"I couldn't decide between Teddy bears, giraffes, monkeys, and bunnies so I bought them all. I had no idea it would be so hard to decide!" Riley admitted, with a nervous laugh.

Piper smiled at him, affectionately and noted, "I think I had more fun watching the internal struggle within you as you wrestled with your decision."

Tori laughed and said, "Gemma and RJ will love them. Thank you, Riley."

"You're welcome," he replied, setting the animals down on the table with the plants and flower arrangements.

"I'm glad you're all here," Tori announced quietly, trying not to wake the twins. "I wanted to tell you all something that I remembered happening during delivery."

"I hope it wasn't something about our case, Agent Cooper," Agent Hunter chastised. "You had much more important things to focus on during that time."

Tori shook her head and replied, "No, nothing like that! Towards the end, when I passed out, I heard someone call out to me, encouraging me to wake up and keep going. It was Karla. She's there with the others just like I dreamt she was."

"You heard Karla?" Reagan asked quietly.

"Yes!" Tori smiled. "She's with Elsbet. She's happy, I could feel it. It was her who helped me in the end. I wanted you all to know because I know how much you miss her and how much you've all been worried about her."

Riley looked over at Reagan, and they exchanged a look and smiled at one another, finally feeling the closure they'd both been looking for.

Then he looked over at Piper and his smile softened. *"It's time to move on,"* he thought to himself.

Feeling his eyes upon her, Piper looked over at Riley, and she met his gaze steadily. In that moment, Tori knew her friends futures were about to change in a dramatic way.

"Thank you, for telling us that, Tori," Reagan replied. "I can't speak for everyone, but I think we would all agree that it helps to know for sure that she's okay."

"Agreed," Agent Hunter nodded.

"And I have equally happy news for you," Reagan advised. "I stopped by to check on Goliath on my way here, and the vet said he's doing exceptionally well. His wound is healing much faster than expected, which I would guess may have something to do with Remy. Have you heard from him?"

Sensing his presence, Tori shook her head and replied, "No, not yet. But I suspect he's nearby."

"Well either way be forewarned, Goliath may not want to leave after the way he's being spoiled by the staff at the clinic. He's completely won everyone over. I swear I saw five of the young veterinary assistants sneak a treat to him while I was there."

"That sounds like our boy," Tori chuckled.

Laughing with her, Reagan replied, "The vet said he should be able to come home in a few days."

"Right about the time we are," Ben noted.

Breathing a sigh of relief, Tori smiled at Reagan and said, "Thank you, Reagan. And Agent Sullivan," she added, acknowledging him. "I can't thank you both enough for taking care of Goliath the way you did."

"You're welcome. I have to admit. I've gotten a little attached to that big, slobbery, dog." Agent Sullivan chuckled.

"Same here," Reagan agreed.

"He's a hero! He saved Tori's life. I think it's time we made him an official FBI agent and part of our team," Piper declared.

"I agree that his heroism should be acknowledged. However I would seriously doubt Goliath would be able to pass the field training of our canine unit," Agent Hunter advised.

"That's true. He's a bit clumsy on an average day," Piper admitted.

Turning to Agent Hunter, Tori asked, "Were you able to find out anything about the man who shot us? Was it Zander like I thought?"

"Let's not worry about that right now, Agent Cooper," Agent Hunter advised. "We'll have time to discuss that when you're ready to come back to work."

"No, I want to know," Tori argued. "I think I deserve to know! We can't wait that long. Ben and Piper won't tell me anything, so I want to hear it from you."

Heaving a deep sigh, Agent Hunter inclined his head in agreement and replied, "All right. We found a partial boot print in the soil where we believe the gunman was standing, but that's all we found. For the time being, he's still at large."

"And still capable of coming after you so from this point forward, I've asked to be assigned to you personally to protect you," Logan declared.

Ben blinked in surprise and looked at Logan with a new sense of appreciation. "Dude! Are you serious?"

Logan smiled at Ben, wryly and replied, "Hey, if that's the only way I'm going to get to hang out with you like old times, then I'm willing to make the sacrifice!"

"I think that sounds like a great idea. Thanks, Logan!" Tori replied.

"I agree! We have plenty of room and a fold-out couch you can sleep on," Ben offered.

"That'll work. But I'm not changing any diapers! I just want to put that out there right now! That's your job!" Logan insisted.

"Deal," Ben laughed.

"And by the way, you did an excellent job adding the new filters to your search program, Agent Cooper. The request completed as you hoped and gave us a name," Agent Hunter praised.

"It did? Tell me!" Tori demanded.

"Our shooter's name is Alexander Wells, and he goes by the shortened name of Zander as you suspected. Agent Nichols confirmed his photo on record with the man from the deli."

Tori looked at Reagan who nodded in confirmation, "It's the same guy."

"Wow. So what's our next step?" Tori eagerly asked.

"WE are chasing down several leads, now that we know who we're looking for," Agent Hunter advised, firmly. "YOU are going to take your maternity leave and enjoy getting to know your children."

"But…," Tori began to argue.

"No arguments!" Agent Hunter scolded.

"Fine," Tori conceded.

"Speaking of which, we need to get to work, and you need to get your rest," Agent Hunter announced, advising everyone it was time to leave.

"You're leaving so soon? I feel like you just got here!" Tori frowned.

"We'll come by the house once you're all settled and ready for visitors. I promise," Reagan smiled.

"Okay," Tori agreed.

"Congratulations again, to you both," Riley added.

"Thanks, Riley," Tori smiled. "Thank you for everything."

"We'll talk to you soon, Agent Cooper," Agent Sullivan promised, waving goodbye from the doorway.

"Thank you, Agent Sullivan," Tori replied.

"I'm going to go too, okay?" Piper asked. "I want to go home and shower and change, but I'll be back later, I promise!"

"Okay," Tori smiled. "Thanks again for everything, Piper. You're the best friend anyone could ever ask for."

Piper smiled at Tori, warmly and replied, "For you, always!"

As Logan was about to leave, Ben jumped up from his chair and called out, "Logan hold up! Let's talk about how we're going to handle things at the house." He turned to Tori and said, "I'll be back in a bit. I just want to talk to Logan. You'll be okay alone for a few minutes?"

Glancing down at the twins sleeping in her arms, she teased, "I'll be far from alone."

Laughing, he admitted, "Right. I'll be back soon."

As the door closed behind him, Tori exhaled a deep breath, secretly happy everyone was gone. Glancing around the room, she quietly announced, "I know you're here by the way. You don't need to hide from me."

Instantly, Remy appeared at the foot of her bed. "How did you know I was here?"

Tori shrugged and admitted. "It's hard to explain. The air just feels different when you're around me. Like it's purer, or there's less static."

"Really?" he mused. "That's interesting."

He looked down at the twins and smiled, affectionately at them.

"Would you like to hold one of them?" she offered.

"Naw, not yet," he drawled, quietly. "They look pretty comfortable where they are right now. Maybe I will a little later."

"All right," Tori nodded, regarding him thoughtfully. "So you heard Goliath is going to be okay?"

Remy lowered his eyes, guiltily and gave a quick nod of his head. "Yeah, I've been to see him."

"I heard," Tori admitted, still watching him carefully. "I remember what happened, Remy."

He looked into her eyes, revealing the anguish he felt, but he still felt reluctant to respond. Instead he nodded at her, guiltily.

"I'm not angry with you," she confessed. "I understand why you couldn't help him."

"Your eyes weren't saying that at the time," he grumbled.

"I'm sorry about that. I really am. I was scared and didn't know what was going on. All I know is he saved my life, and I couldn't bear it if he died because of it," Tori pleaded.

"I know that," Remy replied. "I gave him to you so he could protect you and that's exactly what he did. He's a good dog."

"He's not just a dog, Remy. He's my guardian. And he loves with his entire being, just like you do. It's one of the things I love most about him. He reminds me of you," Tori admitted.

Realizing she didn't blame him as he feared, he asked her, tentatively, "So we're good?"

Tori looked down at Gemma and RJ sleeping peacefully in her arms and smiled. Then she looked back at Remy and nodded, happily. "Yes. We're good."

"Good," He nodded quietly, still not fully making eye contact with her.

"What else is bothering you?" she asked, knowing him too well.

Laughing lightly, he looked at her and said, "You always seem to know."

Peering at him speculatively for a moment, she said, "You went after him, didn't you?"

He laughed again and admitted, "See what I mean?"

"Did you find him?" she asked, quietly.

Remy shook his head and replied, "No. I think he knows he went too far this time. Where ever he's hiding, he's making sure I can't find him."

"When I'm feeling stronger, I'll find him," Tori declared fiercely.

"Are you sure that's such a good idea?" he asked, with raised eyebrows.

Tori raised her chin defiantly and said, "I'm not afraid of him, Remy. And now that I know if I'm killed, my power will help fuel the amulet that makes me even less afraid."

"Well don't go all Dirty Harry on me for goodness sake!" he argued. "Your first priority is to raise those two children of yours. You let me handle Luc, understood?"

"Fine," she relented.

"Okay," he agreed, gruffly.

She watched him for a moment, wondering if he was ready to talk about Elsbet, and decided to test the waters.

"Elsbet still misses you," she said quietly. "She's truly repentant for what she did."

Watching his gaze travel down to the amulet, she noticed his face change. "I had no idea she was in there."

"I know you didn't. None of us could have guessed it was her causing the stone to react the way it does," Tori admitted.

"It makes sense when you stop to think about it," he reasoned. "So that's where Karla and the others are?"

"Only those who have been killed at the hand of another are in the amulet. Do you know why that is?" she asked, curiously.

Remy nodded and replied, "Father told me."

Surprised by his admission, Tori's eyes widened, and she asked, "He finally spoke to you?"

Remy looked at her and gave her a crooked, secretive smile, "He did."

"What's that look for?" she smirked. "What exactly did He tell you?"

"Are you sure you're ready to know?" he teased.

"Well, yeah, when you put it that way!" she demanded. "Tell me!"

Desperately wanting to share his secret with her, his face lit up with a huge grin and he replied, "I know why RJ is here. Why God created him."

Tori gasped in surprise and whispered, "He told you?"

Remy nodded, enjoying the look of pure joy on her face.

"Tell me!" she demanded again.

Giving her a speculative look he teased, "Are you sure you're up to it?"

"Remy….," she warned.

Giving a hearty laugh he relented. "Okay, fine." Looking back at the twins, he quietly called out, "Gemma, RJ, time to wake up, my children."

Hearing him call them by name, both babies began to stir, and they slowly opened their eyes. When they saw Remy standing beside the bed, they both smiled at him in recognition.

"They already know you," Tori marveled, watching them.

"Yes they do," Remy admitted. Addressing the babies again, he told them, "Your mother wants to see what Father showed you. Are you ready to show her?"

Both Gemma and RJ raised their heads to look up at Tori, and they smiled at her and nodded.

"Hello my beautiful angels," Tori whispered, happily.

"Okay," Remy replied, turning his attention to Tori. "Tori, place your hand over the amulet."

Shifting Gemma slightly so she could reach, Tori reached over and placed her hand over the stone resting on her chest. "Okay, now what?"

"Gemma, RJ, place your hands on top of your mother's hand," Remy instructed.

Immediately each of the babies placed their hand on top of Tori's.

Looking at her one last time to make sure, Remy asked, "Are you sure you're ready?"

Tori nodded and said, "Let's do it."

"All right," Remy agreed, reaching down to place his hand on top of hers and the twin's hands.

As soon as their four hands were joined, the amulet burst into an array of white light that filled the entire room, and Tori saw what God had revealed to Remy and the fate of her children.

It lasted only a moment, and when Remy pulled his hand away, she stared up at him with bewildered eyes.

Swallowing hard, she whispered, "Is all that really what's about to happen or what could happen?"

Remy smiled at her and replied, "It's all about choice, Tori. That's all He's ever asked of us, to choose Him."

She looked down at RJ and noticed he was staring at her intently. "So if he chooses, he'll be the one to...," she breathed, unable to finish her sentence.

"Yes," Remy confirmed. "RJ will be the one who saves the world."

Note from the author

This book was a lot of fun to write! Once again, Agent Hunter has a tight-knit solid group of agents who truly care about one another, and they all finally have the closure they needed when they discovered Karla is now a guardian within the amulet. That closure opens the door for Piper and Riley to begin to explore their feelings for one another. I don't know about you, but I look forward to seeing what happens!

And having Logan join the team seemed like the ideal opportunity to allow Tori to take a break from being a field agent, honing her skills as a profiler while she waited out the remainder of her pregnancy.

Speaking of which, what do you think of Gemma and RJ? The Gemini Twins has a nice ring to it, don't you think?

Recipes from Children from the Light

Sweet Hawaiian Stuffed French Toast

Ingredients:
2 – 8oz. packages of reduced-fat cream cheese, cubed
1 round of Kings Hawaiian bread, cubed
1 dozen eggs, beaten
1 tablespoon ground cinnamon
1/2 cup maple syrup
2 cups milk

Directions:
1) Spray an 8 x 12 baking dish with cooking spray and arrange half of the cubed bread in the bottom of the pan.

2) Next arrange the cubed cream cheese on top of the bread.

3) Layer the remaining half of the bread on top of the cheese.

4) Combine the eggs, cinnamon, syrup and milk in a mixing bowl and pour evenly over the bread and cheese.

5) Cover the pan with aluminum foil and place it in the refrigerator overnight.

6) The next morning, remove the pan from the refrigerator and allow it to come to room temperature, about 30 minutes.

7) Preheat your oven to 375 degrees and place the pan in the oven, still covered. Bake for 45 minutes.

8) Remove the foil and bake an additional 15 minutes until the top is browned and bubbly.

9) Remove the pan from the oven and let it rest for 15 minutes before cutting. Serve hot with extra syrup.

Pork Meatballs in Parmesan Broth

Ingredients:
1 pound ground pork
8 ounces of low-fat ricotta cheese
½ cup seasoned Italian breadcrumbs
1 egg
½ teaspoon ground nutmeg
1 generous pinch each of kosher salt and fresh ground pepper
1 cup shredded aged Parmesan cheese
4 tablespoons of grape seed oil
32 ounces low-sodium, natural chicken broth
1 cup chopped, canned artichoke hearts
2 cups fresh baby spinach
16 ounces old-fashioned egg noodles

Directions:
1) Combine the first six ingredients in a large bowl, including ½ cup of the shredded Parmesan. Form the mixture into 2 inch round meatballs and stage them on a plate.

2) Working in batches, heat 2 tbsp. of the grape seed oil in a deep pan and sear the meatballs over moderate heat, turning every 2-3 minutes until they are browned on all sides. This step is important as the meatballs need to be browned and firm enough to hold their shape without falling apart in the broth. They will cook all the way through in the next step.

3) Return all of the meatballs to the pan and add the broth and the remaining ½ cup of shredded Parmesan. Cover and simmer for about 20 minutes, to cook the meatballs through.

4) Meanwhile, cook the egg noodles according to package directions, drain and stage them nearby.

5) Add the artichoke hearts and spinach to the soup and cook a few minutes longer until the spinach has wilted. Adjust the seasoning with salt and pepper as needed.

6) Spoon a generous helping of the egg noodles into bowls and gently ladle 3-4 meatballs into each bowl along with enough broth to cover the noodles. Sprinkle the soup with additional shredded Parmesan and serve.

Sweet Zucchini Cupcakes with Cream Cheese Frosting

Ingredients:

<u>For the Cupcakes:</u>
1 1/2 cups flour
1 cup brown sugar
2 teaspoons baking powder
1 teaspoon lemon zest
1/2 teaspoon ground cinnamon
1/2 teaspoon ground nutmeg
1/2 teaspoon salt
1/2 teaspoon vanilla extract
1 zucchini, grated
1/3 cup olive oil
2 eggs

<u>For the Frosting:</u>
2 (8 ounce) packages cream cheese, softened
1/2 cup butter, softened
2 cups sifted confectioners' sugar
1 teaspoon vanilla extract

Directions:

1) Preheat your oven to 350 degrees and line a muffin pan with paper or foil cupcake liners.

2) In a large mixing bowl, combine the flour, brown sugar, baking powder, cinnamon, nutmeg, and salt.

3) In a smaller mixing bowl, combine the grated zucchini, oil, eggs, vanilla and lemon zest and then add the mixture to the larger mixing bowl. Stir the wet ingredients into the dry ingredients until combined.

4) Divide batter evenly into the muffin pan, filling each liner 2/3 full.

5) Bake the cupcakes 30-35 minutes or until a toothpick inserted into the center of a cupcake comes out clean.

6) Remove the cupcakes from the oven and cool the pan on a wire rack for 10 minutes. Then remove the cupcakes from the pan and allow them to cool completely.

7) To make the frosting, blend the cream cheese and butter together in a mixing bowl until creamy.

8) Mix in the vanilla and gradually stir in the confectioners' sugar.

9) Pipe a generous swirl of the frosting on top of each cupcake and serve.

Mucho Mushroom Fettuccine with Tarragon and Goat Cheese Sauce

Ingredients:
2 pounds Portobello, Shitake and Porcini mushrooms, cut into thin slices
1 tablespoon butter
2 tablespoons olive oil
Salt, to taste
Fresh-ground black pepper, to taste
2 tablespoons chopped fresh tarragon
2 tablespoons chopped fresh chives
1 round goat cheese
1/2 cup grated Parmesan
1/2 cup milk
1 pound porcini fettuccine

Directions:
1) In a large pan, melt the butter with 1 tablespoon of the oil over medium-high heat. Add the mushrooms to the pan and then generously season with salt and pepper. Add the fresh tarragon and cook, stirring, for 3 minutes. Continue cooking, stirring occasionally, until the mushrooms are golden brown, and no liquid remains in the pan, about 5-8 minutes.

2) Combine the goat cheese, Parmesan, milk, and 1/4 teaspoon of the salt. Stir until smooth.

3) Meanwhile, in a large pot of boiling, salted water, cook the fettuccine until just done, about 12 minutes. Reserve approximately 2 cups of the pasta-cooking water and drain the pasta, returning to the pot.

4) Whisk 1 cup of the pasta-cooking water into the goat-cheese mixture. Toss the pasta with the mushrooms, the goat-cheese sauce, the remaining 1/4 teaspoon salt and 1 tablespoon olive oil, the fresh tarragon, and the chives. Add more of the reserved pasta water if the consistency seems dry.

5) Transfer the pasta into a serving dish, and sprinkle with additional Parmesan.